I0748411

THE EXCULPATION OF OBI UDO

IHEANYI ANUNUSO

HANYVISION LTD

UNITED KINGDOM/ UNITED STATES / NIGERIA

ISBN - 978-1-7397772-1-0

PROLOGUE

All eyes were glued to the screens in the arrivals section of Terminal 4 at Heathrow airport, as Obi walked in through the automatic doors, all eyes apart from Obi's that is. His, were fixed on the tablet that he held in his hands, even as he made his way through the crowd, to get to the point where he knew that his brother, Buchi, should be emerging from in the next ten minutes or so.

London, it would seem, was engulfed in a riot. A riot brought about by the boiling over of racial tensions bubbling underneath the surface for some time. The news stations in the country, around the continent and the world in fact, showed images of people, of every age, color, ethnic and religious persuasion, engaging in a city- wide rage of looting.

There had just been a highly contentious, and suspicious, killing of a Black man in the Tottenham area days earlier. Tensions in the North London suburb were already high, with the stop and search police tactics that were essentially targeting black drivers, which Obi knew about from his friends who lived in the area, whenever he came to visit.

The London Met had almost lost control of the situation, engaged in running battles with angry crowds of mostly black Londoners, protesting at their general treatment in the hands of law enforcement officials around the British capital, with the disputed case of the slain man held up as yet another instance of prejudicial police treatment towards people of color.

Obi tore his eyes away from the continuing coverage of the fast-evolving situation, as groups of mostly Black people, started to emerge from the departure gate, informing him that the passengers from the Nigerian flight had cleared their luggage, having come through immigration and customs.

Soon enough, Obi spotted Buchi coming through with a clothing style hinting at a trip to the North Pole. It was his first trip to the colder climes of Europe, infact, his first trip outside their native Nigeria, and like most Nigerians travelling to Europe and the United States for the first time, their travel get-up reflected the warnings of family and friends, about the perils of much colder lands, far, far away.

After the exchange of greetings, Obi led his brother to the car pack from where they proceeded on their journey to Enfield, North London. Buchi in addition to marveling at the smooth roads that seemed to maintain their quality despite the length of the journey, was also watching the news coverage of the day's events on his elder brother's tablet.

"Wow. Dad talked about some of the race relation problems that existed during his time, but I didn't know that things could get this bad." Buchi said solemnly, as he watched the continuing street battles between the police and the protesters.

"Don't worry, though" Obi replied, as he negotiated the usual London early morning rush hour traffic. "We won't be driving through any of those areas; I'm taking a bit of a circuitous route."

"A circuitous route, you say?"

"Yeah, it's called the North Circular. It's an express way built around the outer perimeter of London, allowing you to get to any of the four cardinal points; north,south, east and west; without having to drive through the entire city to get to where you want to go. For example, Heathrow is on the outer auspices of West London, but we're heading to virtually the farthest part of North London, in Enfield. You see the traffic we've had to encounter so far? Imagine if we had to drive through large swathes of London to get to where want to go. It would take virtually forever."

Buchi enjoyed the rest of the ride to Enfield, taking in the sights of well-planned sections of the city, with their different building patterns, the numerous Big Ben buses that plied countless routes, ferrying people from one destination to the other and of course, more white people than he had ever seen together at one place or time. He was also pleasantly surprised by what seemed like a quite diverse ethnic configuration. In addition to the Caucasian population that he noticed, there were large numbers of Black and Asian people on the streets as he passed by, more in some areas and sections than in others, but still a lot more than he imagined. He even saw quite a few people wearing turbans, of whom he would later recognize as British naturalized Sikhs from the great state in faraway India.

Before they got to Obi's place, Buchi requested a stop-over at a McDonald's, for his first fast-food meal, at least one with a different menu from the ones he frequented back home in Nigeria. On Obi's advice, he went for the Big Tasty meal, same as Obi. They enjoyed their meal at the outlet, before embarking on the final leg of their journey, getting to Obi's apartment around 11am, where after Buchi's luggage unpacking was done, they both settled in, Obi to the living room to watch the continuing coverage of the day's events, and Buchi to his bedroom to catch some sleep, after his overnight, inter-continental journey.

Towards evening, Buchi emerged to join Obi in the living room, after he had regained strength and comfort in his body. The analysis of the riots was being debated on TV, but he took a look around the room for the first time since he arrived, noticing a few photographs of people that he didn't know.

"Who's that?" He asked, pointing to the enlarged photo of a pretty, emerald eyed lady.

"Ah, Buchi…" Obi exclaimed, laughing. "That would be the one you would notice first. You still have an eye for the beautiful ladies, I see." A statement at which they both laughed at, remembering times gone by.

"She has made a great difference in my life." Obi continued. "One of those people you'll be lucky to ever meet."

"What about those guys?" Buchi asked, pointing to a photo, which showed four men; two black and the other two White; standing together with Obi in the middle of a half-formed circle.

"Those men, along with the group over there…" Obi replied, while pointing at another photo, which showed one of the men in the photo that Buchi had just enquired about, with two women and Obi. "…was the family that I had over here,which looked after me during the rough times."

"Mum told me a bit about some of the things you went through, trying to use it as a story to let me know that things here don't come on a bed of roses, and to try a teach me to be very careful during my time here."

"It was good that she did that. While we are on the topic of my life lessons, I might as well have a little chat with you before you head off to Leicester to start your master's degree program."

Obi then turned down the volume on the TV and drew closer to his younger brother, as if he was about to reveal the vault combination lock code for the Bankof England.

"Things are not always what they seem here, Buchi. You have to learn, especially as a young black man in this country, that you have to be careful in the way you deal with people, and I mean everyone, both black and otherwise. Things you might take for granted, even something as mundane as having relationships with a female, can lead you to immeasurable harm, if you are exposed to lawful scrutiny,without legal cover or protection."

"The law here says that everyone is equal under God, but you will discover that under the cold microscope of societal prejudice, perception, expectation and tradition here in the UK, that some people are more equal than others."

"I don't want to scare you away from being all that you want to be here or curtail the freedoms that you so want to enjoy, but I am your brother, and it would be remiss of me, to not prepare you for things that you might encounter in the future."

"In the end, nothing might happen that would make you remember the words that I speak to you right now, but just like you, I was a newly arrived young man in this country but with no one to advise me adequately on the fleeting nature of choice in the free world. Everything was going well, until, as mum told you, strange things and coincidences, started to happen…"

CHAPTER ONE

I wake up this morning at 8 am, feeling tired because I couldn't sleep until 5am.Again.

It's been this way for months ever since the trial, and then compounded at an alarming rate by the backbreaking events that have followed.

The job, the house, money and all remaining dignity, all gone...

Why wake up my head says, you're beaten? You can't work because no one will hire anyone like you, and you know what that means- no prospects. Even talking toa pretty woman on the street is beyond you now.

Girls! You're still talking about girls after everything. You're done. If they ever find out what you were accused of.... Well, you figure it out...

The last thought makes me remember why I'm up now- probation. The damned probation, as if the conviction on the most embarrassing and dehumanizing of offences was not enough, I have to find the money out of my meagre unemployment benefit, to catch a bus and journey for an hour every week, to answer deeply personal and perverted questions about my life, my upbringing,my family and anything concerning my past sexual relationships, questions I would be too embarrassed to ask even my own worst enemy.

"Did you sleep with your parents, past a certain age, in the same bed?" "Did you and your siblings share a bed?"

So it goes, on and on, every week, with each probing question, worse than the last. Sometimes I just break down and cry. I try so hard not to, I want to preserve some tiny portion of my dignity, after all, I am a man and a proud one at that. I try to not show how broken I am, try not to give anyone that pleasure in addition to everything, but it's so hard, not with the questions.

It's like trying to clear your head from a horrible nightmare, and then being brought right back to the place you so vividly remember, every week.

Anyone who thinks that their privacy is being invaded by government based on government based on holding people's records or some sort of clandestine surveillance procedure, ought to face the questionnaire I get weekly.

It's my last week in my house, and I plan to make the most of it. Some of the things I took for granted will be no more soon. Simple things like taking a shower when I want to or even cooking my own food, sleeping in my own bed, cold as it is, as I can no longer afford to keep the heating on in the house.

I have no family, never married, and I am grateful, for my current plight is not for sharing, but on the negative side now, I will soon have nowhere to go and already can barely eat properly, but I still will have to go for that weekly probation meeting.

I take my shower, God, how I'll miss my shower, and I get ready to move out. A bus is all I can afford now, trains while quicker are a luxury now, and so I have to be at the bus stop between 925 and 930am to catch a bus going to Brent Cross, just so that I can be on time for the 15-20 min Q&A session of questions ranging from "how are you today?" to the more embarrassing stuff...

My probation officer is nice, I think she knows the torment that the questions bring for me, but it's her job, sometimes she tries to warn me about something she will have to do next week, sometimes she puts it off till the next week.

Maybe it's her job to be nice, but I doubt it, I've generally been a good judge of character, as funny as that might sound in my current predicament and events of the last year, I think I would have been able to spot a fake after a while and it's been six months.
It was probably the only semblance of normality in my whole predicament, someone that was genuinely concerned with my well-being, and I suspected, believed that something did not quite meet the eye with the case sitting right in front of her, but had a job to do…or maybe it was imagination.

Either way, that perception of mine, magnified as it was by the events that had overtaken that last one year of my life, was the lone bright spot that I had that I would remember of the period, a weekly raindrop of human compassion for me, in my sojourn through a seemingly unending desert of relentless misery and hopelessness, the type that could break every man, but make only one...

CHAPTER TWO

ALL RISE!!!

The courtroom is sparse, in fact, probably because my trial had an early start; it's just my solicitor and I, the court reporter, the prosecutor and the three judges.
I look at the faces of the three judges, a woman and two men. They all look like they are in their sixties.
As they approach the bench, my heart sinks, I can see the order that they will be sitting in, as they walk towards their chairs, it's a male judge followed by a female judge and then another man.

Instinctively, I knew that whoever is sitting in the middle chair, would be the presiding judge in this magistrate court. If the reaction of everyone I had seen, who didn't know me, and probably some who did, hear the charges for the first time and look at me, then this was probably going to be more difficult than I had imagined in my worst nightmares.

Earlier in the morning, my solicitor and I, had our pre-trial meeting in the backrooms of the court, going through the merits of my case, what the prosecutors would do, and what kind of decision I would get from the judges. Best case and worst-case scenarios.

"I would advise you to plead guilty" she said. Her name was Carol Tate; she was slim, really slim, not really far off from anorexic, and tall.
She also tended to talk really fast and came across as having a nervous disposition.This nervous disposition made me feel that maybe, this might be her first case, a sobering thought to anyone who found themselves in the position I was in. But who was I to judge what a good lawyer sounded or looked like? I had never dealt with one or seen one live in action in my life. I was just thankful that I had one.

Sobering thought or not, I was glad to have a lawyer from a somewhat reputable firm, even though I had no idea what a reputable law firm looked like. I just saw the office and saw people in different offices, which even though small and a bit cramped, seemed well or reasonably furnished, and thought that looked professional. Still a nagging thought of doubt persisted, but the truth was, at the time, they were the only professional looking law firm that I could afford. I tried contacting others that I had seen advertised in papers and directories, but for a criminal offense, which I was being charged with, the price was always steep.

Welcome to the world of the defendant with limited means, choice is not an option, so from the beginning, you are at a disadvantage. Your limited means and hence, your limited resources for your defense, against the limitless resources available to the prosecution.

Carol continued, perhaps seeing the look of annoyance and dismay on my face,which said "Really? No way in hell". She said, "The prosecution has a strong case because of a couple of factors. You confirmed that you called the young lady in question They got the police officer from your first incident and arrest, who will testify that he apparently told you not to see or speak to her again, and finally, the judges are always likely, especially in a magistrate court, to take the word of a policeman, and they will certainly take the word of a girl who claims to be a victim, especially because of her age…"

At that precise moment, all I could think about was the nightmare playing itself out, right in front of my eyes, and like every truly bad one, had only gotten worse.
It had all started, just over a year ago….

***

"Do you live around here?" she asked. A perfectly innocent question from a good-looking girl, especially a good-looking girl that wanted to know everything about you….
She said her name was Talia. I had what I thought was then as, the good fortune of seeing her one day at the train station.
Tall, dark and slim, wearing a white blouse shirt and black trousers, she had caught my eye; she had a classic African like face, dark, oval and high cheekbones,beautiful and distinct.

As was normally the case when you saw someone on the train, you are usually going to different places and talking or trying to "chat up" is not feasible. For me,with my reserved personality, that was even more of a challenge. For fear of rejection or public embarrassment, I held back from public courting unless I had the opportunity to do so if people were not in the immediate area.

But I remembered her face and knew that I had a second opportunity. I would try to speak to her at least.

Weeks past. My normal route outside my area, either shopping or going out did not include the station I had seen her disembark at, unless I decided to go down to South London which was occasional. This was the case until the fateful day about 3 weeks later.

As it can be with London transport services, there are disruptions to the service,both to the overground and underground services sometimes, which can cause delays. While on my usual path to South London, one of these delays was taking place, causing a stoppage in train service for about an hour or so, through cancellations.

We got going finally and as we passed the Hendon station, I remembered that this was where I had seen the girl and actually about the same time. So, I took a chance and got off, hoping that I might see her getting off the same train, and when I didn't, looked at the next train arrival time which was 15 minutes and thought I'd wait and see if she got off on that one and if not, I'd be on my way.

Fate, I thought, was smiling on me because she did get off on the next train, and I could hardly believe my luck. I walked quickly to catch up to her as she had gotten off a distance from me, composed myself, and made eye contact and smiled as I got closer and stopped in front of her. "My name is Obi, I saw you a couple of weeks ago at this station when we were both on the train, you looked like someone I knew from back home and I wanted to say something but didn't have the opportunity. Hope coming up to talk to you is, ok?".

She looked at me and smiled, not sure if she smiled because she thought I had tried to feed her a line that had probably been used a million times, or if she believed me.

"Where are you from" she asked, noticing my lack of a British accent and probably recognizing that when I said, "from home", I probably meant another country.

"I am Nigerian." I replied. "I was born here but brought up over there."
"I am from Zimbabwe. I was born there but came over here at a very early age with my family."
"Sorry. I actually thought you were Nigerian. What's your name?"

This entire conversation was going on as we walked down the platform and away from the station. After her immediate wariness, when I first introduced myself, she had visibly relaxed and seemed quite comfortable as we chatted about living in the UK and the differences to our respective native countries.

Talia, as she said her name was then, asked, "Do you live around here, and do you use this station frequently?"

"No, I was just passing through your station when I first saw you, I don't normally use this train line unless I'm going to certain places where using this line is more convenient".

"So where do you live", she asked.

"I live in Colindale, not far from here. How about you? Do you live around here too?"
"Yes. Actually, we are quite close to my house now. It's just on this next street."
"In that case, I better get back to the station."

If you grew up in Africa, and especially if, like I did, you came from a conservative society based on strict parenting, there was this unwritten rule about not going girl's place, if that was her parents place, and you didn't know her or her parents that well. It had been especially true in my family home growing up, and I still had a natural recalcitrance so many years later.

As I had just basically met her for the first time, I did not think it appropriate to know her place at this point in time until I knew her better and thereafter, more comfortable with knowing her family when the time was right, if we got to that point.

"Is it ok if I took your number? That way we can talk and get to know each other better". I asked.

"Yeah, that's ok, where were you going anyway?"

"I was going to see friends in south London and the underground was having some delay problems, but I usually use this line when I want to get down there anyway. Is there a good time to call you?", as she put her name and number in my phone.

"You can call anytime, but I've got more free time in the evenings. My college is far from here and I usually get back late around this time. By the time I've eaten and settled down, it's usually around six or seven in the evening. You can try me then".

"Ok, cool. I will ring you later in the evening, when I get back home. I am really glad I met you and it's been really nice talking to you, it feels like I've known you a bit longer. Speak to you later, and take care".

"Alright, bye then" she said as she walked off, while I went in the opposite direction, smiling like a million dollars, thinking how lucky I was to have seen and talked to her and how well everything had gone, just like a dream.........The nightmare had just begun.

***

First, it was the incredulity of the situation, then panic that I had let a golden opportunity slip, then a feeling of resignation.

I had tried to call Talia's mobile number, when I got back just as I had said I would, but it would not go through, I kept getting the non-existent number auto-message.

Annoyed with myself, for not checking the number or, even giving her mine by dialing it after she had given it to me, I checked the number and found out that it had only ten digits.
Doubts started creeping in. Was our entire conversation a charade? Did I make too much of it? The conversation of the evening came back to mind, and I couldn't see it, hell, she actually would have showed me where she lived, if I had wanted, I could have walked her there.
These hardly seemed the actions of someone who didn't want to give out their number, and so that put my mind at ease.

As I sat, thinking of what I should have done better, it came to me. While we were walking down from the station, she had asked if I lived near the station and used it regularly. When I answered in the negative, she said that she used it regularly. She then started talking about her morning schedule and how she had to wake up early in the morning.

"I need to be at the station at about 730am, to catch the train around that time, so that I can get to college on time and its far from here, which is why I have to be up early and get back late. How about you? How early do you need to be up?"

"Well,", I said, "I have to be up at work by 9 am, but leave my house about 815in the morning…"

Remembering that bit of our conversation, I resolved, as this was now the weekend, to go down to her station on the following Monday, about 730 in the morning, on my way to work and hope that I might be able to see her.

That part of our conversation also reassured me, that I wasn't making a mistake with my assumptions, on the friendliness or "realness" of our conversation.

Calmed, I went by the rest of the weekend, happy and waiting for Monday to arrive.

CHAPTER THREE

"We are re-arresting you on the charge of sexual grooming. You have the right to remain silent, anything you say…"

I was in shock. A bone-numbing and heart- chilling shock. I tried to say something as the officer who had come into my cell was reading me my rights.My mouth opened but nothing came out, as he went through with his rendition,turned and then locked my cell door as he left.

The last four hours had been a particularly disturbing horror movie with the difference being that I was in it, with events happening around me and to me that I was hopelessly powerless to stop, so much so, that I might as well have been in a cinema watching it. Ha, if only I was that lucky….

As the gravity of my situation sunk in, shock turned to anger and frustration and then self- pity and utter embarrassment.
I thought of my parents, my family, proud achievers all, and very honest at the risk of prosperity, back home in Nigeria. They had been so proud of me, living without support, sending money back home when I could, trying to help out when needed. At that thought and remembering that it was my father's birthday the next day, I started to weep …

I was Obi Udo, the first-born son of an accomplished man, greatly respected in society. I had grown up trying to emulate him in some way, probably not as intelligent a man as he is, but to have the respect of people around him and people who had heard of him.
Instead, here I was, sitting on a hard bunk in a cell, surrounded by thick walls, locked in by a door of solid steel, with a tiny window high up, my only vision of the outside world.
They take away all your possessions, even your shoes, and ask you to fit yourself with slippers deposited in a bin basket.

As I sat there wallowing in self-pity and weeping softly, head in hands, the extent of what was about to befall me was sinking in fast.
Being of Nigerian heritage and proud of it, I was aware of the undeserved reputation we sometimes have as being somehow the epitome of some criminal enterprise or the other.

I would trade the allegations that I was being accused of, with any charge of financial impropriety and even armed robbery and happily plead guilty.

It was a mild July night, and I was awake for most of it trying to contemplate how it could be, that I was in such a position…

***

The Monday morning came around quickly as it always seems to, the signal that another weekend was over, only this time I didn't mind.

It was the first weekday since I had met Talia, and it was first opportunity I had to try and see her after the debacle of the mobile number. Because I would need to go off my normal work route to be able to see her that morning, I woke up an hour earlier, had a bath and put on my work clothes and was off.

I lived in Edgware, north London and there were two ways to travel by rail to Hendon, but only one true way if you were planning to go to the Overground station, which was where Talia and I met.

Remembering that she said she had to get out to the station by 7:30am, I left my home by a quarter to seven, so that I could walk down to Mill hill Broadway station and then grab a connection going down to her station, which was the next stop. I got to Hendon over ground about fifteen minutes early, being unfamiliar with the train times, and sat in the station waiting till it was 7:30.

Sure enough, she arrived on time, maybe a minute or two out, with me nervously glancing at my watch, knowing that I had a window of opportunity to see her, which was for about 20 minutes, before I had to leave in order to get to work on time.

Sometimes in life, there are times when your sub-conscious self is trying to tell you something, or maybe it's just that "sixth sense".

As I watched her approach from across the bridge that spanned the rail line inside the station, something kept telling me something wasn't right here.

That "something" was right there in front of me, but I just didn't see it or as I thought about it later, couldn't see it, for the simple reason that I wasn't looking for it.

"It", as I would later discover, was what she wore right there in front of me. She wore a stripped blazer and black trouser and some simple black shoes. Sometimes,I smile at my incredible lack of observation, maybe because I've cried enough about it, because, as clear as today, I can remember the thought process when I saw her that morning.

"That looks odd", I thought, didn't make fashion sense and looked a bit little unkempt, somewhat. Most girls in London tended to be fashion conscious. I put most of my uneasiness to meeting her for the first time since the mobile number debacle and not being 100% sure that she wanted to see me again and therefore not knowing what her reaction would be to my presence and tried to relax and talk.

"Hey, how are you doing Talia", I said as we met.

"I'm fine", she said, and "What are you doing here, this morning? I thought you didn't normally use this station.
Yeah, I don't actually. I tried to call the number you gave me, and it didn't work."

"Oh sorry, my mobile phone has problems, and I'm just trying to change it."

. Well, that's it, I thought, it was probably likely that she was being nice, and politely saying that she just wanted us as friends or something of the sort.

"Ok", I said, knowing that my time window for getting back to my work route was closing, "I remembered you said you come out to the station at this time, and so, when I couldn't get you on your mobile, I thought I'd try meeting you here as I didn't have any other way of contacting you".

"But I have to be on my way now so that I can make it to work on time", I said asI prepared to be on my way, "It was good to see you again, take care".

"You're on your way to work?" She asked, "When do you finish?"

Having mentally thought and accepted that this wasn't going

anywhere, and that I had probably miscalculated her interest in me, her question took me aback. Oh well, I thought, it doesn't hurt to find out why she's asking.

"I work for a bookmaker, and we tend to do long hours and so, I won't be finished till about 10pm tonight".

"Wow", she said. "That's a really long time to spend at work, since you said you start this morning. When do you normally have days off"?

"I'm usually off work two days in the week, but I don't do long shifts every day I am at work".

"Ok, I usually come back home around 5 in the evening myself, because my school is far outside London. We can meet up tomorrow or sometime in the week if you are free".

Not quite believing my luck, I said. "I'm doing long shifts today and tomorrow,my first day off will be on Wednesday. Is that ok if we met on Wednesday?"

"I'm not sure how my Wednesday evening will be" she said, "But, we can meet at the station closest to my school, which is Borehamwood around 4.30".

"That's fine with me, I'll be there around that time, got to go so that I can go try and catch my train to work from another station and be on time, it was really good to see you again, I wasn't sure what to expect this morning, but I'm glad I came. Hope you have a nice day, and I'll see you on Wednesday".

"Ok, bye" she said.

As I left the station in really good spirits, all I could think about was the old saying about the benefits of taking risks or making a move even when you are unsure.

In this case, I felt in my gut, that I should have at least given it a try that not having her number didn't mean that she didn't make a genuine mistake. All the uneasiness I felt at the beginning had gone, and I felt good as I made my way to work. My hunch or gamble had paid off; it had been worth it, as far as I could see.

The fact is that there are two sides to every coin and that when gambling, as much as there is an opportunity to strike gold, there is the inherent danger of losing everything.
Contrary to my euphoric feeling that morning, and in fact throughout that day,in the midst of my 12-hour shift, I was about to lose everything that I had cherished the most.

***

The appointed day of Wednesday arrived quickly, I can't remember exactly what went on in the days leading up to it, apart from the fact that I was working all through it. A mind-killing, body- fattening, 12-hour shifts, each day.

On the morning that I was supposed to meet Talia, I slept in till about 12, took a bath, and fried some sausages and eggs, and the day just felt right. At about 2pm, I left my flat and as I tended to do on my days off, do my shopping and laundry. I was trying to do this earlier than I normally would on an off day, to be on time to meet Talia.

I arrived at Mill hill Over-ground Station at about 330pm, thinking about the length of time for the journey and not wanting to be late, only to find out on getting to the help desk and looking at the train route, that the station I needed was only a stop away in the opposite direction that I would normally use. Because I rarely used the over-ground and because I never needed to go in that direction, I hadn't realized how close her station was, when we spoke two days ago, besides she had given me the impression that it was far. However, the lack of awareness would allow me to see something that I might not have seen, had I gotten there at the right time.

Outside of the fact, that I would be getting to the earlier that I would have wanted, it didn't bother me apart from the fact that I might need to wait around for about half an hour or so.

Elstree and Borehamwood Station was about a 6–10-minute journey from Mill Hill Station. I had never been there before, and so being early, I decided to take a little walking expedition along the high street, which ran close to the station.

Compared to most London high streets, Borehamwood was about average, which was about normal for a town basically on the outskirts of Greater London. It had some brand name shops, mostly retail, but not much that would make a casual (and reluctant) shopper as myself, want to have more than a perfunctory look around.

Having left the station to pass the time as I had gotten there about half an hour early, the paucity of the high street meant that I was back in the station with 20 minutes to spare. I remember sitting on the seats along the platform, waiting for the time to elapse to 430 pm. I didn't think much of it at the time, but there was a sight that would become significant in the following minutes and hours.

It's funny that among the dozens of people who got off the train in that 20-minute span, I would remember only him, a community police officer in the distinctive yellow jacket, bald headed and stocky of average height. He stepped of the carriage by himself; they usually tend to work in pairs and seemed also to be the only one to get off from that particular carriage too. He looked up and down the platform and then walked straight into the ticket hall.

Sometimes, I think fate has a way of laughing at us, making fun of our inability to truly comprehend events that will shape our lives, even though we might be looking right at it, watching with growing amusement, as we wish in our minds, what we could achieve if we could only see our future and fate.

Just like the morning that I set out to see Talia, I had been looking at clues to my coming fate, looking, but not seeing.

Unlike that morning with Talia though, I don't remember having that strange feeling in the pit of my stomach, a sensation that would usually convey a feeling of dark foreboding. Maybe, because I was already uneasy about waiting for a while at the station, any extra sense of foreboding, would not have registered.

As I think back, it is significant that I would remember that one person, that one face, but only after the fact, just like the morning with Talia.

It's like the audience of great magician or escape artist who are left amazed by the performance. They, the audience, are there the whole time seeing only what the magician/escape artist, wants them to see. They are looking at everything, or so they think, but seeing nothing.

You can never truly see things you are supposed to see, no matter how obvious they are or not, if you have no idea what they are, or what you were supposed to be looking for in the first place.

CHAPTER FOUR

4.40 pm.

I had arrived at the station almost half an hour early and was now waiting 10 mins past our meeting time, and still no sign.

It was starting to get a bit awkward, hanging around on the platform, while people got on or alighted from trains, every 15mins or so, especially, as it was approaching rush hour. As the time started to approach 4:45pm, I took a look at the time for the next train out. This being my day off, I usually tried to get as many things as possible, cleaning, visits, cinema and other stuff. The next train back was arriving in 3mins, so I decided to have a look outside the station, one last time and if I didn't see her, I would be getting on the train home. I went through the barriers, to take a look outside the station, and as soon as I came out ofthe exit/entrance and looked right, there she was…

That feeling I had felt when she approached me from across the rail bridge at Hendon over ground station on that fateful Monday morning, when I had gone to see her, returned, much more forcefully. It was a feeling of a sudden chill in the air,and an added weight in the pit of my stomach. I was instantly very afraid. The scene I was looking at was one I would remember for the rest of my life.

She was there alright, standing next to the community support officer I had seen alight from the train about 20 minutes ago. Our eyes met for a few seconds, Talia and me. The community officer hadn't seen me as he was standing at an angle, slightly backing me, in what seemed like conversation with her. Talia looked me right in the eye, without much emotion, probably apart from recognition, and looked away.

The first thought in my head, when I saw her, was that, maybe there had been some kind of trouble, and that would explain the delay. But the feeling in the pit of my stomach, as well as the voice in my head, told me of a danger or trouble that might be a lot closer to home, but I could not understand what such trouble could possibly, but a slight drumbeat of panic, was thumping in my chest.

Confused, I decided to do what we had planned in the beginning, meet up at the station platform, and if I didn't see her, catch that next train, but I think deep down, something was telling me to get out of there, the drumbeat of panic, which I did not understand the reason for, increasing every passing second.

I had never been in trouble before, with the police, but always had an aversion tothem based on what I had heard over time, about the police in Great Britain.

I was about to get a first-hand experience.

***

I had barely been on the platform for two minutes, when someone approached me from behind and tapped my shoulder.

"What's your name, Sir?"

I turned around to look, and found a man I hadn't seen before, wearing a white t-shirt and jeans, short blonde hair and about my height. He repeated his question a second time as I turned to face him.

"Who are you, and why are you asking my name" I asked, the air around me seeming very still, and it seemed that everyone on the platform seemed to disappear, even though it had seemed crowded with a burgeoning rush hour cluster of people only a moment ago...At this point, a vague realization had started to set in, not totally complete in knowing what was going on, but the sinking feeling in my stomach, was setting off red warning lights in my head, that I was in some kind of danger.

"Ok, you're being difficult, you're under arrest". With that he pulled out a police badge and a pair of handcuffs.

I must have gone into shock for a minute, but I remember asking a question as he turned me around, taking my hands around my back, and putting the handcuffs on.Filled with embarrassment, shame and still in shock, I offered little resistance, aside from asking the question that reflected the sheer confusion and panic in my head.

"Why are you arresting me? What have I done?"

"You are being arrested for harassment" he said, as he led me away from the train platform, through the barriers, where I saw Talia, standing somewhat sheepishly to one side, on the other side of the barriers, and then through the door leading to the inner recesses of the station.

As we got in, he started using his radio to talk to someone, who was a lady from what I could hear.

"I got him".

"Where?" She asked.

"At Elstree & Borehamwood Station" he replied.

"Borehamwood Station? What was he doing there?"

I remember that conversation like it was yesterday, it would be significant later, when I thought about it, but at that moment, all I could think about was, how in the hell had I gotten myself into such a predicament and what was going to happen next?

"Did you say that you were arresting me for harassment? I couldn't have been harassing her. I was told to come here."

"You can explain all that, when we get to the police station, I would advise you that anything you say now, can be used against you in court. I will take you to the station and interview you, there; you can say what you want, on the record".

The radio came alive again, and it was the lady's voice again. As I drifted off in my thoughts, wondering why she (Tania) would do this. I started thinking back to the conversations we had on the occasions that we met, when something I heard snapped me back to the present.

"Tell her mom that everything is fine, nothing happened to her" said my arresting officer to the lady on the radio.
The feeling in the pit of my stomach disappeared, everything stopped in fact. It was as if, all the warning signals the human body can emit in times of crisis realized that their work was done, and that they did not need to be there anymore.

A new sensation arose in its place, a feeling of dread. You hear when people describe a certain feeling they have, in moments of sheer terror and horror, when either they have a seemingly out of body experience, where they hear themselves screaming or open their mouth to scream, but nothing comes out.

Mine, was the experience of my brain, trying to connect dots, making a billion calculations, and then, arriving at the only plausible question that it could ask. A question it feared, it already thought it knew the answer to.

“How old is she?” I asked the officer.

“She’s fourteen. Did you not notice the school uniform or the badge on her coat?”

It all started to come together, as my mind started to assemble the pictures and remember things, from the very first day I had met Talia.

The gut feeling that I had that morning when I first went to look for her at the Hendon overground station, that feeling of something not quite right, when she walked toward me across the station bridge that morning. I had thought about the odd color combination of the coat, I remembered thinking how it looked out of fashion, for a London girl at the time.

It wasn’t about her being unfashionable that my sixth sense was trying to warn me about that early morning. Alas, too late, I now knew it was the fact that she was wearing a school uniform. The fact that I hadn’t grown up and gone to school here only compounded my abysmal lack of observation. But as I later reflected, I probably wouldn’t even have picked up the significance of that, having worn a uniform myself, till I was seventeen, as was normal in Nigeria.

But I was warned, which was what that feeling was, a warning of impending danger. I could hear a voice talking to me, or was it fate laughing at me.

“I showed you everything, the “mistake” with the phone number? Of course, it was deliberate you fool. That should have told you something, but oh no, the eternal optimist in you, chose to interpret it another way. That was your first clue.I tried to warn you at the station that morning too, but you didn’t notice what was staring you in the face”.

It's the master conjurer's trick, that life, or is it fate? plays on us mere mortals. It had been "fair". It had showed me everything I needed to know, in order to make the right decisions.

I had looked at everything put in front of me, and I had seen nothing. But unlike the audience of a great magician, that pay in advance to be entertained by their lack of observation, this lack of observation on my part was going to cost me a lot,long after today's act was over.

Fate, and the master conjuror's trick, that is our life path.

CHAPTER FIVE

The officers I met as I got into the station were very friendly. As I would get to know that is the way they conducted themselves, to make the process of booking and logging arrested persons as hassle free as possible.

It made sense for the processing policemen, to be as friendly as they could be, to get the full cooperation of people brought into the station, based on the situations we all have seen on some movie or TV program, over the years.

The officer, whom I was brought off, seemed quite jovial/light-hearted, and that relaxed me almost immediately, and I did not mind answering his questions concerning my name and address.

I had been made to wait for an hour, first inside the train station and then in the police car that later arrived, before they drove me off to the station, in a place outside London called Hatfield. The wait had only served to increase my embarrassment and anxiety at my situation.

All I had wanted was, to get the opportunity to explain myself, in what I could only think of as being a horrible misunderstanding, clear my name and go home. Itwas the only thing my mind could think of, right there.

Meeting what seemed like a neutral face helped me calm down a bit, under the circumstances, as I thought I would soon be getting the opportunity to give my side of the story and thereby clear myself.

First though came the procedures, the things I had to go through, from processing,making sure that I knew my rights and of course finger printing, then electronic printing as well as, a mouth swab for my DNA.

When they read me my rights, they asked if I wanted a lawyer present at my interview. At this point the PC (Police Constable) who had arrested me jumped in.Thc PC knew that I had been eager to tell my side of the story, all the way from the beginning, in order to clear my name, so he suggested that if I was serious about clearing my name quickly, then hiring or asking for a lawyer would be counter- productive.

The worst thing about the choice I made, wasn't really choosing the no- lawyer option, no, the worst thing was that I hadn't realized the situation I was putting myself into, so much so that I would actually make that same mistake twice, the second occasion even more damaging. As I look back on my incredible naiveté, time after time, through this chapter of my life, it is so painful, because I could see a lot of things I could have done to change the course of my life, and I kept making the wrong decision.

But, at the time, wanting so much to clear myself, as quickly as I could, to put this horror episode behind me, I could only think of it as being the best option,and told the duty sergeant of my decision not to seek legal advice.

Whenever next, you hear of a rich or well-connected/experienced person, standing behind their legal team, to fight charges in court, no matter the public perception of whether the person is guilty or not, they are doing what a person's legal right allows them to do, and that is very important.

Most of us have grown up with the perception, usually perpetuated by television shows, that when the police arrest you and question you, they are doing so with the sole intent of finding out information to ascertain, if you are guilty or not, or looking for clues for their investigation.

Sometimes, if you do not know the law or your rights well, unscrupulous policeman and prosecutors can take advantage of you, when they realize that fact. Like a lot of people tend to do, the easiest option is preferred. Solving a case can be painstaking business, and not everyone is cut out to do it. The worst possible thing for any accused person is to have such officers in charge of your investigation.

You have to realize, that it does not cost the police or prosecution any personal funds, to bring charges against you, but it will cost you a substantial sum to defend yourself. The more serious the charge, the more it will cost you to defend yourself by hiring lawyers.

It's a cruel quirk of the modern justice system, that in order for a person to truly take advantage of the right to defend oneself against allegations, baseless or not, such a person must have the necessary resources to uphold that basic human right.

Just as, human beings prefer the easiest possible route, so we also tend to overuse and abuse that which is free.
This is also the tendency, of the unscrupulous police officer or prosecutor. It costs them nothing to press charges, even if there is not enough evidence.

I think, the more cases that officers can generate and "solve", which lead to prosecution, the more they are recognized as doing a good job. It's just as result oriented as your commission pay sales job. The more you sell, the higher your pay goes up and you rise within the organization. There is a direct correlation between the sales reports and your upward career path.

The same thing happens with a police officer. Ever heard of a police officer, who wasn't good at solving cases being promoted upwards, to the top jobs? I doubt it. The good officers will have cases and diligently solve them and be upwardly mobile in the department. They have no need to manufacture cases or evidence.

I had the misfortune of having my case, fall in the hands of the dubious lot, and then showing them that I was naive, in my lack of knowledge about the importance of my rights.

As soon as I told the duty officer, of my intention not to seek legal counsel, I remember the arresting officers being immediately friendly, asking if I wanted to have some coffee, water or something.

The completion of the arrest process went fairly quickly, photographs and all, and then, I thought everything was ready for me to do the interview and begin the process of explaining myself and clearing my name, but the "games" began.

"If you could just wait in that cell, over there" said my arresting officer, whose name was given by him as PC Theo, "there is nowhere to wait around here, and we have got some paperwork to file, which will only take 20mins, and I will be back here so that you can give your own side of the story. All we want is a statement, so that we can deal with this matter quickly". The "we" included the community officer, whom I had first seen at the train station, and who accompanied us to the police station.

Happy that my situation was about to be looked at, or resolved in some way, I didn't mind going in for a few minutes and then doing my interview.

I sat there in my cell, simultaneously afraid at the situation, I had put myself in, and calm that somehow, now that I was going to be given a chance to explain myself, everything might turn out fine. That later thought perfectly encapsulates my usual optimistic view on life and circumstance in general.

Your wristwatch is one of the possessions that are usually taken away from you,before you go into the cell. So, as time passes, you have no idea of the time.

But I had an idea, of what 20-30mins felt like! And after what felt like close to two hours, especially with the light fading, and with my earlier calmness quickly dissipating, I went to the intercom, which was situated next to the door, to enquire as to the whereabouts of my arresting officer, and also as to what time my interview would begin, as had been earlier stated.

The person on the other side, said he had just come on duty at the desk and would enquire about my arresting officer, and get back to me. Two minutes later, the duty officer called back on the intercom, to deliver the next big shock, in a truly horrendous day "The officer who arrested you is no longer in the station. He left some time ago and is on the way to your house."

Now when I was arrested and also when I was being processed, the charge that had been made by my arresting officer was that of "harassment of a minor", and among the things asked of me, which made me uncomfortable at the time, as to their motivations or rather, their seeming desire to see if there was anything I could be found guilty of, was, their enquires as to my immigration status and where I lived.

I also handed over my house keys and my phone, along with anything I had in my pockets including my travel card and bank card, unwittingly handing over full access to my property, along with my agreeing to my lack of a need for legal advice.

"What!!! In my house?! What is he doing there?" My outburst emphasizing the incredible shock and surprise that went through my mind at the time.
The calm patience that had been in me, that had set in about an hour into my arrest ordeal, vanished, and that empty-like, falling in feeling in the pit of my stomach, which usually warned me that something wrong was afoot, came back with a frightful vengeance. I would not ignore that warning this time.

"I want to see a lawyer immediately! I want to see a lawyer now!"

There was a sound of commotion, on the other side of the intercom, like someone quickly coming across, and a new voice came on, I would recognize this voice as that of the person, who seemed in control of the station, and who was first briefed about my arrest, as soon as, we came in. Maybe, he was a police station manager of some kind.

"The officer is on the way to your house to search and take possession of some of your property. An officer will be on his way to read out a new charge to you, and a lawyer will be made available to you, shortly."

I was more furious about being tricked by the arresting officer, than shocked at the turn of events. My gut feeling which I had ignored, when they were checking into my immigration status, was that they looked like they were looking for something else in the way of additional charges, was turning out to be correct.

My cell door opened shortly after, with a new officer, whom I had not seen before, coming in. He motioned and bluntly asked me to move to the far corner of the cell, while he stayed near the door, which I thought odd, considering he wore body armor and was armed.

"You have been additionally charged with sexual grooming of a minor…"
"What!!!" I exclaimed.
He went on to read me my rights and then left my cell immediately.

When I was first arrested and taken to the police station, and the charge of harassment was read out to me, I was confident that I could prove that I was innocent of such a charge, once I told the truth about the facts, which would show that there was no evidence of such an occurrence and would point to a complete misunderstanding.

But, after the charge of sexual grooming was read out to me, I knew I was in trouble, because the only way such a charge could be determined, was if someone had decided to manipulate the facts with confidence, in which case, the truth wouldn't matter.

The only thing was that left me confused, was how they could be allowed to officially charge me with something, which I was absolutely sure that the evidence which was needed to charge me was non-existent.

I had read books and watched those crime television shows, where I would remember police officers having to go to a judge, in order to get the permission for a search warrant or anything that would involve a serious charge, or that would somehow invade the privacy of an individual, and then, the judge would ask to see or hear some kind of evidence that would warrant such a request.

I was absolutely certain that no such evidence could possibly exist to make any such assertion, for the simple reason that there wasn't.

All I could think about was that, if they had managed to put that charge on me without any corresponding evidence, what else could they do? I couldn't wait to see my lawyer.

"Your lawyer is on the phone for you" said the man on the desk, via the cell intercom about 30 minutes later or so I thought, and I was let out of my cell shortly after.

My lawyer was a Greek-Cypriot named Dan Papadopoulos, as he had introduced himself on the phone. He told me that he had been contacted by the police on my behalf, as was legally required. I asked him the time as I had lost track, since going into the cell, and he said that it was 8.37pm.

He then asked me to tell him as much of the full details of my situation as I could of what had transpired that day culminating in my arrest. I did, and then asked him the question that had been troubling me over the last half hour or so.

"After they had arrested me and processed me, they said they just wanted to interview me, but then while I was waiting in the cell as they asked, they left to go to my house, and then charged me with sexual grooming. Can they just do that, without any evidence?"

"Having listened to everything that you have told me about the events that led up to today, it's obvious that when they would have checked your phone, as I am sure they would have immediately after you went into the cell, they would have found no evidence of any interaction between you and your alleged victim. They would also have checked your oyster card and found that you have not previously been to Borehamwood, or at least no evidence there to support that notion, especially as you don't drive. If you have told me everything exactly as it happened so far, they have no evidence to pursue that charge of harassment," said Dan.

"What they have obviously done is ask the Station Chief, as they can in the U.K,if they can charge you with sexual grooming. This charge allows them access to your property to search for any evidence that could link you to the charge. They are trying to find anything incriminating between you and the alleged victim or something else. Now, I have to ask you some questions. Do you have the right to stay in this country? And do you have any type of pornography in your home? If you do, it will be used against you.

"No" I said "I keep no such material at home, and I was born here" my confidence and calm starting to return.

"That's fine then" he said "I can't come over to the station until, the officers get back and notify me that they are ready to conduct an interview. Hopefully, they should be ready in about a couple of hours or so, and then, we can see what they are really saying and get you bailed."

With that he said not to worry and said he's goodbyes and we ended our conversation. I was then led back to my cell by a young officer, who looked about 21 and remarked, "You guys seemed to have a lot to talk about". I wasn't entirely sure if he was being sarcastic or if the normal time for conversations between detainees and their prospective lawyers, tended to be much shorter, but I couldn't really care at the time.

My shellshock at the turn of events had started to wear off, now that I had an idea, through my lawyer's explanation, about the processes that were at play, and the police officers had been trying to do to me.

As I sat back down in the cell, the first thought that came into my head was, "this sure isn't like the movies and television shows", where the police would get you in, trying to know the truth and would want to know your side of the story, in order to ascertain your guilt or innocence.

Here instead, it seemed that for whatever reason, the police were almost hell-bent on finding something on me, even though they didn't have any initial evidence to support their charges, and could tell from their records, that I had no previous arrests or record.

The second thought that came to my mind was about some people's lack of trust in the police, usually refusing to tell them anything.

I had worked in a betting shop, and because of the tension and anger of losing money, and sometimes drunkenness; we had to call the police to deal with certain situations. In the aftermath of these incidents, and especially in some of the low income neighborhoods in London, where most of these betting shops tended to be located unfortunately, just like the way access to drugs and gun shops tended to belocated in low income and black neighborhoods in the United States, during the 60's and 70's, there was that look of "you don't know what you are doing with these guys, they are not your friends, they would do the same to you without hesitation"

Sometimes, those feelings would be communicated to me verbally, and if it were felt that we had gone over and beyond with trying to give up information, to try to help police enquires, especially if the matter did not involve any problems to us personally, but I never usually took any notice. While I had been brought up in Nigeria, where the police where corrupt, there never was a thought that they would go out of their way to gather evidence to incriminate innocent people of some kind of crime. They had a hard enough time, investigating real crimes anyway.

After my conversation with my lawyer, I understood what they had been trying toget across to me; I had always held pride in my having a British passport, being a part of an “advanced society” where all rights were protected, especially those of the innocent. I wondered if what was happening to me right now had anything to do with my skin color and a perception that people like me don’t always know our legal rights. I resolved that should I ever be in a position to turn in someone else, I would be demure, unless it was something truly horrific.

But, even more perplexing, I knew that what had gone down today, here, could never happen to me back home in Nigeria. Someone would want to find out the full story and my side too.

What was the point of living in an “advanced society”, where all was “fair”, if your rights could be so easily circumvented if you didn’t know them all exactly,especially if that was done by the people who were supposed to uphold them?

George Orwell had the famous sentence “everyone is equal, but some are more equal than others”, I wondered if similar contradiction could be made of the “advanced society.”

…Everyone has equal rights and are “free” …as long as they know exactly what those rights are, and all the various ways those said rights can be compromised….

CHAPTER SIX

I waited till what I thought was about midnight, hoping to stop my mind from thinking too much about my situation, by trying to mentally count minutes and hours; before I was convinced that the police officers weren't coming back. I gave up playing the time game a while later.

Being that it was late in the night, my intercom buzzed, with the duty officers trying to find out what I would eat. Hardly in any mood to eat, I refused, but asked what time my arresting officers would be coming back. I was then told that they wouldn't be back that night, and that the interview would now take place the next day. Wondering why, I tried to settle down and sleep, with the day events on constant replay in my head.

The morning came quickly, I barely slept and watched the daybreak in the sky, it was the only thing I could see from the tiny window, high up in the cell, and it held new meaning for me that morning. An appreciation of a simple phenomenon that I had always taken for granted. I thought about people who spent time in prison, wondering what it must feel like to wake up every morning, for a period of time, to a sight such as that. Your sight of beauty and freedom of the world, limited to the size of an inaccessible tiny window.

Daybreak came with new realizations and problems. I, as shop manager, was supposed to be opening up that morning. There were contingency measures that could be taken if such a situation, in which I could not open up on time or not at all, but none of those measures could be put into motion without phone calls being made.

This brought anxiety to my mind as soon as I saw those first tell-tale signs of light. Try as much as I could, I could not remember a single number, either of the other shops or of my colleagues. I called up the front desk on my intercom, trying to see if I could get some help retrieving numbers on my phone, which was in custody.

The voices were different from the officers who had been on duty when I had last called the previous night. There had been a shift change. Sometimes even amongst horrible circumstances and people, you find good people, and I was very lucky that the two people on that early morning shift, a man and a lady, both about my age or maybe a bit younger. They tried to find my phone, in the evidence room, only to find that, it had been taken away, by the arresting officers. They then tried to find the phone numbers of the shop locations, whose street names I could remember, but to no avail, as the phone numbers were not listed...

Finally, the lady officer went online to the company website and found a number for the head office. But, as it was still quite early in the morning, about 7am, it was decided that the phone number will be tried again after 9am, by which time the office should be open. It had taken about an hour to find the number, with communication going back and forth, between the officers at the desk and me. Iwas extremely grateful for the help, I got from them. I am not sure; I would have gotten that help from anyone else

I wasn't sure what was going to happen to me, but I did not want it to affect my job. I had no one else to rely on and had always been independent and couldn't afford to lose my job. They asked if there was something that I wanted in the meantime, and I requested for water to drink and some toothpaste, mindful of the fact, that I was supposed to do an interview that morning, with my lawyer and thepolice.

I was allowed to come out of the cell and make the necessary cover arrangements on the phone, and then taken to what looked like a bathroom area and given something like a chewable toothbrush, with some toothpaste, and then taken back to my cell to wait for my interview.

I had been arrested at about 5pm the previous day, and then taken to the station by 6pm. It got me thinking because, I had believed that the police could not hold anyone for 24 hours, without an interview or questioning, and I asked my lawyer about this, when he got to the station about 12pm, which was when the police offices indicated that they were ready to conduct an interview (this being about 1pm, a good 20-21 hours after my arrest), he expressed surprise that the police had detained me for that long without questioning.

He then told me that they had obviously used their new powers to detain people for up to 24 hours without questioning, powers they had been given to deal with potential terrorist threats. I, never before arrested, and with no evidence to support the charges, had been driven and dumped in a station outside London and left there, for almost 24 hours without questioning, just the same way, a potential terrorist, would have been treated.

My lawyer and had asked for us to sit down together in a room before the interview, so that I could go through the events, as they happened, and he could then advise me of my rights and tell me what to expect during my interview. After making sure I understood that I should ask him questions, if there was anything that was ambiguous or I didn't understand fully, during my interview/interrogation, we told the police that we were ready.

There were two people preparing to interview me when we got to the room, and to my surprise, the officer who arrested me was not one of them, in fact, I never saw him again. You would think that someone who had made the arrest and made the plethora of charges to invade my privacy even more, would have at least have the courage to conduct an interview with me, which had been his whole premise in asking for my cooperation "so that we can get to the bottom of this". My guess is that he must have realized that he had no evidence, after taking my phone and house keys and going through and thrashing my flat, as I would later discover, and passed on the problem to someone else.

In his stead, a man and a woman, made excuses for why I had stayed in the station overnight and for almost 24 hours, without an interview, taking place. They said there had been "traffic" on the way to my place from the station, and that by the time they had been through my place, and taken the evidence to the station, it was "late", and they then decided to "leave it" to the next day.

Considering, that it was a maximum journey time of between 30-45 minutes from the station to my place, especially in a police car in a police car with sirens and Sat-Nav, and that I had been processed by about 18:30, which was the last time I saw him (the arresting officer), I thought the excuse laughable, especially as this was 13:30, the next day.

But these were serious accusations/charges that were being levelled against me,hardly a laughing matter, and I wasn't sure what the two officers in front of me were going to come up with, so I let it pass without debate, and went ahead, as I was asked, with my statement.

I told them how the events of the previous day had come to pass, all the way from the first time I had seen her and waited for their questioning. They started by going through the items taken from my flat- my laptop, my digital camera, sim cards found, and then most discomforting, with a powerless feeling of my being somehow violated, my sister's leftover belongings and most horrifyingly, my niece's passport documents and clothes.

When I saw that, I felt a deep shame and total disgrace. My sister had come over,to spend the holidays here in London, with her infant daughter, my only niece. It had been a moment of pride for me, having to provide and take care of someone else for the first time; the responsibility of that two-month period had been very welcome.

As I sat across the table, from the police officers questioning me, a deep anger arose in my heart. This situation had been brought great shame to me, however it came about and however it might end, But I could deal with, as long as it was just me, after all, the decision making had been mine and mine alone.

Seeing what had been taken from my flat, changed all that. It felt like not only my privacy, but, the privacy of my sister and her family, and in particular and even worse, the privacy of my little niece, had been violated, and I was utterly powerless to stop it, the very worst feeling in the world.

But it would get worse. Their control over my private property grated me, I hadn't killed or harmed anyone, and they had no evidence whatsoever, on the charges I was being accused of. My lack of knowledge on my rights in this situation, annoyed me, even though I had no use of that knowledge or a lawyer before now. Surely, the police couldn't just walk into someone's home and take whatever they wanted, without some kind of legal permission?

The final stripping of whatever dignity I had left was when they started asking me questions about my niece, insinuating type questions....

I hated the police from that very moment. I hated the power

structure that had given them such authority, to do what they had done. But I reserved my most hate,for these officers, especially the coward, that I never got to see again, who had violated the deepest sanctums of my privacy and dignity.

***

The interview concluded about an hour later, after cross-examining my statements. My lawyer had initially asked that I answer no comment on all but the most innocent of questions, but I answered almost all anyway, as I had nothing to hide, unless they tried asking probing stuff that had nothing to do with the charges.

I was then subsequently bailed to re-appear in a month's time, and with my lawyer having left already, had to find my way home, from the unfamiliar area outside London. I had no travel pass, as that had been taken by the police as part oftheir investigation, I had no cash on me, and no phone either, as that had been taken also, and there was no cash point in the area. That left me with no option but to ask the officers to take me back into London, as it was on their way, and as they had dumped me here in the first place.

It took us about half an hour to make it back to London, which I checked considering my arresting officer excuse for not making back on time last night, was that it was a long journey between my house and his station and coming back.

They dropped me off as soon as I could recognize my surroundings, and I walked the rest of way for about twenty minutes, trying to find the route with the least likelihood of passing by anyone. I was well aware that, having not taking a bath or cleaned up since the previous morning, I smelt badly, still wearing the clothes full of perspiration from my ordeal, in the middle of a hot summer July day. I had lost a lot of my dignity over the previous 24 hours, but I was determined that strangers on the street, and definitely not friends, could know, by just passing me on the street, just how low I had fallen.

CHAPTER SEVEN

Months after my ordeal, I couldn't sleep. I had come back to the station after thirty days, as was mandated and they had found no evidence to prosecute me on the charges...which...didn't surprise me.

What did surprise me was that they refused to give me back my property, as soon as the investigation was over, claiming they needed to check it more "thoroughly"(my laptop), and that my sister would have to come forward and claim her daughter's property.

All this dragged on for at least a month, primarily because I couldn't afford a lawyer, who would force them to do the legally right thing. I was told to call back almost daily to find out if they were ready to hand over my property. This went on and on, until I got tired and called the law firm that handled my station questioning, and asked if there was anyway, they could help me without taking a fee, pro bono work if you like.

The associate I spoke to kindly told that I didn't need to pay anything, because as they had handled my initial interview, this problem was still related to that same case. He said he would make enquires to the police, as to why my property was still being held, long after they had decided not to pursue charges.

It took all of about 10 minutes, for him to get back to me, telling me to call the police back immediately to arrange for my property's collection, which brought that particular issue to a close.

But even as time passed by, days going into weeks, I could never forget what had happened and why it had happened to me. I was ashamed to tell people what had happened, not knowing how they might judge me. I mean, someone stealing from the bank or from other people, could say he/she was greedy, or could even say they were hungry, and that they just needed the money, and then could claim contrition for their faults, and say they would change for the better.

If on the other hand, if you were accused of causing harm to an underage person,it implied some deep structural fault in moral fabric, which cannot be explained, and maybe...never forgiven.

The rest of the year went very, very slowly. Even though I was convinced that I had done nothing that could have upset the girl, I tried to remember every look on her face, to see if I could see her looking afraid, or upset, but couldn't. As time continued on its intermittent march, all I kept thinking about was, if I did. Pangs of guilt about what might have transpired that maybe I hadn't noticed. Was she scared when I came to the station that morning?

Everything changed, especially, anything that to do with women. Meeting new girls was never the same, because I felt that I was going to have to lie at some point, especially if it looked like it was going in the right direction.

One day I was going to have to tell this person, the thing that shamed me the most, because they would need to know Whereas, in the past, I would go into relationships, just to make friends and see taking things as they came, now there was a mental burden I bore. Going into a relationship, or in my case, trying to get into one, felt like I was going to live in a house that had no doors or windows.

The closer I got to the point where I thought, I might want to talk about the things that had happened, I felt this insane urge to tell someone, I felt like I had just gotten out of the shower in the door-less, window-less house, with the chilliest winter wind passing right through, and shivering, I would run back into the innermost part of the house, seeking refuge from the stiff wind.

I wondered why I felt this way; I had done nothing, deep in my soul I knew I had caused no harm. But something kept eating at my soul, wherever I was and whatever I was doing, work or at home, it didn't matter.

It hit me finally one day, when weeks and months, I decided I wanted to re- arrange my flat. I had left it the same way the police had turned it over, the travelling suitcase I could never use, because the handle had ripped off, clothes in the wardrobe, everything.

I thought something was missing, and then remembered what it was. My sister had left some of her daughter's clothes for winter along with some of hers, as she expected to return to London and didn't need it where she was going.

The police had taken them and not returned them claiming that they were not mine, and I never was able to get them back, they had apparently done some kind of test on them...

I realized why I felt so naked and depressed. I had always craved my privacy and kept my thoughts and possessions to myself and the people that I trusted.

That feeling of privacy and personal space had been totally destroyed by that incident, and I would never get it back, and I wanted to know what really happened, because for the life of me, it never made sense after months of introspection and re-collection.

As fate would have it, I got what I thought was my chance almost a year later.

***

I had never been in a courtroom before, so even though I was in this predicament,I looked round, trying to match the scenes to the ones I always saw in the television dramas and the movies.

First was the silence, like in a library, only quieter, which until the case was ready to be heard, gave me an eerie feeling of foreboding disaster. It was the kind of silence one might expect, just before something bad happened in a horror movie scene.

Second thing was that there was no big crowd (which I had been dreading); in fact, there was no gallery. There had been one at the arraignment case, where the charges against me were brought to court, but not in this room. We must have waited about 15mins or so for the judges to come in, but it felt like an eternity, before we got the "all rise" announcement. The crown prosecutor then stated the case against me to the judges and for the record.

"The case brought against Mr. Obi Udo, states that on the 4th of April 2010, he approached Miss Talia Dube, and thereafter, called her continuously over a period of time. He has admitted to knowing she was wearing a school uniform, on the day he met her, but still called her phone, even though it was obvious that she was under-age. He has been charged with non-violent harassment".

The presiding judge then asked what my plea was. "Not guilty your honor" I said standing up, as I was asked to do, by my lawyer.

Thereupon the prosecutor indicated that they would want to call Talia to give evidence in the trial. Because of her age, there was some kind of provision, where she was supposed to give evidence from another room. We had to wait while that room was set up, in order to allow videoconferencing, so that she could be seen and heard from our courtroom.

Her evidence began with the prosecution asking her questions, on the events as they transpired. I, being short-sighted, tried squinting at the television set, which was about 6 feet away from me and must have been about 12 inches, to see her face as she spoke. Conspiracy theories popping up in my head, I still didn't believe she would back up the falsehood in the police report. But she was about to put those conspiracy theories in my head, to rest.

"Talia", the prosecutor said, "Could you describe the events of the 4th of April2010?"

"I was coming back from school at about 4:30pm on that day, when I saw a man across the street from me, coming in my direction".

"Could you identify that man as being in this courtroom?" asked the prosecutor.

"Yes" she said, "He is sitting over there next to the lady" pointing towards me. "He came across the street and followed me, and I kept on walking and wouldn't stop. Eventually, I stopped, and he asked me if I remembered who he was, and I said yes. He asked for my number, and I felt afraid, and I gave it to him. He then left, and called me around 10pm, but I didn't pick up. He tried the next day as well with a different number, and then finally, he met me two days later, where I told him that, I didn't want to see him again".

"Did he ask you anything about lawyers?" the prosecutor asked.

"He did not look intelligent enough, to talk to me about lawyers."

A gradual haze descended on my mind with me desperately looking at the tiny screen, to see if this was really happening, and then sitting back in frustration, because I couldn't see anyway. My lawyer had her opportunity, to ask questions about the evidence statement that had just been given.

"Did you at any time, send a message or indicate to my client, that you did not want him to contact you anymore?"

"No" said Talia.

"Did you and my client ever have a phone conversation?"

"No"

"What were you doing on the 5th of April, in the evening after school, which was the day after he saw you?

"I was meeting with friends".

"But according to the statement my client gave to the police, when he was arrested, he had a conversation on the phone with you, about the issue the two of you had spoken about the previous day, on the question of you, speaking to his lawyers. But you could not continue with the conversation, because you were talking with your friends and did not want to elaborate on that conversation there?

"I don't remember having such a conversation".

"Then, Miss Dube, how did my client know what you were doing at that time?Do you mind if we check your phone records, to see if you actually called his phone as well?"

With that she left the room, and any hope I had about the truth coming out, along with whatever was left of my tattered self-pride, left with her. Two people that I assumed to be her parents, who were ushered in when, she was about to start her testimony,

left to the courtroom as well.
The court then took a recess for lunch. I left for the backrooms of the courthouse and recounted every moment of that fateful second meeting....

***

"Mr. Obi, you may take the stand". We had come back from the recess, and the prosecution processed to finalize the fine points of their case, to argue for my conviction and then it was the defense's turn to argue against and then I was calledto the stand.

"Do you swear to tell the whole truth and nothing but the truth, so swear to God.
"I do"

"You may proceed."

"Your Honor" I started, "On the 4th of April...

CHAPTER EIGHT

It was a nice warm spring day, and even better, I was off work, after a period of five days on the trot. Being that most of my workdays consisted of long hours of staring at the screen and dealing with sometimes aggressive customers, willing to take out their daily frustrations on someone, preferably the person standing behind the counter taking their money.

The hours were usually long, generally starting from 8am and ending at 10pm every night. The only reason that the people running the company couldn't get us to stay longer, was probably on account of the labor laws or government legislature, that they hadn't yet managed to turn or lobby around, yet.

The labor force generally consisted of early school leavers or graduates and others with some form of higher education, who all constantly thought that they were never going to stay in such a sometimes mind numbing and eternally listless job, and that it was only a temporary stopover in life's journey.

I had been here seven years now and had made such declarations at every opportunity too, but as I looked around me at my fellow staff, every one of whom,had been around for almost the same amount of time, I realized that we had settled. Stuck in a job with no satisfaction but needing the money because of commitment and priorities.

In these frustrating circumstances, every day off was viewed as a blessing, valuable time away from the long hours of unappreciated and underpaid, and abuse-filled work. On such days, it was my opportunity to catch up on domestic chores, cook the food I needed for the rest of the week, see friends or whatever I fancied doing with my spare time.

This particular day in April, was early spring, the beginning of the Hollywood summer box- office season. I, being big movies fan from as long as I can remember, always checked out the advertising to see which films worth were seeing.

Having done my cooking, after my traditional off day lie-in and the entire housecleaning that needed to be done, I checked the show-times of movies at my local cinemas and then was off to the Staples Corner Cineworld.

It had been a year since the incident with Talia, and I had not seen her since, even though my closest cinema was in the same area where we had met. It wasn't my favorite cinema, primarily because of the size. It was one of those cinemas, where the watching crowd seemed to like to entertain themselves (noisily) while the movie was going on, and there were always distractions with people getting in late and walking along your sight line, because the floor was flat and there were only two passageways, one on each side of the room.

With this being my day off I did not want to spend too much time travelling and spend only the minimum amount of time going there, watching the movie and going back. But most importantly, the closest show time was happening there. So,I quickly got dressed, and headed out to the train station to catch the train going there.

Over ground trains arrival times can be annoyingly unpredictable sometimes, and on getting to the train station, I found that the trains were running late, which would cut into my arrival time for getting to Staples corner, making it almost certain that I would be late.

Trying to consider the amount of time that the adverts would run, I hoped to be able to catch the movie actual start time, but by the time I got into the cinema, the movie had actually started running for about 10 minutes, meaning that I had missed the beginning bit.

Fortunately, this being a major picture and having just been released, there was another showing in just over an hour, and trying to pass the time, I decided to take a walk. Sitting by myself in a screening room, watching a film was one thing, sitting in the lobby by myself for an hour, waiting for a movie to start was quite another.

I hardly had walked 10 minutes up the road when I saw her; I couldn't quite believe my luck. The chance to find out, what exactly had happened the previous July, which had bothered me ever since. I waved from across the road, and she did likewise but in my mind's eye now, less enthusiastically.

I crossed the road and asked, "Do you remember me" to which she replied, "Yes,what happened to you? The police refused to tell me or my mum, anything.

"Well," I said, a bit cautiously, as I had never really understood how everything went down in its entirety," The police arrested me because they said, you reported me as harassing you. They also said that you were underage, that you were fourteen".

She looked surprised and said, "That's not possible; I never told the police that you were harassing me".

I wasn't upset, I just thought "Well, that's ok, while I might never know what truly went down that fateful day, I could see that she wasn't scared of me. Who knows? Maybe someone saw me and reported it to the police, but at least, it wasn't monstrous thing that I could have said or done without noticing, ass had bothered me all this time. You made a mistake, now just deal with it and move on".

These were the thoughts going through my head as she spoke, until her next sentence, brought me back to the present.

"Besides, I never told them that I was fourteen anyway, because I am about to turn seventeen, this year..."

It was the answer she gave about her age that completely threw me, because she didn't need to say it. I had assumed the police statement as being largely hers and hadn't thought that there could be any ambiguity between the two. Her answer now brought new questions to mind about the authenticity of the whole episode. Still digesting the implications of what she was saying, I asked the first coherent question, my mind could come up with.

"Are you sure?"

"Yes" she said, "they told my mother and me, that we didn't need to know the details".

"Please, I don't have my lawyer's office number on me, but if I went home immediately and got it, could I ring you, so as to ask when and if you can give a statement to them basically telling them exactly what you have just told me. It will really help me."

"Yes" she said, "that's ok", as she gave me her number, and after making sure she had mine, I took off running back to the station. It was almost five in the evening, and I had no idea when the law firm that had handled my bail and police interview,shut their offices, and I desperately wanted to get answers to the questions in my head about the possibilities of my situation, in the light of what had just happened.I was so excited, I literally ran all the way, not caring what people thought, as I maneuvered my way around them on the pathways, at speed. I couldn't quite believe my luck and couldn't wait to tell everyone what had just happened, or rather, the few that I had the courage to talk about the incident.

There were no warning feelings, just pure exhilaration.

***

"Sorry, we can't help you on the previous basis, on which we handled your bail interview, the law only allows for the right of representation at that stage, anything after that, you have to take care of yourself.

Besides, I don't think that you will be entitled to any type of compensation or some kind of redress, because you did not spend any time in prison. It will also be difficult to prove if, the girl in question does not collaborate what you have just told me exactly. If you are to have any chance of seeking any redress through the courts, you must be in a position to take care of any legal costs involved and the girl has to make a statement under record".

I had gotten home in a record 20mins after I left, having taken of running as soon as I left her, running across the rail bridge and bounding down the stairs to catch a train that had just pulled in, and then going flat out from the station to my house, all the while praying that the law office hadn't closed for the day.

Thinking back, I have no idea why I needed to speak to the lawyers that very evening, I could have easily spoken to them the next day I guess, but in all the excitement, all I wanted to do was find out what the possibilities were ASAP. I had gotten home, and then desperately tried to find where I had kept the card the lawyer had left with me about a year ago. Five frantic minutes and a totally disheveled room later, the card was found, and not minding that I was going to blow up my phone contract agreement, by calling at the time which wasn't allowed; a remarkable feat in that penny pinching stage of my life; I dialed, and it was picked up by a secretary, who answered my rapid-fire question about their closing time, telling me that they would be open for about another half an hour.

The lady then passed me off to an associate who she said could help me after listening to my query, having found out that the lawyer who originally handled my case was in court somewhere. It was he, who now informed me of my options, painting a picture of the legal process and possibilities.

I sat down trying to digest the information that I had been given, and what the chances are that I could achieve something reasonable. I knew I had very little in the bank and could not afford a lawyer anyway. Besides, that little amount was going to be depleted further, thanks to the near 30min off- contract conversation that I had just had with the law firm.

My first decision was to call the girl and tell her what had just been discussed and if she was still willing to give a statement on record of what she had told me, even if she might want her parents or a third party involved, from her own side.

I called the number, and she gave me, this time, with my money sense having kicked back in, as I started to relax, with another Sim card I used for emergency purposes, just in case I needed to make an out of contract call but there was no answer. I didn't mind. I thought I'd leave a text, as she might not recognize the number, and then happily checked when the next showing for Ironman 2 was. It had been an unbelievable day I thought, absolutely magnificent.

I had just made a massive, life-changing mistake.

***

"So, Mr. Udo" the prosecutor said, "you went on to the movies that night, but inthe girl's statement, she said that you rang her repeatedly that night, and left text messages. How do you explain that?"

"I did call her that night before I went to the movies as I said previously in my statement, and I called again, after she called me back, a call I missed because I was in the cinema".

"That statement cannot be corroborated by anyone else, and the records don't show any evidence, that she ever called you".

"How can you say that, when you claim that her phone is missing" I countered.

"It does not matter what you think or say, Mr. Udo. What matters is that there is no evidence of in front of the court to back up your claim, and I am certain that I can prove that you were told not to see Miss Dube by the arresting officer after the first incident. A warning that you ignored."

"Your honor, said my lawyer standing up," there is no evidence that such a specific order or instruction, was ever given. My client definitely does not remember such a specific order."

The judges seemed to deliberate among themselves for a minute, after my lawyer sat down. Then, we were asked to recess.

***

I had not seen one of them in almost a year and the other in about three months. As I sat in the hallway, during the recess, the two officers, each of whom, had been responsible for arresting me, on the two occasions that led to this trial, passed me as they walked towards the crown prosecutor; further down the hall; for what seemed like a chat before they were supposed to give testimony in court.

PC Ahmed actually gave me a wink as he went by, DC Adams; the one who had interviewed me alongside his female colleague, the day after I spent the night in the cell; casually looked in my direction for the briefest moment. The wink annoyed me, especially coming from an officer who had been especially arrogant and condescending during and after my second and crucially damaging arrest.

But he was not important today. From my understanding of the evidence that the prosecution was using, DC Adams' testimony was going to be used to state that, I had been specifically told never to approach or speak to Talia, under any circumstances, a specific instruction that I never heard. But if this testimony was believed, it would almost certainly negate the arguments my lawyer and I were trying to make.

This had been why Carol had implored me to take the guilty plea, in the hope of getting a reduced punishment; of which she was sure, baring the unexpected; there would be a conviction. As she put it, the combination of the evidence of a minor and the confirmation of instruction from a detective, was a virtual no-hoper.

I just couldn't give up that way though, it was after all, my life and reputation, and letting it all go without a fight did not sit right with me, even if the odds were stacked against me. I was probably hoping for a miracle of some sort, maybe a crisis of conscience, forcing someone to own up to what really went down. With each passing minute of the trial however, that hope continually diminished.

***

It was never in doubt, my conviction, once DC Adams testified that he had indeed told me to never contact Talia. As soon as his testimony was over, the lady head judge decided that all my evidence was inadmissible; phone records and all; because the officer's testimony proved that according to the judge's assessment, that I knew beforehand, never to contact the plaintiff.

The question, that the officer's testimony might be false, or that there was no evidence to back up that claim apart from his word, was never even considered or contemplated, just as my lawyer had feared.

I was convicted on the charge of non-violent harassment, in short order, and then asked to return at a later date for sentencing. I left the court in a bit of a daze. A different set of possibilities were on the horizon, very different from the ones that Ihad considered on that fateful day, when I ran home after meeting Talia again.

On that day, as I had turned my flat upside down, looking for that complimentary card, the exciting possibilities swimming in my head were, the option to sue the police for defamation and breach of my civil rights or at the very least, an apologyfor their conduct towards me.

Today, only about four months after, as I trudged slowly out of the courthouse, a beaten and scared man, the possibilities lurking in my mind, were starkly different. Was I going to jail? What would the court fine me and could I afford it?I had borrowed money from my bank to cover my legal expenses but losing like I did today, also meant that I would have to pay the court costs as well, without exception or argument.

But the one thing that I couldn't shake was that I had been stained for the rest of my life. Some things I took for granted, might never be available to me again.
Opportunities and avenues I could never again consider. Worse still, my own family and friends and whoever was going to be my wife would have to know something that will probably change their opinion of me forever.
What about the society? As I felt that the people, who knew me, might never quite look at me the same way, I was absolutely certain that I would be totally condemned by the greater society. If I had any ambition or desire to do anything in the public sphere, such dreams and desires vanished the minute my judgementwas handed down.

I looked back on my life, all the things that I had always wanted to do and had never done or had postponed waiting for the "right time", and I just thought, what a waste. Everything, every dream, I had not fulfilled or tried to make good, was either gone or almost impossible to achieve now.

I kept walking, on and on, ignoring the buses that could get me on my way home and the train stations, just thinking about and regretting, every single thing that I had wanted to do and had never done. I got home about midnight, tired and exhausted. The judgement had been read out at about 4pm…I had been walking for about eight hours. I didn't feel hungry, even though I had not eaten at all, that day. I decided to take a shower, forced myself to eat something, because I still had to work the very next morning.

Finally, I got into my bed, closed my eyes and silently wept till the first light of the morning.

CHAPTER NINE

PRESENT

9.25 AM, I just made it. I could see the bus just rounding the corner. I had this habit of being on time, not necessarily early, but just right on time. I could have a lot of time to prepare to be somewhere or do something, but would always leave it,just so that I could be at the appointment at exactly the right time. I was hardly ever late and have always done things this way. My mother called it the fire brigade approach to life. I tended to do things when it was exactly necessary.

It was a forty-five-minute bus ride to the building where I had to go and serve my community service order. Three months had passed since my sentence was announced. I had been given the maximum punishment for the offence I was convicted of, a one-year community service sentence, which involved me going for "counselling". I also had to pay all the court costs. That combined with settling my legal fees, cleaned out my current and savings accounts.

The terms of my sentence stated that I had to go to see my advisor/parole officer,on an appointed day every week, which meant that I had to accommodate my work schedule into it, without daring to tell anyone why I, for the first time, needed to have a particular day off, every week. However, being as broke as I was, needed to work as many extra hours as I could, sneaking them in, either in the morning or the evening, depending on when my appointment was. I after all, had a large loan to pay off.

Today though, there were no extra hours available, and so after my appointment, I could at least try and get some rest. The meetings usually took about 20-30mins.
At first, it was simply asking if I knew what I had done wrong, to which I frustratingly answered in the affirmative. Of course, I knew I had made a grave mistake, I was re-living the mistakes and the costs just about every week.

Gradually, the questions turned more cryptic. Enquires about my parents and other members of my immediate family, my sexual orientation, and habits, gentle but obvious probing into my personal life and habits.

This was the twelfth week of these meetings now, and I felt a weight come over me, when it was time to go. But there was no alternative and postponements only made things worse, or so we were warned at the very first meeting, where a lot of us came in for an induction.

The routine was always the same. I would take a fifteen-minute walk from the final bus stop to the front entrance of an ordinary looking three-story building, with no large signs announcing its function (this I was grateful for, the very first time I got there, constantly looking around to see if someone recognized me).

I had to push the front door buzzer to get access into the building, where I would then have to identify myself to the receptionist, who sat behind a solid glass partition. Dionne was almost always the one in the receptionist's seat. Slim and of Caribbean origin, she seemed to be sympathetic to us; the people coming in to serve their sentences or whatever was being required of them; or at least all the ones I had seen come through the door at the same time I did.

Once you had identified yourself and the advisor that you were supposed to see,you were then buzzed through to a waiting area, where along with whoever was waiting to see advisors at about the same appointed time, you stayed.

The people that I met in this room were of all types. Some, you could tell from a mile away that they had been in prison, likely very recently. They had a kind of hardened demeanor. Some were women, not sure what their offences had been, but they looked all right. Others were young, probably about the age of eighteen,probably serving out a sentence for some juvenile misdemeanor.

While the personalities in the waiting room were of different backgrounds, the one constant was the silence in the room. It didn't matter if there were ten people in there; as happened occasionally; or just a couple, there was very little or zero conversation at all. It was as if everyone was blind to everyone else and completely unaware of their existence. No one wanted to look too closely at anyone else. For my part, I prayed silently and constantly, that I would not meet anyone that I knew, either on my way there, or my worst nightmare, inside the building.

When I later tried to understand the phenomenon of total silence in the room, realized that maybe everyone was hoping for the same things I was, not seeing anyone that might recognize them. We had all made some mistake or another, some maybe worse than others, but it was probably a chapter of our lives that we wanted to be done with and try to forget ever happened, hoping to never make the same mistake again. To that end, it was imperative, that we keep this circumstance away from as much of the public as we could, in the hope that we might avoid frequent reminders for the rest of our lives and, that it might not affect future options we might choose to pursue.

So, there we would all sit, eyes staring continuously at the ceiling or the floor or,at some very important and never-ending pseudo-text message that we suddenly found on our cell phones, until mercifully, we would be called in through a third door by our advisor, hopefully sooner rather than later.

This was the twelfth or thirteenth time, I had come here, every Wednesday, meeting my advisor Karen (another nice Caribbean lady), and everything played out the same way, that was until today.

I had just finished my session with Karen, this was one of the more pleasant ones, where I wasn't asked about some aspect of my personal habits; their favorite being of some sadistic sexual nature; just the usual "do you have a girlfriend now", "what type of woman do you fancy" …pretty tame stuff compared to the usual. I always wondered when they would bring up a question about my parents' habits, in the supervisory board's favorite realm. I didn't blame my advisor though. I think she was trying to do her job as mandated by her superiors. Besides, she tried to give me fair warning about when the particularly brutal side of the questioning was coming up.

But today was not one of those days, and so, after we exchanged goodbyes and she escorted me to the door, I walked out to the waiting area, through which we had to leave the building. There was just a single guy in the room.

"Are you just starting your sentence? I haven't seen you in here before".

It was the first time I had been asked anything directly by anyone in the building,other than by the receptionist and the advisors. But, what a first question to be asked! It was exactly the type of question, I hoped never to be asked by anyone who knew me and definitely a secret I would never want known by a complete stranger. While I was trying to figure out what response was best to give him, he started speaking again.

"By the way, my name is Jermaine".

"My name is Obi, and I started about three months ago. How long have you got left, to serve on your sentence?

That came out with ease, and to my surprise, with some kind of relief. In a funny kind of way, I didn't really mind telling him my name. Maybe, it had to do with the way he approached me, with a good vibe and no pre-judgement.

"Well," said Jermaine, "I got out of prison a few months ago and I'm on parole. I have to report here occasionally, but it's not consistent. They change the times of my appointment, as well as the location on short notice. It's almost like they want to catch me out. My parole agreement is very strict and if I miss out on an appointment for any reason, I will be sent back to prison immediately. I think they are trying to break me or force me into a mistake. You should be very careful with these people".

With somewhat alarm, I had never thought of or seen that side of the probation service, I replied, "I will try to be, and good luck with your situation. Hope you make it". And for reasons, I don't remember, we shook hands, and I left him and went out of the building, wondering what his offence might have been, but thinking that he didn't sound that bad.

I would get to know so much more very soon, a whole lot more than I bargained for at the moment of our first meeting, but a very welcome change from what had been a pretty lackluster and predictable period, a change, which was really needed.

The very next week, my usual morning appointment had been switched to an afternoon slot because, I asked for a time change when I realized that there would be extra hours available, a week in advance. So, having come from work, which was a much shorter distance travelling distance than coming from home, I found myself arriving about twenty minutes early.

While wondering what I would do with all this extra time on my hands and definitely not wanting to spend that much time in the "meditation" atmosphere of the waiting room, I saw Jermaine, coming round the corner, from the parole office building. We recognized one another immediately and there was no hesitation or seemingly awkward moment this time. Even though we had met and talked for about five minutes previously, an onlooker might have concluded otherwise, probably thinking that we were good friends.

"Are you coming from an appointment" I asked. It was obvious that was most likely the case, but I was trying to find a topic of conversation to start off with.

"Yes, I truly hate those things, but it is keeping me out of jail right now, and I would do anything not to go back there".

My curiosity eventually got the better of me, having been debating with myself,while he was talking, about whether to ask him why his parole conditions were that stringent. It was a difficult thing to ask, mostly because I had never really wanted to tell what my own offence was, to anyone in the first place.

But I sensed that he wanted to talk, maybe even from the first time we met and probably more so now. So, I made up my mind and hoped for the best.

"I've been thinking about what you said, and I don't understand why your conditions are so stringent, since they thought it fit to let you out of prison. I hope its ok that I ask, especially as you hardly know me. I can't judge you either, I think sometimes, what I was convicted off is more humiliating, than anything else I can imagine."

"What are you serving for? It is a community service order, right? Looking at you, I thought you might have done some silly traffic offence or something".

I had no idea why I told the truth. I could tell he had been willing to talk, but before that moment I had no intention of telling anyone, anything about what I had been through for the past two years, neither friend nor stranger.

But there I was talking, I told him everything, intently watching his face for any reaction, any sign of the pre-judgement that I feared from others. There was none,actually, he was quite impassive. I think he had heard worse stories than mine and perhaps had lived through even worse. If I hadn't looked at my watch just before we met, I would have sworn that I had stood there talking for hours.

Instinctively looking at my watch now however, I could see that I was five minutes late for my appointment. I had spent almost twenty-five minutes talking, and I felt that I could have gone on and on. But it was probation time now, and as much as I hated it, just as he did, I did not care to be a part of an alternative, which I was sure, would be worse.

"Hey Jermaine, I'm late for my appointment, maybe we can chat another time. It was really good to meet you again though".

"Same here, brother…erm, what was your name again. I know it sounds like a name from "Star Wars" ….

"Ha-ha, its Obi", and then I remembered that, in all my effusive might in telling my story, I had forgotten to ask him what his crime was. "Hey, by the way, I forgot to ask you what you were on parole for."

"I assaulted a police officer and almost killed another."

CHAPTER TEN

JERMAINE

The council estate of Grahame Park was the largest North London and one of the worst for living conditions. The buildings were clusters of large impassive looking structures that welcome inhabitants and visitors with all the homely feeling a ship's crew felt when they approached large chunks of rock, dangerously sticking out of the water on their pathway to shore.

There was the solitary and almost obligatory presence of a police support office, right in the middle of the estate, which was basically where all the shops were. Just like the commercial/retail buildings in its vicinity, it had opening and closing times and even days when it didn't open, which was laughable considering the extensive criminal activities that went on around the estate.

Inhabitants of the estate generally belonged to three groups. The first and original group were the people who had settled there a long time; most likely from the early seventies; when the criminal element had not discovered the usefulness of the planning structure of the buildings, built close together and inter-connected.They would usually lament about the time when the estate was clean and safe, and you could raise a nice family in it, which quite frankly, looking around at the buildings, is a time you couldn't quite believe, ever existed.

The second group were the less privileged and state housing dependent. This group was not as fond of the estate or have much pleasant memories of it, but don't have much choice other than being here. The combination of a lack of adequate affordable housing in London and, the ever- rising cost of living brought them here. They were mainly minorities or immigrants arriving here due to different circumstances and trying to make the best of what they had.

The last group and the only ones that were quite happy about the current state of things, was the criminal element that lived in and around the estate. There was a huge drugs and prostitution culture there, controlled by different gangs and factions. Their activities were aided by the plan of the estate, where the buildings were linked together and massive, meaning that it was possible to evade detection by entering and exiting, through a multitude of entrances in the expansive area.

Most of this group were members of under privileged families, moved here so that they could be housed. They were basically members of the aforementioned, second group. But as is so often the case with under-privileged families, especially the second generation and onwards, they desperately wanted to get out from under the poverty line. With the opportunity for a more conducive environment made up of a secure location and a market for the produce of criminal activities, drugs for the people who wanted to forget their problems and stolen goods for the people that wanted the nice things of life but could not afford the market price.

It was a mutually beneficial arrangement for the people (inhabitants and others from the surrounding neighborhoods) who wanted the goods and services, and other inhabitants who used the trade to get a better life and a ticket out of the estate.

Jermaine's parents had come to the estate in 1980 about a year after he was born.They were of West Indian heritage. Darren, his father, worked on road construction crews and Mary was a checkout operator at her local supermarket, or that's what they did before the horrible austerity period of the late seventies. The limited income from both their jobs and the birth of their first son, gave them no other avenue to progress in, but to register and enquire as to the availability of housing relief.

They split up after a couple of years the pressures of raising a child in a rough neighborhood, with no work available; at least nothing permanent; becoming increasingly heavier to deal with for a young couple. Darren was 22 when he left the flat, he had shared with Mary, who had just turned 20. He never meant it to be permanent, he just did not want to be nagged through the night yet again and decided to go back to his mum's place in Kingsbury, just for the night. But as handsome young men grow to find out, there will be plenty of opportunity to stray, and so, his came in the morning on his way out to the shops, making him decide to stay back at his mum's for just one extra day.... he never came back. An out of wedlock baby and her demanding mother, made sure of that.

That left Mary, barely older than a child herself, to look after Jermaine. With the never subsiding pressure of low income and even lower employment opportunities, while at the same time watching her unmarried mates going about with their lives; fun, parties and events; unburdened by responsibility, she searched for help. Two drug-runner boyfriends later she found it. With the proliferation of drug use on the estate aided by its structural planning, for a burdened and impressionable young girl, it was only a matter of time.

Jermaine learnt early how to look after himself and his half-sister Salma the daughter of his mum's second drug runner boyfriend, who was a drunk himself. While he couldn't do much for his mother, as she slowly but surely became entirely reliant on Jeremy, he did his best to protect himself and Salma when Jeremy came around drunk or when junkies were looking for their dealer.

He's early life troubles forced him to grow up quick, but more importantly while watching his mother's health deteriorate, taught him never to experiment with drugs, personally. That decision was important, when he opted for, like a lot of his friends on the estate, to participate in the illegal drugs trade, pulling himself out the poor living conditions he was born into.

By the time he had turned twenty, he had bought himself a nice second-hand Honda civic and a small apartment, where he moved both Salma and Mary, out of the reach of the drug culture. Jermaine had steadily gotten help for his mother, as he became affluent enough to get her on therapy programs, as well as being influential enough to control the supply of drugs to her, gradually cutting it off. However, that kind of influence on the drug supply on the estate unfortunately brought him to the attention of the undercover drug police squad in the area. He was arrested three times by his 21st birthday and under constant surveillance around his flat.

The cat and mouse game continued for years, until the police got their breakthrough courtesy of Jeremy. Jeremy had been caught with quite a large quantity of cocaine in the boot of his car during a police surveillance operation, which had been the result of a tip-off. When he was offered a deal to reduce his punishment by helping the police land even bigger fish, he gave up all he knew on Jermaine's activities, having always hated him for reducing his hold on Mary,as well as knowing Jermaine's very apparent disdain for him.

Armed with all this new inside information, the undercover squad lay in wait for Jermaine at his pick-up and distribution points without success. Jermaine had never trusted anyone while growing up, including for obvious reasons his own mother, and constantly changed his routine. Frustrated, the two lead detectives, DI's Patterson and Johnson, decided to pay a visit to his flat on a "routine check",under the guise of following up "important leads" on the drug operation in the Colindale area.

Mary, while being "clean" for a while had been into drugs for almost fifteen years, and in that space of time had also developed friendships with people who were fellow addicts, a natural sequence, if a group of people all patronized the same spots or meeting points.

When she finally did give up on drugs, not all those friendships ceased to exist. Most of those friends still visited her, and now that she lived outside the estate in Jermaine's flat, they found their way there reminiscing about old times, glad that at least one of them had "gotten" out of the estate.

Not all of those friends were "clean" however, and on that fateful day that the undercover drug squad decided to make their "routine check", Davis Leroy had decided to pay a visit to Mary.
DI Jack Patterson was forty-two years old with a twenty-one-year service career in the police force, which in his mind had been rather uneventful, without some of the major news crime stories. The absence of these marquee achievements he felt,had hampered a faster rise through the ranks. His wife also thought he should be much higher than where he was (telling him so every day), wanting to stand out, whenever the police officers' wives met for their regular meetings.

DI Derrick Johnson, on the other hand, did not have a slow rise. He had only been in the service for ten years, but it had been whispered among his peers quietly over the years, that his rise was only the result of his family connections. He knew of these rumors, which were true, though he would never admit it. He wanted to be part of a big headline crime bust story, to justify his position and quash the rumors, or as he called them "the haters".

The Colindale police station and the Grahame Park unit had garnered itself a reputation in the police community as a major drug running operation area and a place where illegal drugs, prostitution gangs and the police were fighting for supremacy. Arrests happened every day, and for anyone ambitious and looking for a big publicity police bust, this was it. DI's Patterson and Johnson had requested transfers here, hoping for that big publicity case that would advance their careers, for different reasons, but with a similar end result, respect among their families and peers and justification of what they thought was right.

They arrived within months of each other and after working together on a few operations/raids, and discovered that they had a few things in common, not the least of which, was their ruthless pursuit of objectives at all costs. They carried out their operations with ruthless efficiency, not worrying about any human costs, this attitude due partly to their complete disregard for the "immigrants and blacks clogging up this area of London". They tried to operate as much as they could on the edge of their authority, believing that everyone in the estate had something to do with the criminal activities in the area. They did not care much for informers either, jettisoning them as soon as they had made use of whatever information they could get from them, never liking any personal association with any such "filth" that came out of the estate. Surveillance work was more to their liking, as they could easily infringe on personal rights, as most of the "druggies" were too incoherent to understand them anyway. Besides it kept them from making promises to criminals awaiting justice, that they had no intention of keeping anyway. Jeremy was about to get the full punishment for the numerous charges that had been filed for his crimes, but he didn't know it yet.

And so, at 3.15 in the afternoon on that Friday, the two of them along with two community support officers, arrived at the corner of Annesley Avenue, just a few doors down from Jermaine's flat. They decided to do just a bit of neighborhood surveillance/reconnaissance work for a short while before going to the door, as DI Johnson remarked "you never know what you might find". The community support officers were barely out of the car when DI Paterson thought he recognized a man coming towards them from the opposite end of the street.

When the man turned towards the doorway of Jermaine's flat, Jack immediately remembered where he knew that face from, as one of the clients of a small-time dealer he had busted just over a week ago. “Well, well, well” he said out loud “what have we here?” Signaling to the community officers to come back towards the car he decided that the team was going to go in now. What better motive to get into the house than a “druggie” going into the house of a suspected drug dealer’s flat, that was under surveillance.

Davis had known Mary for over fifteen years and secretly had always admired her. But they had met while she was at the height of her addiction, when looking for places to acquire illegal drugs. He stood no chance when Jeremy came on the scene, him being able to provide Mary with the thing she desired the most at the time, in return for her affection.

After she was taken out of Grahame Park; and from under the influence of Jeremy; Davis continued to visit her, as he had always been liked (and pitied) by Jermaine, who thought he was a good man who had just fallen on hard times and even worse company. Mary knew he still used drugs in spite of his protestations of innocence and having lived that life of being with someone who had access to drugs, she wanted nothing of that sort of life, but just prayed that he would kick the habit somehow.

While Davis had stopped using the expensive and more destructive drugs like heroin and cocaine, he still smoked cannabis quite a bit, and on an occasion like today, when he had just been to his dealer, carried around a substantial amount. Whenever he had the opportunity, he bought in bulk because in the idiom “you never know what tomorrow brings”. He just made the mistake of bringing all ofhis “tomorrow” into Jermaine’s home on that fateful day.

Mary and Davis had barely sat down in the living room, when there was a loud series of knocks on the door and then a loud voice asking for “Mrs. Adams”. Mary instantly recognized that tone of voice and the whole scene as being that of law enforcement, based on past experience from the old council estate, but went to the front door anyway, curious to find out what might have brought about the visit. She opened the door and was met by the face of DI Patterson and three other unformed men, none of whom she recognized from the amount of time she had spent on the estate and in run-ins with the police.

"Good afternoon, madam, are you Mrs. Adams?" asked DI Patterson, even though he knew that she was, as his team had kept a dossier on the family, in their efforts to penetrate Jermaine's operation.

"Yes, I am".

"We have some information that we are following up on, and we would like to search these premises, madam".

Now if Mary knew her rights well enough, she would have asked to see a warrant before letting them inside the house. But she had been in trouble with the police before because of her association with Jeremy, at the height of his drug-running operation and did not want a repeat scenario. Besides, she knew that the house was clean because no one who lived here, used drugs and Jermaine was always careful to never bring any drugs or anything illegal, anywhere in or around the house, and so there was nothing to hide.

"That's ok officers, we have nothing to hide, come in."

The team came straight in, and in accordance with their plan, but to the complete surprise of Mary, they made a path straight for Davis. DI Patterson had made a callback to his unit to confirm something he thought he could remember about Davis. During one of their surveillance sweeps of the estate, they had picked up on the fact that Davis would have a substantial amount of cannabis acquired from one of the major dealers on the estate. It was only when they became convinced that he bought this for his own pleasure and not for distribution, did they decide not to move in on him, instead deciding to keep tabs on him and the dealers that he frequented, hoping to use him to track which dealers were the biggest distributors on the estate.

They knew when he made the substantial buys that he did, usually on his payday which arrived on the final Friday of every month, from his job as grounds man for the local council of Barnet. Knowing that today was the final Friday of the month, and also knowing from Davis's past history that he bought in substantialterms, DI Patterson thought there might be a good chance that he had something on him and could barely hold his excitement at this unique opportunity, and so he came up with the excuse to search Davis, while he was in Jermaine's home.

“Mrs. Adams, we followed this man (pointing at Davis) here, as we were warned that there was a major distributor in the area, and he is a big buyer of illegal drugs.“Could you please stand up, sir”?

Davis was already shaking with trepidation before the last statement by DI Patterson and had been that way since the police entered the house. He knew what he was carrying in his pockets, having come down to Mary’s straight from Gabriel’s; the dealer who had been his supplier for the last two years.

DI Johnson who had been intently watching him all through the conversation that went on between DI Patterson and Mary, had seen the profuse sweat gathering on Davis’s face and knew they were on to something here for sure. But the target was Jermaine, not Davis, and now came the delicate dance that had to be done to get Davis to, willing or unwittingly, implicate Jermaine.

With a nodding gesture to the community officers for help, DI Johnson began the search, while the others secured Davis. Mary, seeing the terrified look in Davis’s eyes, felt her stomach sink, with that scary premonition, that something bad was about to occur here and now.

It took only a few seconds for the first packages to emerge, wraps of cannabis, stuffed in his trouser pockets and on further investigation even more in the inside pockets of his coat, which was beside him.

“Well, well, well. What do we have here?” Jack Patterson said. “You’ve got quitea haul there”.

“Looks like we found our distributor, Jack” said Derrick Johnson. “This is big.What’s your name Sir” asking Davis.

“It’s Mr. Davis Lloyd, officer, but I am no distributor, I just was holding this for a friend…who’s trying to quit”.

“Sure, Mr. Lloyd, Of course you were,” said DI Patterson. “We get all kinds of excuses from people in your position. But that,” pointing at the drug haul that had now been placed on the floor, “is enough to be seen as for distribution purposes, and that’s a possible long jail sentence if you are convicted. My fellow officers will take you to the car outside, and I will be there to join you shortly, to take you to the station, just as soon as I take care of some business here”.

As the protesting Davis was led out by the two community officers, DI’s Patterson and Johnson, stayed behind with Mary. “Mrs. Adams” said Jack Patterson as he sat down on the living room sofa, “We would now like to search you and the rest of the house as we believe that Mr. Lloyd probably came here to make a pick-up, and so we would like to start that search right now”.

Jermaine was coming back home and only a few meters from his front door, when the two community officers emerged from the house with Davis in-between them in handcuffs, and then walking in the opposite direction. He almost considered walking on past the house or turning around in the direction he had just come from, until he heard the raised voices coming from inside the house, which he recognized as that of his mother and an unknown male voice.

He quickly went up into the house, ignoring his instincts to stay away, the protective instincts he had developed early in his childhood taking over. Jermaine came into the living room to see his mum struggling with two men, he did not recognize. Instinctively he jumped right in, punching the first man he got in contact with, which happened to be DI Johnson, knocking him to the floor.

Derrick Johnson immediately got up from the floor and looked for the first thing he could lay his hands on to subdue Jermaine, who Derrick now recognized, as Jermaine tussled with Jack Patterson. Jermaine noticed out of the corner of his eye, as Mary scrambled from the scene, Derrick raising the huge flower vase that his mum loved to keep in the living room with freshly picked flowers, towards the couch where he lay on top of the struggling Jack Patterson.

Mary had been having some of her favorite home-made strawberry cake when Davis arrived, and both the cake and the small knife she had been using to make slices out of it were still on the living room table, and Jermaine grabbed it to confront the advancing Derrick.

“Police” screamed Derrick, as he saw the knife, and Jermaine hearing that immediately put his hands to his side and then asked for identification. DI Patterson immediately got up and hit him on the back of the head with a side stool,knocking him unconscious.

Jermaine came to, a few minutes later to find himself and his mum in handcuffs,he recognized the men he had been fighting with, along with the uniformed ones who he had seen lead out Davis from the house along with several more. They read him his rights and told him he was being arrested for resisting arrest, assaulting police, and possession of illegal substances. With his instincts returning, he decided not to say anything and counselled his mum to do the same as well, seeing her bewildered expression.

They were taken to the Colindale station, where the charges were officially read and they were both remanded in custody, until they could be interviewed and then if allowed to, be bailed. Mary was bailed after her interview in which she said nothing. Jermaine was held longer, as he was charged with trying with violent assault towards a police officer and possession of a class B illegal substance with intent to distribute.

After two days of interrogation, Jermaine was finally bailed to appear back in court in a month's time to answer the charges brought against him. He was brought home by his mum and his half- sister Salma, and as soon as they were in the safety of the back garden (Jermaine was convinced that the police might have left listening devices in the house, as they seemed to be conducting a drug distribution operation and could get authorization to do such if they proved that it might be big), Jermaine asked his mum to tell him exactly what happened on that Friday afternoon.

"Davis came for a visit, and shortly after the police came in saying that they were looking for looking for a drug dealer in the neighborhood and asked to search the house."

"Did they have a search warrant? Did they show it to you?" asked Jermaine.

"No. They never showed me one, and I never thought to ask for it at the time, everything happened so fast, and I never had much time to think about things properly. One minute I was chatting with Davis, the next minute there were four policemen knocking loudly at the door."

"I wonder what brought them to the house and I doubt they had a warrant" said Jermaine, wondering out loud. "I have never done anything illegal or criminal that might bring any attention to the house. I wonder if they were just fishing for something and got lucky. Go on though, tell me the rest".

"Well, I thought that there was nothing to hide in the house, and so I let them in and allowed them to search. I'm really sorry about that, I should have thought about it better. Anyway, instead of searching the house, they immediately went to Davis and started searching him, and things just started getting weird after that".

"No mum, I think things were already very weird by that point. First, they come into the house without showing a warrant, and I'm sure they did not have one, then come right into the house of a guy they suspect of drug-running and the first thing they do is search Davis, almost like they knew something or rather were absolutely sure of something. What happened next?"

"They started finding small packages in Davis's coat pockets, quite a number of them, I had no idea he used that much, and as soon as the police found those packages, they took him downstairs and tried to proceed to try and search me, which is when my wits returned, and I asked why they were doing that and refused to be searched. At that point they tried to get physical with me to get me to comply, saying something about me being known as a "drug user" and my being connected to "drug gangs", which is when you came in.

"That's ok, at least I know what went on at the house now, I think they will try to scare us with police assault charges, but I don't think they have much of a case, if it is proved that they had no warrant in the first place, which is why they tried to scare me into taking a plea deal, telling me that drugs were found in my house. We just have to be patient with the legal process, just like my lawyer advised, and ride out this storm".

Jermaine and I decided that we would meet up on a weekend, and just hang out together, in a way he was one of the few people I was comfortable with after the whole Talia episode. We met up at the McDonalds in Brent Cross, got a table for two and proceeded to chat about the paths our lives had taken, our future plans and what are chances were of achieving our goals…

"So, what happened next?" I asked, as he had gone on to tell me his story about how he had gotten to this point. "What happened with the charges?"

"Well, it turned out that they had no warrant to search the house, and because they had no uniforms and not supposed to be in my house, anyway, my lawyer argued successfully that I had just reacted to the sight of two strange men attacking my mum and had backed off when they identified themselves. However,they managed to stick me with possession of a class B drug, it was cannabis that Davis was carrying, because they would have charged my mum with that and that was the only way to let her go, in the form of this plea deal. Davis was not so lucky; he got a four-year sentence for possession of a Class B drug, which is exactly what I got as well."

"However, on appeal, my lawyer managed to prove that the drugs found on the scene, were all from the same type of packaging, and since I was not in the house when the drugs were discovered on Davis, it was only logical to think that they came from the same source. That's how I got off my sentence after serving two years, but under strict conditions because of my past. Needless to say, the police were not very happy and are waiting for me to make the slightest mistake."

"Wow. So how is your family doing?" I asked.

"Right now, everybody is okay. When I was in jail, it was different. We thought we might lose our house and I was worried that my mum might move back into the estate and fall back to her old ways. But I think, when she saw what happened to me, it made her even more determined to make something of herself. She and my half-sister Salma have a contract to clean some offices, in the name of a small cleaning company they formed. They are basically looking after me now".

After that day we kept regularly in touch, always meeting up every couple of weeks. When I lost my job and needed some money, he introduced me to his mum and was added to their staff of cleaners, as they had gotten even more offices and residential apartments to clean. It was very convenient, with me not having to bother about criminal record disclosures and also being with good people.

It was on my way home from one of those cleaning jobs that I met the first lady I would talk to in almost a year. With my new job came travelling, the jobs Mary's company got were spread out through London, and the only way to get to the different locations on time was by the London over ground/ underground train network.

On my way back from a job in Ealing, West London, across the seat from me, sat a beautiful slim, raven-haired lady, sitting cross-legged in a mini skirt. I noticed her as soon as I got on the train, and also noticed that every man was looking at her. She was stunning.

To my complete surprise, when I did catch her eye, her emerald eyes locked with mine and she actually smiled, and she didn't look away either, I did. When I finished pretending to look elsewhere, and look back at her, her eyes were still there, looking at me, with a slight smile forming on her lips.

Her name was Delia.

CHAPTER ELEVEN

DELIA

One of the great things about London is its transport system, the buses that crisscross through the different sections and zones of the city, but even more important, the train network. The over ground and underground train systems were made up of routes/lines that were built at different times during the 20th century.
The one annoying thing with it, is its lack of consistency and reliability which runs across the entire network.

That annoying trait is more noticeable or less, depending on the length of time that has elapsed since that particular line was in service. For example, the Northern line which was completed in 1941 is almost consistent in its ability to have some delay or other, while the Victoria line officially opened in 1969, is so much faster and efficient. Having lived in North London for most of my time here, I had to endure "the misery line" as the Northern line was once called, because it was the quickest way to get across the area to my various work locations, especially during my early work years in London, when I worked at multiple locations in the same time period.

That line however, had nothing on the Circle line, which just seemed to have some kind of fault or delay just about every day, and delays that could take large amounts of time to put right. I am exaggerating of course, but it felt like this whenever I was using it. Unlike the Northern line that I had used because it was purpose built for the London region that I lived in and my work travel routes, this line, aptly named for its circular route (when it actually functioned optimally), was one I took to fulfil one of the genuine pleasures I had in my life at this point in time.

As I counted the stations to my destination, Euston square, Baker Street… I thought about how often I had made this exact journey over the past two months, usually forgetting about the stresses of the day or about even the seemingly never-ending journey, that it was all going to be worth it, when I looked at the beautiful woman I was going to meet at the end of my journey.

Finally pulling into Paddington Station, I followed the same path I always took, walking through the interchange walkways that connected the different underground lines that used the station, as well as the busy over ground station. The station was one of the large ones in London, like Victoria and Kings Cross but a bit smaller, where you would find fast food kiosks and other small-space business stores.

The walkway from the station, went through the side of the over ground train tracks, with trains pulling in and out. It then ended in a large square space that poured out to the main street which always seemed to have revelers or some sort of party crowd, either going into or pouring out of one of the numerous restaurants that lined the high street.

I would turn right just as the square met the high street, and just keep on walking straight down towards Delia's home, always entertained by the activity on the streets on either side of me, but never impressed enough, to ease off on my pace. Whatever it was that made them happy, whatever it was that they were celebrating, I was sure that at the end of my destination, I would have much more to celebrate than they.

As I reached the door leading to Delia's apartment, about to press the buzzer to alert her to my arrival, I thought of the circumstances that had allowed me to meet her, that night, on a late train going home.

My job had just mysteriously disappeared, soon after the trial, in the most head- scratching fashion, my crime being that having been left alone on a twelve-hour shift on a Saturday; I decided to send all excess cash in our banking facility, next door. Being that it was a directive from the head office, to get rid of all excess cash on Saturdays, due to a lack of banking facility on Sundays, it came as a shock to everyone and left me utterly devastated.

If I hadn't met Jeremy when I did, I would have surely ended up homeless; it was always going to be fairly difficult to get another job that would involve financial responsibility, once I had a criminal record and the place, I lived in was leveraged on the salary level I was on, anything substantially lower just wouldn't do. While the pay rate from Mary's cleaner contract wasn't big, there was a lot of work to be done and thus, quite a lot of money to be earned on aggregate.

Most of my days and nights, week after week, were spent trying to do as much work as I could, to pay the bills at the end of the month, with little left over for much else. I would never complain to Jeremy or Mary, but I was unhappy. I felt that something was just not quite right. The rest of my life would surely not be all about living from paycheck to paycheck, just because of this one incident. Surely, the humiliation of the trial was enough. Was I going to be continuously at a disadvantage, even when I strived at what everyone took for granted?

This was the state of thought that I was in as I sat on that train, looking around at the people in the carriage, wondering if there were any of them in the same boat as I was. People who could never, have a bank job, be a manager, or even, dream of being involved in politics, for fear of what you might have to reveal about your past.

I was thinking about how much I really wanted to be in politics, about how I would do all I could to make sure that people who had some criminal record or anything similar, would have something that allowed them not to lag behind society if they wanted to come back in and contribute, to not feel that they continuously owed the rest of society a continuous life-long apology, for wanting to live a good life, after they had served a sentence or paid some other debt to society.

That is indeed what I was thinking…until my eyes met the emerald ones of Delia,and instantly forgot how much I wanted to be the President of the United States…or was it the Prime Minister of the United Kingdom? Whatever it was, it did not matter anymore at that moment in time. At first, I thought I might be imagining things; it had after all been a long time after all, since I had even spoken to a girl, never mind…other things. If it wasn't for the "I caught you looking at me" smile on her face, I would have convinced myself that I was blowing things out of proportion.

But the smile stayed on, and her eyes continued to linger occasionally on mine, train stop after train stop, and after a while, a new anxiety arose. I was in my situation, in fact I was on this train at this hour, and due to circumstances arising from the last time I thought I'd met someone good. Sure, she looked in her twenties, but looking at her reminded me of all the things I wasn't sure I could do anymore. The things I could no longer afford; I was barely hanging on as it was; the secrets I could never reveal.

My work that night was to clean a floor of offices in Ealing Common, the kind of cleaning I didn't actually mind because the offices were generally well taken care of anyway, it was a new contract that Mary had secured through a friend who worked there, and all I needed to do was make sure the toilets were clean and all the waste, taken outside. After that, the polishing and carpet-cleaning to make sure the office was neat and tidy for the next day's business hours. The only drawback in doing the job was that I couldn't start until 9, as the office only shut at 8:30pm.I had moved out of my apartment, and moved into the spare room in Colindale, and my journey time to and from Ealing was just over an hour and a half. With my normal time to complete the work being the contracted one hour, it meant that I usually got home about 11pm.

My usual journey plan was to take the train from Ealing Common, which was on the District line, and take it all the way to Victoria station, then changeover to a Northbound Victoria line train and then finally, changeover at Euston, to the Northern line for a train home.

As we stayed on the train for the third station in a row, I knew I had to talk to her or I would never forget or forgive myself, for what might have been, if I had never tried. I anxiously started waiting for the next station and hoping that she was going my way, at least to Victoria station, it was getting late already, and I didn't want to arrive at Jermaine's house too late at night.

We pulled into Earl's Court station next, and my heart sank as I saw her start to get up and with one quick look at me, moved to the carriage doors. As the doors opened and with my pulse racing, I knew I had a decision to make, one that had to be made before those doors shut in about 30 seconds, I was going to be home late and depending on how positive a yield my next move was going to be, it might be really late, as I had no idea where she was going. Also, my stomach started churning as it realized that I had already made my decision, the type of decision that had so nearly landed me in jail, just a few short months ago.

I could already hear my father's voice and that of my primary school teachers, reminding me all those years ago "You never learn your lesson. I thought you were told never to do that again". Those statements were usually followed by an elongated twisting of my ears; large out-hanging ears that always seemed to meto have some type of enticing "pull me" effect on people, friend, or foe.

It had been a long time since I was that hesitant to speak to a lady, and sometimes I think that because I had such a short moment to think about the decision and any possible ramifications, I didn't have enough time to get scared enough to talk myself out of it. I quickly, and as calmly as possible, got up from my seat and made my way to the door just as it opened and got off on the platform, alongside her. She must have sensed me behind her as we got on the platform and turned around as if to see, who it might be. Upon seeing me, a quizzical look appeared on her face, softened a moment later by a half- smile, seemingly waiting for me to state my business.

"Hi, I'm sorry to bother you at this time…but…I …couldn't help notice you on the train, and I just wanted to say…hi".

She looked at me for a moment and then burst into a nice easy laugh that I would become accustomed to in a while, but still looked down the platform and was glad that there wasn't anyone else on the platform, at that moment. She then spoke to me with a delightful and seductive throaty voice, a voice that sounded just about as beautiful as she looked.

"I thought you were coming up to me to sign the photograph that you had taken of me in the carriage, on the way here".

"What photograph?" I asked, quite confused.

"You were looking at me for so long in there, that you had to have taken one" She explained, laughing.

"Well, I wasn't the only one looking" I countered, smiling.

"Are you claiming that I was checking you out" A sudden frown on her face.

"Oh no…I meant to say…. you…I was only joking" With a sudden dread that I was about to blow this thing.

But the frown disappeared just about as quick as it had come, and she smiled mischievously, “I was just messing with you, I think you are going to be easy to….eh, what is the term for it, cross-up?”

“I think you mean, mess about” I said smiling again,” My name is Obi, but what may I call you?”

“My name is Delia. Are you really going in my direction as well or are you stalking me now? She asked, with that mischievous look playing up again in her eyes.

“Well,” with a happy confidence, starting to creep in, “I was supposed to continue on with that train to Victoria Station, and from there, get on trains that would take me to Colindale.”

“Colindale...? Where is that?”

“It’s up in north London, quite some distance away from here. I know that we have only just met and that you hardly know me, but I knew that if I did not try and introduce myself to you, I might never get that chance ever again. I don’t know how polite it is of me to ask for your number or anything, but I will like the chance to see you again sometime, so that I get a chance to tell you more about me, if that is, okay?”

“Where are you going now, are you in a hurry?” She asked.

“No, no. I just didn’t want to inconvenience you”.

“What do you mean by that…Oh I get it; my English is still improving…No, what I mean is that. You say that you were going to Victoria Station? Well, I can’t just give you my number just like that. What I will do is take you up to that station and then we can separate and go our different ways. I’ll decide there, if I want to give you, my number.” This last bit was said with a slight smile, which made me want to know her even more. “So, you have to really impress me, and your time starts now, just like in the game shows. No?” she continued, smiling.

I started telling her about me, just as the next train going towards Victoria, got to our platform. The next few stops to Victoria Station went by too quickly, just like everything that is nice and that you enjoy, seems to. I told her that I was coming from work but told her that my friends and I had contracts to look after office spaces across the city, under a company that we formed together. She frowned slightly but let me continue. I told her my name, and about its ethnic origins and meaning, which was “heart”.

We got to Victoria shortly after, and as we got up to leave, she looked at me and said, “You lied to me about your work and ordinarily, I wouldn’t bother, and would just not see you again. But there was this sadness I saw in your face, when you were talking about it. It was like… there is something, you can’t yet tell me. There is nothing to be ashamed about, if you are cleaning places, at least not with me. I used to do that when I first came to London.”

“It’s not necessarily shame Delia, but I do want to impress you. There are reasons that I am the way I am now, but I want to look the best I can be, in your eyes. I’m sorry for lying” I put my hand out to shake hers, and started to turn, as if to leave, thinking about how I could never win, when she spoke again.

“It looks like in addition to not being open; you also don’t listen very well. I said that ORDINARILY, I would not bother about you again. Obviously, I am thinking about making an exception. What is the matter with you? You’re not good at taking hints as well?”

“No” I said, with a tight smile, “I just don’t want to disappoint anyone else, especially someone that I think, or rather that I know, I am going to like…very much. But still, I would very much like the chance to try to impress you, somehow”.

“Disappoint me? Obviously, you have some issues. I have problems here as well,but I deal with them and don’t carry them around with me for the whole world to see. I think you are a nice guy, but may be if we meet again, you will have a more, shall we say, uplifting manner.”

With that, she shook my hand, and walked off down the platform, probably looking to get a connecting train to wherever she was going. Dejected and defeated, I walked in the opposite direction, looking for my own connecting train, home.

I spent the rest of that weekend and most of the following

week, replaying the entire episode in my mind, wondering where I might have gone wrong. Maybe I thought, I looked too hard or was too flippant in my manner, thinking I was already on my way to a spectacular "catch". She maybe thought that I might have been over-confident at times. But, as I continued to remember that night in detail, I started to think about the things that she had said, and take a look at myself, from her perspective.

She had mentioned something about my demeanor. I seemed to remember her saying something about me not being the only one who had problems, and not having to carry them around everywhere. This got me thinking, "Why did she notice, anyway?" Maybe there was something there, she probably thought that I might be lying about something major, and she was right on that count, even though she might not guess how major.

There was no way that I could tell her about the things that happened to me in the prior months, but I realized that I didn't want to be by myself anymore. Even if I wasn't yet ready to thoroughly confide in anyone, I still wanted someone close. I wanted a girlfriend. I wanted someone like Delia. I had always been attracted to strong, beautiful women. Women, who spoke their mind but still, had a good heart, and I suspected that Delia had these qualities, with the way she observed me on the train that night, and I desperately wanted a second chance to try and woo her again. But this was London, and you never got those sorts of chances, in a city of its size. The odds were just too great.

Mary and I had decided to divide up the cleaning jobs that we had, with me being the younger person and with probably less responsibilities (or maybe less of a social life and circle), having to take up the jobs that were a bit further out of north London, while she primarily dealt with the ones closer to home.

The only cleaning jobs we got outside North London were located in Ealing, and so I came to agreement with Mary, that I would take care of the Ealing end of our work schedule. I didn't really mind the travelling, I hardly went out much now anyway, and I relished the opportunity to travel and see different people every time I went out. I guess it was a substitute for going out, for me.

The work that followed the travelling did not really take much away from me physically. Maybe it took away some of my pride, based on the fact, that for all my years of study, I had somehow managed to wind up, having to clean toilets and wash dishes, to make a living, and to survive. Physically not a problem, but emotionally and psychologically, humbling.

I also didn't mind the fact that I worked in relative silence, with virtually no one else around most of the time. I actually preferred to work alone, that way I didn't have to share my feeling of despondence with anyone else. Whatever shame or impotent feeling that I harbored; I was always glad that no one else knew about itor could see me do the work that I did now.

After I had met Delia, the previous week though, the only thing that I thought about was how I was going to see her again. I became more aware of my timing in the building. The contract stated that we would be paid on a fixed hourly rate for every day that we cleaned the office, and we were allotted two hours every night between Monday and Friday to get the job done.

I never really bothered that much about finishing on time, as I had the keys and access to the office, and could get in and out on my own, without need of assistance from a third party. But now however, I made sure that I finished within the one hour that I was contracted to, not just because that was the contracted duration within which my work was actually paid for, but because I actually wanted to be on my homebound train by ten minutes past ten at the very latest.

The night I met Delia; I was certain that I remembered getting on a train at about that exact time. After I had spent the next night on my way home from work, standing at the platform for a few minutes longer (okay maybe it was a little longer than that), hoping to catch another glimpse of Delia sitting in a carriage on her way home, I decided that I would not stand on the platform hoping for another glance of the face I so wanted to see again. No. Instead, I would make sure that I would be on the train that left the platform at around 1015pm. It was a one in a million shot that I would ever see her again, probably a fruitless and hopeless task, but at least it was better than standing on a platform looking hopeless to anyone who had the pleasure of passing through that station consistently at that very time, night after night.

I did just that, exactly. Night after night, I would stay for about 15mins on that platform, sitting in the middle of the platform, and at other times, sit at the end of the platform where I knew that the train would appear out of first. All of this being my strategy for seeing the most carriages on the incoming trains and, in my mind, the best chance of catching a glimpse of Delia.

This went on for about three weeks, with me convincing myself that this strategy, or rather, this fantasy of mine, was sustainable. Eventually though, it dawned on me that this was a hopeless quest, that the only way that I would see Delia again was, if it was fated to be that way.

My "underground misadventures" though, had other consequences. Where, over the past year I had learned to insulate myself from society, and feel comfortable doing that, now, I started looking back through my old cell phone contacts, looking for old girlfriends or acquaintances that I had in the past. I wasn't quite sure what I was trying to accomplish when I started, but I began calling them up,starting up conversation, however perfunctory.

They never led to much more, maybe a visit or rendezvous arranged just to talk, I never had quite realized or remembered how much my female friends had talked to me, but obviously they had remembered, and while like I said, the meetings and visits hadn't led to much, it kind of let some of myself, my old self that I thought I'd forgotten about and barely remembered, back into the present.

For the first also, I became aware of the singles and adult adverts at the back of the local newspaper. I'd seen them before, but there was so much going on in mylife; work, relationships, friends and all types of new people to talk to and get to know. Now, I was just curious or maybe I was just looking for the easiest way to find company. Whatever the reason was, I started calling the numbers in those adverts randomly.

The first time I actually called was on a Saturday, one of the rare Saturday's when there wasn't an office or building to clean. The number had been listed on the page advert as belonging to the "butterflies massage agency" and a lady whom I assumed was the receptionist, picked up the phone.

I was polite as I could be, which I always was generally, but on this occasion, I wasn't quite sure what to say or ask for. The receptionist seemed to realize that I was new to this quite quickly and tried to assure me that everything was alright and not out of the ordinary and promised to do her best to "accommodate" me.

First though, she wanted to know what I was looking for exactly. What type of girl? Did I want her to visit my place, and if so, at what time? She then proceeded to describe the ladies that they had available that night; white, black, East European, tall. I wasn't sure who wanted, and so she recommended an East European girl named Eva. She then took my name and number and said she would get the girl to call me.

The call came about five minutes later. Her voice was part deep-throated and part-raspy, that distinctive Slavic East-European kind of accent, that commanded or demanded attention, but still very sexy at the same time…

"My name is Eva, what's your name and how are you doing tonight" she asked.Thinking fast about for whatever reason, not wanting to give my name, I replied.

"My name is David and it's nice to meet you too. I'm sorry for bothering you…I saw the number of your agency in the paper... and I called".

"This is your first time calling the agency?" she asked with a small laugh and a hint of excitement and surprise in her voice.

"Yes" I said suddenly wondering what I was doing, but nonetheless, very excited that I was about to meet someone. There was this thrill of excitement about not knowing about not knowing what was going to happen exactly next.

"Okay David, what do you want to do tonight?"

Suddenly, there was this confusing fear that went through my mind. What exactly did I want to do tonight? I hadn't really thought about it in exact terms…

"I'm wearing a short black skirt, a white sleeveless top and black open toe high heel and I can be with you in the next forty-five minutes, if you want me to come over to your place."

I wasn't confused anymore all of a sudden; I didn't know the exact details of what would want to happen that night, but I knew I wanted her to come over.

"I would like you to come over… you sound quite nice".

"Well, thank you. You sound like a nice guy too. How old are you, if I may ask?""I am 32".

"Where are you from? You have an accent that isn't British but sounds really nice. I can't really place it and I've been wondering about it since we started talking."

"I'm British-born, but I'm of Nigerian parentage and grew up there as well."

"Okay. I knew you sounded a bit different, but it does sound nice though. I am Romanian myself and I'm sure you can hear my own accent".

"Yes" I said laughing now, "I heard it and it sounds really nice, and I mean that. It's nice to meet you, Eva."

"It's nice to meet you too, David. Okay, I guess you want to see me? How long will you want me to stay?"

The receptionist I spoke to earlier, had told me the price that I had to pay for companionship, depending on how long I would want her to stay. What we did with the time was entirely up to us.

"One hour, I think. Is that all right?"

"Yeah, that's fine. It's about 7:30pm now; I should be there by about 8:15pm. Once you give me your address, you will need to call back the lady at the reception desk, who you spoke to earlier, to tell her that I have been booked by you."

With that the conversation ended and I proceeded to call back the receptionist, to finalize the arrangement, and then wait for Eva to arrive. For some reason I made the bed and tidied the room like I would do, if I was expecting a real girlfriend to arrive for a real date. My room was on the ground floor of the house and was accessed through the side of the house, by a sliding glass door. It had been renovated this way to allow for access by the occupant without necessarily using the front door to the house. I'm pretty sure that this had been done Jermaine's benefit, but now it suited my purposes nicely, as I didn't need anyone else to know about the "event" that was about to take place tonight.

I had also told the receptionist that Eva was to call me as soon as she arrived, so that I could direct her as to which entrance, she would take.

She promptly arrived at 8:15pm, a Volvo Saloon probably black or some other dark color but couldn't tell with the lack of natural light at that time of the night.The driver had called my phone from a bit further down the street, just as I had asked. I had been on the lookout since about 8:00pm from my window and had seen the car go by a few minutes before slowly, and then come to a stop just past the house, just like it would, if the driver had just spotted the house number, he was looking for. So, I was ready when the call came, after the car had continued down the street and then reversed direction. I told the driver, what entrance to come towards, after she passed through the little gate at the front.

Eva came through the gate wearing a black fur coat that came to her knees.I could see her approach from my window perch and got up to open the glass sliding door before she got there. "Hello Eva?" I said, like there might be some doubt, but I hadn't seen her before anyway and it was the first thing that came tomy mind to say, anyway.

"Hi David" she replied, as she dresses exactly as she said she was. The black skirtstopped around her thighs and revealed a pair of shapely, long legs. I would say she was about 5'7, with raven dark hair, an oval face with high cheekbones and a certain glint in her green eyes.

She looked around the room, at the lone chair, and then back at me with an unspoken question, understanding what she was trying to say, I immediately motioned her towards the wooden chair that I had slightly pulled out from my reading table. With it being the only chair in the room, the only other place to sit on was on the bed, which is where I sat down.

"You look very stunning, Eva. I think you were being modest when youwere describing yourself" I said as she settled into the chair, cross-legged.

"Thank you, David" she replied laughing, her eyes sparking. "Did you say that you wanted to me to stay for an hour?" Gently bringing us back to the business at hand with a cursory look at her watch which immediately made me realize that, for what she was doing, every minute counted.

"Yes" I said, "I agreed to see you for one hour, should I pay you now?"

She smiled immediately "Yes, of course. I forgot it's your first time. It's always best that way, and besides, I have to confirm with the driver and the office, that I have received the money, to make sure everything is alright."

I handed over the money that I had withdrawn from the nearby cash point and watched her count it, wondering about my next step of action. She finished counting, put it in her bag and then proceeded to call the "office" and her driver that everything was above board. She had taken her coat off earlier, and now she looked at me...

"What would you want me to do, David? I do kiss and sex with a condom..."

I barely heard most of she said next or recognized the terms of expression that she brought up; code names for sexual acts, I would later learn. But at that moment, I didn't quite know what I wanted her for. I had a beautiful lady in my room, but I knew instantly that I didn't want to have sex with her, definitely not with some one that I had just met for the first time. So, the question was what to do exactly?

"I can tell that you are slightly nervous, and its fine, we can talk in the meantime.How old did you say that you were again?"

"I'm 32"

"You look 27" she said.

"Thanks, am sure you'll still look 23 when you get to my age" I replied with a laugh.

She laughed right back, settling back into the chair, re-crossing her legs and I noticed that she was wearing some kind of stocking, for the first time. She really had nice legs…

"You like my legs?" she asked, with a mischievous look on her face, snapping me out of my thoughts. I only then realized, red-faced, that I had been starring.

"Yeah… they are really… um...nice. Sorry if I was staring."

She laughed again, with those green eyes twinkling, got up from the chair and walked slowly to the bed, where I sat, sat down next to me and crossed her legs again , watching me all the time.

I couldn't take my eyes off her, and I knew that she was looking at me and that this was a tease, solely for my benefit. No one had done that for me before, and I think my excitement palpable, even if I wasn't exactly going into meltdown mode,but I'm sure that she could tell. I was looking into her eyes now, and she without now, without breaking her gaze, sought out my hand and took it in hers, then drewmy hand to her thigh and knee, rubbing it along and across her stockings.

"Do you like that" she asked, and then taking off her shoes, she turned towards me, so that she was sitting across from me on the bed, with her thighs across mine.She then raised her knees and crossed her legs again, looking at my face all the time.

I was aroused now and rubbing my hands on her legs and feet. She was smiling widely now, and I kissed her lightly on the cheek, just about the same time as she tucked her foot into my crotch, gently rubbing.

"I think you might have a foot fetish" she stated matter-of-factly, still smiling.

"It is supposed to be the fetish of the intellectual. Are you highly educated? I mean like going through university, postgraduate and everything? You're not about to tell me that you are a type of young professor or something? Sorry for being so direct" she said laughing softly; clearly enjoying the effect that she was having on me.

I barely cared anyway, with the way her foot was moving, along my penis and crotch area; I had unzipped to relieve the pressure; gently moving her foot at a quicker pace, every few moments. I had known that I wouldn't have sex with Evain the conventional sense, but right then, I also had no doubt that in a few minutes, and I was still going to be satisfied, one way or another…

"Yes, I went to university and everything" I said, a bit relieved that I wasn't doing something weird or strange, but still enjoying myself massively, nonetheless.
However, I was starting to feel guilty that, I was the only one being satisfied and thinking that maybe, I should do something…

"What do you like, Eva? I mean, is there something I could do to please you insome way? I'm feeling really… happy because of you; it's only fair that I do something in return?"

"Shush, it's okay David." She said, still stroking me with her foot, but seemingly on second thought, or perhaps seeing the unconvinced look in my eyes, she started to unbutton her top and motioning me over with a smile "Maybe, you can rub my breasts a little, but like I said, it's okay, you don't need to. I'm here for you…

I rubbed her breasts and then kissed them gently, looking at her face every few moments to see if it was alright. She noticed, and maybe as a way of encouragement, she pulled my head closer in, for a few moments allowing me to gently suck on her nipples. Then she suddenly got up, gently pushed me down that so that I was now lying down on the bed, face up. She then rolled off her stockings and then took me between her feet, moving them up and down, until I came.

"Do you have tissues" she asked, almost like nothing had just happened. "Or actually, never mind. I have quite a bit right here" she said, reaching into her bag,on the floor right next to the bed.

As we cleaned up after ourselves, an awkward short silence ensured, especially as I wasn't sure what to do next. I offered her use of the bathroom, which she took. I looked at my watch,8:45pm, what was I was supposed to do with the extra 30mins. I realized that we could probably do some other type of pleasurable act, if I so desired. But somehow, I thought it a little rude… what the hell? Why was I feeling guilty about having sex with a lady, I had just paid?

She came out of the bathroom smiling, and then I realized why I was having conflicting thoughts. I wanted to know more about her, not just as a client that she had during the night. I guessed that maybe, a lot of other men had tried the same thing, but there wasn't any harm in trying, seeing that there was more than half an hour to spare.

First though, as she sat back on the bed, I excused myself and went to properly clean up in the bathroom too. I asked if she needed to go, after I got back out, to which she replied that she would stay as long as I wanted her to.

"How long have you lived in England" I asked.

"I've lived here for just over three years now, but I will be leaving to go back to Romania, in about a year's time."

"Why?"

"It's just time for me to go, I want to buy a house back home and live, and maybestart a business, something good and nice. I have been doing this thing for three years now and I don't want to do it much longer. I want to start the next stage of my life, sooner rather than later."

"That's really nice and good luck too. I hope everything works out well. For me,It's a pity though, I was hoping to see you again sometime…"

"We can still do that. I have about a year still to go, before I leave." She then got her phone out of her bag, saying as she did that, "This is my personal phone number. I like you, and if you want to meet up, just call me on this number, and we can meet up. You will still pay me (a smile appearing on her lips), but not as muchas you were paying through the agency, and even then, only if I am free. My first obligation is to the agency, and I can only do what I do if I am not interfering with my agreed schedule with the agency. I suspect that you are not rich" she said laughing, "But you look like a nice guy, so when you can, give me a ring."

That was so perfect; I thought I might be dreaming. I knew that I couldn't really afford to see her for quite a while, but I knew I definitely wanted to see her again. This arrangement was the best I could have hoped for, and as the hour time-limit wound down, I kissed her on the cheek and we agreed to the arrangement that she had proposed, promising to see one another again.

As I watched her car drive off, I was filled with a terrible feeling of loneliness,and the house felt just really empty, but as I slept and remembered the events that had taken place just a short while before, a satisfied smile played on my lips and I slept easily and peacefully, for the first time in months.

***

We met a few more times over the next couple of months, always at my place, but after a while, the excitement of the first night gradually wore off. I think I eventually realized that I was basically just paying for the hope of a relationship that's never going to materialize. It wasn't about me being tired of casual sex, kissing and the close proximity of a beautiful woman. No, I wanted more. A lot more than a few encounters, when I could afford. A lot more than trying to, save as much money as I could every month, so that I could try to see her as regularly as I could. A lot more, than feeling so alone immediately after being so happy, in animated conversation and embrace, with Eva.

It had nothing to do with Eva. She had promised me nothing other than, the chance to meet up and be together for what whatever period possible. She had a plan for her life, and she was happy with it. I also eventually realized that I was one of a number of men helping her get to where she wanted to be eventually, in a mutually beneficial way. I wanted a relationship without limits or restrictions. ButI still wanted somehow, the thrill I felt the first time I met Eva.

Eva left the country about six months later, to go home to Romania. I didn't get to see much of her in those final few weeks, partly as I still had the rest of my life problems to deal with and sort out; money, housing, work (something professional). I was starting to feel uncomfortable with my living arrangements.

When I had no "relationships" or visitors and not much interaction with anyone outside of Jermaine's family, such things as privacy, personal space and convenience hadn't mattered, but my clandestine meetings with Eva had changed that and made me hanker for those small privileges and think about the future.

After I realized the fallacy of waiting for a relationship to happen with Eva, I decided not to tie myself down to fantasy. I still wanted to meet women, but I wanted those meetings to have a chance, no matter how little, of growing into something more. I started calling the agency numbers again. This time though, I knew about the ones that had an online presence, with pictures of their ladies displayed.

The cleaning business that Mary ran had grown a little bit in the last few months,and with it, my disposable income. It allowed me some extra flexibility in my spending habits, and while I couldn't and wouldn't go crazy, it meant that I didn't need to wait weeks or months, in-between "dates" now.

I chose girls that looked like Eva, inevitably. She was a very beautiful woman, and while our arrangement had not been what I really wanted, she had been quite nice to me, and I had always enjoyed her friendly banter, calm demeanor and sharp intellect.

I had become aware of the online agencies through Eva. During some of the periods when we stayed together, and either we didn't do anything sensual or very little , depending on the way I felt, we would pass the time by surfing the internet, checking out interesting things to entertain ourselves with. On those few occasions she would confide in me, some more private details about her life.
Apparently, she was not exclusive to the "butterflies' agency". She was listed on few others as well, under different names of course. The difference was all the others were online and had her pictures on them.

She tried to look different on each with different hairstyles and angles. It said a lot about the rapport between us, that she trusted me enough, to want to show me which sites and her profiles…or maybe she just didn't care if I knew…

The online sites had pictures and statistical descriptions of dozens of girls, from different nationalities, all very beautiful with ages ranging from 18-35. Most of the girls were of East- European origin, and as Eva explained to me, had usually the same journey pattern that got her into the "world's oldest trade". Eva had worked for as long as she did, to pay off the debt she owed to the people that had made it possible for her to get here. Her main goal was to make as much as she could for herself after she paid her debt, but she still had to give the agency a percentage, every time she saw a client. Whatever was left was used to pay her rent, at the apartment that had been procured for her at a price, and then living expenses and savings. This was why she tried to get clients that she could trust to come to her personally, just so that she could keep more of the money herself and speed up the path to her target.

It was cheaper to go to the places of the girls on the online agencies, than it was getting them to come down to mine. This meant journeys into central London, which I didn't mind at all. There had never been much need for me to go into that area, through most of my time in London, apart from the odd "club-night" or shopping trip, and these had largely occurred in my earlier time here. So, it was a welcome distraction for me, having to learn my way around places like Marylebone and Earls Court. I rarely ever saw the same girl twice. There was always something not quite right with them. The girls were beautiful, mostly brunette, but sometimes blonde. Whereas with Eva, I had waited for a relationship to take form, this time I had lost that naiveté, and generally could tell if there could be anything more if we would "meet" again.

This pattern went on for a while, with me looking for something, not finding it,but at the same time, not quite sure what or whom I was looking for, until about three months after I had last seen Eva.

I had called up a new agency that I hadn't used before, and looked through their site, looking fora lady that might catch my eye. I saw one that I thought I liked, slim and raven-haired. She had her hair cover about half her face, but I could see her eyes had an emerald color.

I thought her face reminded me of someone I had seen before, which is probably why I chose her. She had the look of the girls I usually wanted to see; beautiful, slim, dark haired and of good height.

As was custom, I got the address to go to in Paddington, from the receptionist,after she had confirmed the lady's availability and time. The lady went by the name of Mia, according to the site page description, and after I had dressed andcleaned up, I left for work.

My plan was to do my cleaning jobs for the day quickly, which started at 5:30pm.They were all located in East London, Stratford, Ilford and Canning Town. Unlikesome places that I had cleaned, they provided their own cleaning equipment, which meant that I wouldn't have to carry mine around, from job to job. All I had to do was carry a bag with my cleaning clothes, use them at the job sites, and when I was finished, put back on my evening clothes, with a dab of perfume. I always liked to look presentable, when I went on any of these "dates".

The offices at Ilford and Canning Town were the furthest away and also the easiest to clean. They were on the small side in comparison to some office spaces that I had worked in, and I believed that I could do both within the allotted of one hour for each one and then travel to Stratford with fifteen minutes to spare.

You always out-do yourself when you are motivated to do something, and I was in the Stratford office by 7:50pm. It was twice the office space in either Ilford or Canning Town and had a time allocation of an hour and half. I had arranged to see Mia at 10:45pm, thinking that would be enough time for me to finish my work and travel all the way to Paddington.

I finished up at 9:15pm having thoroughly gone through the entire office. One of the reasons that we got retained by our clients was the fact that, I always liked to do my responsibilities well, whether at home or work, and people always appreciate that. So, while I was pretty fast doing the job that night, it was still done well.

There was still ample time for me to get to Paddington from Stratford by 9:15, for my meeting with Mia at 10:45. I took my time to change into my evening clothes and freshen up and get going towards the Stratford Underground Station. The route I had to take was fairly straight forward. The Central Line on the

London Underground Network ran through the Stratford Station. It was probably the second fastest lines of the London Underground, behind the Victoria Line. I took the westbound train from Stratford, all the way through to Notting Hill Gate Station, literally about a half-hour journey. I then switched on to the Edgware Road bound District Line train, which was towards the other end of the scale for speed, compared to the Central Line.

I got to Paddington Station, with about twenty minutes to spare, after which, came the problem of trying to find the address itself. I had been told that it wasn't far from the station, and after I had gone in the wrong direction twice, I finally located the street.

The house number was a bit further down the street, and locating it wasn't easy at 10:40pm, with poorly lit doorways and numbers jumping from one side of the street to another. Finally, I found the door with an intercom system next to it. The number I was given had been 22, and a female voice answered, when I pressed the buzzer on the intercom.

"Hello?"

"It's David; I'm here to see Mia?"

"Okay" she replied, and I could hear the buzzer mechanism that opened the door, as the intercom connection cut out.

I walked through the door, into a corridor, with doors along either side, and as I glanced at the numbers on the doors, I remembered the apartment number that I was going to and instinctively realized that it would have to be a room upstairs. I climbed up the first flight of stairs I found towards the end of the corridor.

Apartment 22 was a bit further down the second-floor corridor and I knocked on the door a moment after getting to it. A lady opened the door, in a white bra and lingerie, with black stockings and open-toe high heel slippers. Her green eyes looked at me quizzically at first, as if she thought that she might have seen me before. A range passed through me as well, first shock and surprise, and then ting of embarrassment, as I realized immediately who it was standing half-naked, right before my eyes.

“Hello David, nice to meet you”, she said, as she ushered me inside, “Have we met before? I feel like I have met you somewhere.”

“Yes, we have, but not here. But I’m glad to see you again, anyway” I answered,and seeing the questioning look in her eyes, I thought it best to re-introduce myself, with sudden feeling of relief and happiness, filling my mind…

“Hello Delia….”

CHAPTER TWELVE

There are a number of things that change through life, things that happen that you never knew were there, things in your life and character, shaped by or brought through events and people you meet. I had never been on a date or relationship with an East-European lady before I met Eva, or knew I had any particular preferences when it came to sexual activity. I had never spoken to any Caucasian lady that I hadn't previously known on the street. My slightly muscular build, always seemed to set off THAT startled look, that strange black men with unknown intentions get sometimes, and I never wanted to talk to anyone that had that look. I saw that look as one that fronted misconceptions, and those misconceptions were dangerous and hazardous for a black man, if caught in the wrong place and time, especially in a foreign land.

The first white lady I met, who didn't have that look in her eyes, even though I was a complete stranger, was Delia, the first time I saw her on that train platform.

As I lay on Delia's bed, looking at my watch now as she showered, I thought about how far we had come in the past few weeks, during which we had begun to see each other regularly…

"What do you want to do?"

This was the first thing that Delia said to me, after we got into her room. I sat down on the bed that she had directed me to, trying hard not to smile, or worse, laugh at the turn of events. It wouldn't have been laughter because I found the situation funny, but laughter of happiness and relief. It was my thinking that I lost her that had first put me in a spiral of depression. That missed opportunity made me realize how lonely I was and led me to desperately seek human companionship. That search for human companionship had ironically led me in a circle, right back to her.

I also realized that during the search, I had been able to find something of myself,which was important, to help me appreciate her more and understand what I mightwant in a relationship.

"You don't need to pretend now" she continued, "You came

here to be with me,so we might as well start. It's your time and money that you are wasting".

I could tell that she wasn't really comfortable with me, in fact, I felt certain that if she knew who I was when the arrangements were being made, she would have definitely refused to see me.

"Please don't be angry with me or anything. You are right, I came here for some form of companionship tonight, but I'm definitely not wasting my time right now.I thought I would never see you again, after the night when we spoke at that train station, and I can't believe that we met and am really glad."

Comprehension dawned in her eyes as she gradually remembered and recognized me, and I could see her start to relax a little, even if she hadn't let down her guard.

"I remember our conversation now, I don't remember the details, but I rememberthat it didn't end well. But still, what do you want to do now? I have someone else coming here in about 50mins." She said that last sentence, looking me dead in the eye, like she was trying to shock me, implicitly trying to convey a message that said that she had seen and done it all and didn't care what I knew or thought aboutit.

I had been thinking about how to approach her in this situation. I wanted to see her again, but under slightly different circumstances, or at least, if those circumstances wouldn't change straight away, the groundwork for that change would have been laid.

The problem was how would I lay down that groundwork or effect a change? Myfirst instinct was to try and continue or bridge the conversation that we had started about a year ago. Tell her everything about myself including the things I couldn't bring myself to tell her back then. Basically, trying to do the things I would do normally, when I met a lady for the first time, show my good side and potential.

Then I realized two things. First, I was sitting on a bed, in an apartment building about to complete a transaction for sexual companionship. This wasn't a normal situation far from it, so every normal thing I usually did, had to be out the window.

The second thing I thought about was, Delia was exposed, and not just physically,but her whole personality in my eyes. I knew things about her now that I wouldn't normally know. I felt in that moment, as long as that situation remained unbalanced as it, things could never progress properly between us.

The only way that situation could be remedied or balanced out, was if I exposed myself to her so that she could see me for everything that I was. This wasn't hard. I was right in her apartment, in the process of a transaction…

"Well, we have got about an hour, so we might well do something then" I said.

"Yeah, like you didn't want to do something all along" said Delia, "So what would you want to do, as in, what were you thinking about doing here before you knew that it was I, that you were seeing tonight?"

She had a stern- like look on her face, which initially worried me, until I remembered that she mischievously pulled faces the night we first met, to throw me off-balance, and wondered if she might be doing the same thing now, while actually looking for a reaction from me. It was the small glint in her eyes that made me wonder if her curiosity was aroused, and that maybe this was as good a chance that I was going to get, to make a good first impression the second time around. What could be the safest, least intimate, but still erotic request that I could make? Then I smiled…

"You have really nice legs" I said, looking at her thoroughly and very obviously.She was sitting right next time to me now, on the bed.

"Is this what you really wanted to do tonight" she asked, "You don't need to pretend for my benefit. You are already in my bedroom and…. actually, you haven't paid me yet. You are here for the hour, right?"

"Yes", I said, as I handed over the money, all £150, as I had been informed by the receptionist. "Do you remember the night, when I first saw you?"

"Not really", she replied, as she counted my money to ascertain that I had paid the right amount.

"Well, you wore a short dress on the train that day, and it was your legs and your beautiful eyes that attracted my attention. When you decided that you didn't really want to know me, it hurt me in a way that I didn't quite understand, then. I had been through a lot, at the time. I thought that I had an unbelievable opportunity to meet someone nice and then just like that, you were gone. I came to that station every day after work for days, until it became clear that I wouldn't see you again. After a while, I started to look for girls that looked like you, in a way, which is how I ended up here, I think".

"So, I am the one to blame for you seeking to pay for sex? Is that how you want to justify this scene, right now?"

"No, I'm just saying I have been looking for someone like you, because I thought that I would never see you again. This is not the first, second or even third time. I don't blame you; this is my fault. All I'm saying is… I was looking for a pair of mischievous green eyes, a beautiful smile and the best pair of legs that I'd seen inmy life, all of which I thought I would never see again".

She smiled then, she had finished counting the money, and had come back to sit beside me on the bed. I made a motion to move my hand across to her crossed legs but hesitated for a second and looked up to her for some kind of permission to proceed, which she gave with a slow nod. As I touched her thigh, she asked,

"You want me to take the rest of my clothes off now?"

"No, I'd rather you stay the way you are. I rarely ever have sex, when I am on one of these visits. In fact, I have only ever had sex with one person, the first girl I met, on my very first "time. Her name was Eva."

"She sounds like she was a great lady."

"Yes, she was. But more importantly, she understood me and was great company for me during one of the worst periods of my life, if not the worst. She didn't stay long, and she wasn't obligated to me, but she gave me her time and I was always grateful for that."

"Did you love her?"

"In the end, I think, probably not. I realized that I wasn't the only person seeing her and definitely not the only person who might tell her that they were in love. But most tellingly I think was that her plans for life never changed. She had planned to leave for home when she had acquired a certain amount of money, and even though we had some semblance of a relationship for a while, she never discussed any future scenario that I might be a part of, and I grew to realize that would always be the way it was going to be with us. So yes, I didn't love her, I knew what the score was, but she was the right person for that exact time in my life. She isn't here in the U.K. anymore, but we weren't really communicating much at that point, anyway. I think I also knew that maybe with the way we met, there would be no future in it."

With that I stood up. "Whatever, you feel about tonight, I am really glad I got to see you again. I don't really want to do much of anything. But I thought I'd never see you again, and the fact that I have is more satisfying than anything that could have happened tonight."

"You are leaving because of the way you found me. You came here tonight, looking for company and some fulfilment. Now, without doing anything apart from stroking my thighs, you're satisfied. Are you ashamed or are you disappointed in me, because either way, I don't really care? Just don't cover it up in fanciful words, for my benefit."

Delia said this with anger in her eyes and a slightly raised voice. It was virtually the same look that she had, all those months ago, when we first met and talked in that train station, when she thought, quite rightly, that I was either lying or holding something back. I thought she looked like the most beautiful thing in theworld, at that very moment…

"Believe me Delia, when I tell you that shame, is the very last thing that I feel for you right now. Right now, I think you are the most beautiful woman in the world, not just because of your physical presence, but the way you talk, the honesty, the passion and fearlessness. Sometimes I wish I had always shown those qualities, and I see now the second time around, confirmation of what I probably noticed all those months ago. That honesty, confidence and fearlessness is as attractive as your vivacious beauty."

"The only regret I have is that I wish I had met you again under different circumstances, not because I feel any kind of shame or reproach towards you, but because, I think the circumstances that contrived to make this reunion possible, will also make it impossible for us to remain in contact or have a future relationship, which I would dearly like to have, just like it happened with Eva. Thatis my regret".

"I am not Eva" Delia said with a sudden smile, "And at this moment, I can't see any possible relationship with you, anyway."

"Will it be okay, if I asked you out sometime" I asked.

"That depends".

"Depends on what?"

"If you plan to continue frequenting my kind of business and if you are going to be judgmental and bothersome, about what I do?"

"You do realize that if I truly want to be with you, I will eventually try everything to make sure that you were with me always?"

"I wouldn't be surprised but it will only be done on my terms. Agreed?"

"Deal." I said smiling broadly. "Can I ask you out tomorrow evening, then?"

"Don't be cheeky, now. I don't really like guys that are a little too confident." But she was still smiling, and the tiny mischievous glint was back in her eyes. "But you can try again sometime next week, maybe?"

"I never got your number the first time; I would like to be rather more successful,in getting it this time." I said still smiling broadly "By the way, I'm not being cheeky or overconfident, I'm just really happy."

"Give me your phone" she said as she took the cheap Nokia phone that I had always carried, just a newer one of the old version 3410. I refused to be a part of the new cultural phenomenon of buying "the latest high tech" phone, that would become "obsolete" in about six months, because a newer version was on its way,either made by the same company or another. A commercial rat race of being the ones to have the "latest" thing, a race I had always refused to run.

"This is my number, please don't call in the evening and late afternoon and expect an answer, for now. I would prefer you sending me text. It was good to see you again too" With a smile, she said "I just remembered that you were the first person that I gave my real name to the first time I'd met them, and I don't think I've done it since."

With that, she went to put her clothes back on, we said our goodbyes and I left. As I got home, the usual pang of loneliness, failed to materialize. I usually felt it after I had been home by myself for a while, either after a visit by a lady or after I had gotten home from a travelling out to meet a lady.

The feeling would usually stay with me until I was about to sleep or until I allowed the memories of the encounter to overwhelm me. But tonight nothing, I took a bath and lay down to sleep confusingly content. There were no memories to overwhelm me, except the sensation I felt when I touched her thigh, for the very first time. No, I was content, alone in my bed but happy for the first time in ages, with the thoughts of the things to come in the future with Delia, a future confirmed with the scant physical evidence of an eleven-digit number. Delia's…

Our first date was to see a movie, a cinema date. We met up in Leicester Square, to watch a movie but decided to arrive and meet up half an hour early, just so we could chat for a little while before the start of the movie. She wasn't working that night, and so we chose an 8pm showing of "Dances with Wolves" which was on a limited run at the Mezzanine cinema in the square. We strolled around the square,checking out the revelers in the square, which was bustling with activity, as it always did at this time of day. There were teams of tourists and locals moving around the square, from one restaurant, theatre or cinema to another, or just passing through and enjoying the sights.

By silent accord, we didn't ask about work, either mine or hers. But she did ask where I was going to or coming from, the night that she saw me for the very first time. So, I began to tell her my story, about all the things that had happened to me in the last two years. I told her all the things that I couldn't possibly tell her the first time around. The half an hour passed by pretty quickly and none too soon, too. It had been the first time I had told the story in such detail and all the emotions came rushing back too, and I was surprised and embarrassed, that I had started welling up. I was certain that she had seen it, but she said nothing as we hurried back towards the Mezzanine. I had already picked up the tickets before she arrived,and so we could beat the queue and go directly to the screening room.

The screening room was a bit cramped, and the first time that I had been to that cinema, and especially with it being in the huge landmark that was Leicester Square and I being used to larger cinemas, it caught us by surprise. While the room was not wide enough to accommodate a large audience, it was perfect for a cinema first date, dark and a little cramped, with only the absolute necessary space between seats.

It was in perfect contrast to the movie we were watching, an absolute cinematic masterpiece, filling up the screen with the wide-open Great Plains of the wild and untamed mid-19th century Western United States, the grand ambitions of John Dunbar (played magnificently by Kevin Costner, who also directed this epic), and the adventurous, dangerous and yet wonderful lives of the proud Lakota Sioux, Indian tribe.

It was my favorite movie of all time, right from the first time I had seen it, at about the age of eleven or twelve, and now living in the concrete jungle that was London Metropolis, it reminded me of home. The wide expense of land, the freedom, the adventure, earth with its people and animals at its absolute finest.

When I was a kid, I dreamt that I was John Dunbar, riding his brave horse, with"Two Socks" his wolf companion, going forth into the dangerous unknown, to discover the hidden treasure that is life at its unfettered, utmost best.

Delia wasn't much of a movie-going person, rarely going to the cinema, and so she asked me to choose. All she asked was that I choose a nice movie, but not some all-action, bomb-exploding vehicle. So, I scoured the web looking for cinema show times in London, which is how I found “Dances with Wolves” on a limited run.

When Kevin Costner walks Mary McDonnell through the woods, steadily but silently gesticulating for some type of physical contact with his newly discovered soulmate, I felt like it reminded me of my love life through the past year, looking for my perfect woman through the forests of eroticism and trees of desire, with limited success, but continually and desperately trying to get her attention.

When “Stands with a Fist” finally relents enough to allow “Dances with Wolves” a long passionate kiss and embrace, from the cover of a tree trunk, I moved my hand to grasp Delia’s lightly, and she gripped right back. I had been stealing glances at her as she watched the movie, trying to gauge her reaction to the scenes and storyline, and I could see that she was enjoying it.

As she sat there smiling and enjoying the romantic chase scene, set to the background of John Barry’s magnificent musical score, whilst still gripping my hand, I confirmed what I felt all those months ago on that train to Victoria Station.

I had found my “Stands with a Fist”.

CHAPTER THIRTEEN

The shutter rolled down slowly as the darkness started to cover the concourse. It was 7pm in Grahame Park and for the lone police station, or some would call it a police outpost, in this deprived and over-populated section of Colindale, London, and closing time beckoned. The rest of the businesses on the concourse took their cue from the police closing timetable, after all, why would you take risk of staying open, right in the middle of one of London's more crime-infested neighborhoods, without at least the perception of a police presence. After all, everyone knew the police never showed up on time, for reported incidents on the concourse, unless they decided that the incident was "serious" enough to bother responding to.

Most of the youth in the area knew about the police response times and enjoyed the "coming of age ritual" of causing mischief and mayhem, and then just waiting around, like they were playing a game of "chicken", before escaping just before the police turned up, if they did at all, because they were quite certain that they could time the police response.

Tonight though, unlike most other nights, the single floor building wasn't empty.DI Jack Patterson and DI Derrick Johnson had come in and stayed in the building,unannounced and in plain clothes, with as much discretion as possible, about half an hour before the station's closing time.

The police station/community outreach post was remarkably low-key and low tech and sparsely decorated with furniture. There was barely enough for ten people hanging around at the same time. There was very little weaponry and even less ammunition was stored in the structure, because while the police officialdom were almost certain that no one was stupid enough to break into a police station, albeit a tiny one, they couldn't quite take the chance of leaving weapons and other criminal activity-facilitating goodies, anywhere in a not-totally secure building, right smack in the middle of a drug-fueled crime infested neighborhood. All it would take would was one drugged-out looney to complicate an already delicate environment.

Jack and Derrick had a reason for being here on this Wednesday evening, having arranged to meet with Jeremy in about an hour, under the cover of darkness in the building. It probably wasn't textbook undercover police work, but Jack and Derrick didn't really care, especially about convicted felons like Jeremy. It didn'tmatter that Jeremy was actively working for the police since he left prison, putting himself and his family in harm's way. He had a new-born son with a lady he met barely a year ago, having come to the terms with the fact that he could never be with Jermaine's mum again.

No, to Jack and Derrick, whatever Jeremy had decided to reincarnate himself as, he was still the drug dealer who had helped swamp the council estate with drugs, making loads of money for himself while reducing dozens of others to quivering masses of helpless addictive tendencies. Not that the human suffering of the addicts "those un-employed human siphons of public funds", as the duo thought of them, moved them to any kind of sympathy, anyway. They were all part of the same unwanted group of miscreants. The miscreants that drove the DIs to do their work with a passion, were the ones driving around in their luxury cars and basically living life to the fullest, while they, the police officers, had to struggle with their mortgages and family expenses on their salary. Nothing made Jack and Derrick happier than to put those people away.

DI's Patterson and Johnson had never quite gotten that big case that they were looking for when they transferred here but were hoping that things might start to change after tonight. That was the only reason that they had come out to the estate,where Jeremy lived with his partner. The police station on the concourse was nicknamed "Prison Island" by officers and deployment there was seen as a waste of time or a waste of resources depending on the time of day. Mornings and afternoons tended to be bereft of activity, while evenings and weekends tended to be filled with prank-like activity, from the teens in the area. If there were any major crimes, like armed robbery, it was usually handled by the main police station in Colindale.

Jack looked at his watch, quite certain that he had spent three hours in this hellhole, and got annoyed when he saw the time was 8:10pm.

"That little p--- was supposed to have turned up about ten minutes ago. What the hell is he waiting for? A carnival?" he asked.

"You know their type" answered Derrick, "They never show up on time. The d---head is probably still sleeping in, just like he does all day, apart from when he's busy snorting stuff."

"Seriously, Derrick, what were the exact arrangements for tonight's meeting? Are we sure the dim-witted ex-con didn't understand our rather simple arrangements? We didn't use any fancy words like rendezvous, did we? The very last thing I need is to spend an extra minute more than necessary, in this place."

"The plans were simple enough, Jack" said Derrick laughing. "Meet at the police station in Grahame Park at 8pm on Wednesday night. Knock three times, on the back door that leads to the car park, and when prompted for a response, answer "It's Jeremy Kyle".

"I'm not feeling so confident about his ability to understand the word, prompted"stated Jack, half-laughing, "Maybe that's what's holding him up. You know he can't read properly, the half- wit. He's probably off somewhere, trying to figure out what the word means. We'll give him a bit more time and if he doesn't show up, we get the hell out of here. I'll make us a cup of coffee while we wait, this could take a while. I can just picture him now, trying to figure out the word, prompted." With that he and Derrick burst out laughing…

***

Jeremy got out of Colindale Underground Station at about 8:25pm, turning left on his way out the station entrance/exit, to walk towards Grahame Park.
He knew he was late for the rendezvous with DI's Patterson and Jackson, but didn't care for them or their attitude, "the pigs could wait". He knew they would wait, however disinterested they pretended to be, because he knew how much they wanted to land a big case, and Jermaine Adams, was a big case. He remembered the brief pause on the phone line, when he had first mentioned during the regular week to week briefing updates that took place on the phone on Saturdays evenings. Even though Jack Patterson had feigned only slight interest on hearing about the tip, Jeremy knew how much the DI's hated Jermaine, especially after the big case against Jermaine blew up in their faces, unraveled when the

"mistakes" made during the investigation were uncovered.

Jeremy made his way down the station road, which still had some activity, as students from Middlesex University, lived only about five minutes from the station. He turned left at the roundabout and then suddenly darted across the road, walking through one of the many side- pathways of the Grahame Park estate, and a poorly lit one at that. He glanced quickly behind him as he walked, checking to see if he was being followed. DI's Patterson and Johnson could care less about his safety, and he was well aware of that fact, so he knew that his personal safety would be up to him. The meeting at the police station, right in the middle of the concourse in Grahame Park, was hardly ideal, but the location of the meetings wasnot his call, and according to the terms of his secret amnesty deal to get out of prison early, he wasn't in a strong position to argue, until now.

His path took him through a few apartment blocks, round the back or front of some others, constantly looking around to check if anyone was behind. He was counting on the fact that he knew where most, if not all, the look-out spots were situated, mostly because, either he helped set them up or knew about his rivals' operations, when he was still a major drugs distributor on the estate. Jeremy's evasive maneuvers turned what was normally a fifteen-minute journey into a twenty-five minute one, bringing him to the car park at the back of the police station at about 8:50pm, and then after a cursory look around the car park, walked quietly and quickly to the back door of the police station and knocked.

"Who's there?"

"It's Jeremy…"

***

"Isn't that Jeremy over there?"

Moyo, Riccardo and Suli, were on the way back from the park, after a game of football that boys in the neighborhood, organized amongst themselves on some evenings when everyone had finished with school, or whatever it was that they did till about five in the evening. It was about a fifteen-minute walk from Grahame Park and about the same distance form Burnt Oak, enabling as many guys as could make it, be able to play. It was also a particularly good meeting point for the boys to get their distribution packages enroute to their various locations, for a late evening drug-sale run.

Moyo was a second-generation British Nigerian of Yoruba heritage, his family having arrived in late 1993, at the height of the M.K.O. Abiola election debacle. With heightened tensions, and arrests being made, Moyo's father, who had worked on the campaign, asked for and received, political asylum status from the UK, and brought his family along with him.

Ricardo's family was Portuguese and had a more straight-forward arrival into the UK, with Portugal being a member of the EU, his family decided to come over to the UK, hoping for better economic opportunities for himself and his family.
Portugal was one of the earliest countries in the Euro zone, to be hit with a recession, prompting massive job cuts and a significant Portuguese community in the UK.

Suli, which was short for Suleiman, had the hardest path to the UK. The difficulty wasn't in the process, but literally in the path taken by Suli's family from Eritrea, fleeing famine, political uncertainty and the disease-ravaged camps, where his family got shelter. He lost a sister there to malaria, too sick and too weak for her body to fight it and too far gone along for the medicine, given on their arrival to the camp, to save her. He never forgot about that day, and it drove him to never allow his family to be that helpless, ever again.

All three arrived around the period spanning, late 1993 to the summer of 1994, and gradually became embroiled in the illegal drug trade pervading the estate, with all three of them joining for the same reasons, but slightly different degrees of desire.

Moyo generally only wanted the extra cash, which could be used to get a car to impress his friends. Riccardo only wanted enough money that he would need, to marry his girlfriend and rent a place out of the "hellhole" that he thought of as the estate. Suli, on the other hand, wanted everything he could get from the business. He had joined earlier than the others, and had left school earlier too, to do as much selling as he could possibly do, and consequently, had risen up the ranks quicker.

All three had lived in the same apartment block and had gone to the same school.They had been close friends for all that time and, while at different levels of involvement in the hierarchy of Jermaine Adams gang; they still tended to move around together, just as they were when they spotted Jeremy, while on their way home.

Spotting Jeremy in Grahame Park wasn't anything out of the ordinary, after all, he had lived there longer than any of them. What caught their attention was the furtive way, in which he seemed to move, looking around and walking in the shadows as if he didn't want anyone seeing where he was going. So, for nothing more than curiosity, they followed him, careful not to be seen by him. It was only when he got to the car pack located round the back of the police station that they suspected something was up.

Suli, the risk-taker of the three, went closer to have a better look, crouching between cars to keep hidden, and with the silence around the area at that time of the night; people generally liked to keep away from any un-lit areas of Grahame Park, once darkness approached; Suli clearly heard Jeremy identify himself as"Jeremy Kyle" and saw the door open, recognizing DI Johnson before the door closed.

"Did you guys see what I just saw" asked Suli, after he had made his way back towhere Moyo and Riccardo lay waiting, on the outskirts of the car park.

"Yeah, we did" Moyo said, "What was that all about? Did you see who was inside?"

"He met DI Johnson at the door" said Suli, "I don't know if there was anyone else inside, but you guys know who DI Johnson is, right? The guy, who is really tough with us, trying to do everything to aggravate us, whenever we come across him? Well, he is usually with the other DI, I think his name is Patterson? Maybe he was there too, but I couldn't see inside."

"You know we have to tell Jermaine about this, as quickly as possible" said Riccardo, "I'm not sure what's going on there, but Jeremy has always known a lot about the drugs business on the estate, even if he doesn't run a gang anymore."

"Should we go over to his place, right now, tonight? Asked

Moyo "Especially now, when we suspect that he is still under some kind of surveillance? We are not sure what the significance of this information is, and we don't want to add to Jermaine's problems."

"Alright, you've got a point, but I still think that Jermaine should know what happened here, tonight, as soon as possible." Suli said, "I'll go alone to Jermaine'splace, so that it looks like a normal friend's evening visit. If all three of us went there together, then it might look like some kind of activity, to anyone watching. But I really think Jermaine needs to know what happened here tonight."

With that Moyo and Ricardo made their way back to the apartment block, while Suli went off on his own, towards Jermaine's house in Colindale.

***

Jermaine opened the blinds in his bedroom room, trying to see if he would spot either the patrol team that seemed to walk through his street about every half an hour at times, or the "anonymous" unmarked police car, that would stay packed a little further down the street. He saw neither, and proceeded down the stairs for dinner, which his mom Mary, Salma and new girlfriend Isabelle, were already settling into. It was his favorite dish, the West Indian culinary delight of Rice and Peas, with curried goat, prepared delightfully as always by Mary. As he joined everyone at the table, especially as he didn't want to miss out on having as big a portion as he would want, he thought about the way things had gone over the past year. The Colindale police, having failed to reinstate his jail sentence in the aftermath of "Botch-gate", as Jermaine's drug possession trial was called, instead maintained a heavy clampdown on his activities. They did nothing illegal, but they made sure that any illegal activities would be hard to organize, sustain, or if they were diligent enough, not even commence. This had been achieved by using the afore-mentioned ultra- regular patrols and vehicular surveillance teams aroundJermaine's known haunts, as well as, giving Jermaine a tough community service schedule to adhere to. All the surveillance and time constraints of community service, had forced Jermaine to widen his chain of command and diversify his operation, bringing young boys like Suli, higher up the chain of command, with more responsibility to deal with the day-to-day decision-making of running his operation.

He now had a bit more time for personal things and had met Isabelle at a rave in Neasden, and with the way things were progressing, she looked like she might be the "one". However, he wanted to do things the right way. The last thing that he wanted was for any of his kids, to live the life that he had growing up, or end up with the life he had now. Even his friend Obi, or "Obi- wan" as he called him, seemed to have found someone to settle down with, Delia, if he remembered correctly. What a story that was. It was probably the reason Obi wasn't at dinner tonight. He hadn't checked the door downstairs earlier, but vaguely remembered Obi, saying something about staying out that night.

"I've got to organize some sort of dinner or outing, so that we can all get to know one another and get her comfortable coming over here." Jermaine thought to himself, as he finished off a second helping of curried goat, while the ladies chatted away about some TV show or the other.

"Ding-dong" The front doorbell rang, with its steady, grandfatherly but loud resonance. Jermaine had always liked the old school doorbells, from the old movies shown on daytime TV, and had gotten one for the house, when he procured it.

"Expecting anyone?" Jermaine asked to no one in particular, as it was 930 in the evening.

"No" All three replied, prompting Jermaine to get up and take peek through the living room curtains.

"Never mind" He said, as he closed back the curtains and moved towards the door, "It's Suli. He probably just wants to ask me something."

As he made his way to the front door to meet Suli, Jermaine wondered what would bring him over, and at that time of the night, especially as it had been agreed, or rather, had been an instruction from him, that any talk or meeting that had to do with "business", would take place elsewhere.

"What's up Suli? What brings you here by this time?"

"Hello Jermaine. I didn't really want to bother you, especially at this time of the night, but Ricardo, Moyo and I, saw something on our way back from football just a while ago, which I thought you should know about."

"What was that?"

"We just saw Jeremy sneak into the police station in Grahame Park, and I saw him meet DI Johnson..."

CHAPTER FOURTEEN

The smell of freshly made coffee and leftover pizza, hung in the air inside the police station. Di's Patterson, Johnson and Jeremy, sat in a circle in the main office of the police station, it was almost ten at night and as Jeremy had expected, Jack and Derrick were very much interested in his information concerning Jermaine's recent activities or "apparent" lack thereof.

"So, Jermaine has been in business all this time, in spite of our best efforts, albeit in a much smarter way than before." DI Jack Patterson said out loud, as the briefing came to an end. Some of the briefing had been about the other things or situations happening on the estate; any new gangs trying to set up in the estate, possible leads on wanted suspects, and any new types of drugs appearing on the scene, and so on. Jeremy having lived and run a gang on the estate for many years,was invaluable to the invaluable to the police, when it comes to information about the criminal activities and individuals that the police are interested in, on the estate.

"We will need more than the information that you have given us, We might know the names of the people doing the actual day to day running of his illegal drugs operation" said DI Derrick Johnson, "But we would like to find a particular activity, that would tie directly to his operation. If we did that, not only would we convict him for drug-running crimes, but it would also constitute a major violation of his parole terms."

"I'll see what I can do," said Jeremy. "But you know that he doesn't trust or even like me, and quite frankly, neither do any of his trusted people. We were rivals in Grahame Park, both in business and also personally, and I know that I was suspected to be part of the leak that compromised his operation, the last time."

Jeremy resisted the temptation to cite "botch-gate", which he knew still rankled, the men sitting around him. He smiled inwardly as he remembered their reaction to his telling them that he had credible information that showed Jermaine was back in business, in spite of all their efforts. They had immediately ordered Pizza, in anticipation of a long and extremely rewarding chat. He could see that they were extremely eager to catch Jermaine this time, in part he thought, probably to put a stop to the occasional ribbing that they got from fellow officers, but more importantly, to land the major scalp and publicity they thought that their efforts deserved. They would definitely need him now. He had them in the palm of his hand.

"Well, that's what we need to find out, so we'll be waiting for any information that brings us closer to catching Jermaine in the act.", Jack said, getting up from his seat in a signal that the meeting was over.

"Thanks for what you've brought us today, and hopefully we will see you nextweek, with some more information." said Derrick.

Jeremy grabbed the last piece of pizza, as he got up to leave. "There's no truth to saying, hopefully. According to my parole terms, I have to be here next week." He said smiling. "But thinking that I'm going to get the information you need about Jermaine, that quickly? Well, that would really be hopeful."

With that, he walked through the door that Jack held open, and disappeared into the night.

***

Life is filled with upward and downward shifts in momentum. When things are going your way or looking up, you are happy and comfortable. You are in charge of your own destiny or so it feels, if you want to do anything, you just go ahead and do it. Holidays, parties, shopping, it doesn't matter. The resources always seem to be there, and it's only a matter of fitting it into your schedule, which is always full of things to do, but still flexible for even more.

When things are on the downward slope, there is a change in perspective. Everything seems to come around at the wrong time, too soon or just a little too late. Things that might have been opportunities suddenly constitute a burden on your time or on your expenses. Every little thing needs thoughtful planning and calculations on a priority basis, to fit into a schedule that had little in it to start with.

For Jeremy, the upward slope was being the "man" on the Grahame Park estate. Virtually everything illegal or stolen came to his attention. He had his pick of the girls and was invited to virtually every party. He could go on vacation at a moment's whim and drove his custom- made, personal license-plated Range Rover, because money was no problem, and time was there for life to be enjoyed to its fullest.

As Jeremy contemplated his morning schedule, he knew that he couldn't take the meagre offerings that life at this moment presented him with, for much longer.

He had an 11pm appointment with his Job Centre advisor, Mark. There, the usual question and answer session would commence, "Did you try to find work today, over the past week? "Yes". "Have there been progress, with your previous job search, or interviews or anything of that sort?" "No".

Every week, for the past six months, it had been like this. Every Friday, sometimes in the morning and at other times in the afternoon, he would make his way down to the Edgware Job Centre for his appointment. He was bound to be there on time, and he always was, just to make sure that he could spend only the exact amount of time needed to complete his appointment. However, the office always managed to contrive to create a fifteen-to-twenty- minute wait, in a small room that could fit about twenty people.

The occupants of the room spent their time in that space trying to avoid looking at anyone, lest they recognize anyone or be recognized. No one truly liked to be known to be on welfare to avoid the stigma and personal embarrassment that came with that status. This fact is why Jeremy believed the small waiting room to be a sadistic ploy by the powers that be, to induce shame among recipients, "the sadistic b… "

As Jeremy left his front door, with the sound of his son crying and his girlfriend reminding him that food supplies were running low, yet again, he thought "This is what trying to make an honest living is worth to me right now, absolutely nothing. This path was never for me, not like this."

***

Over time, as emotions faded, Jeremy realized that he did not really hate Jermaine. All the petty differences between them did not matter so much now. Jeremy and Mary weren't an item anymore and were never going to be again. Nor did Jeremy care for her as he once did.

No, Jeremy just didn't particularly care for Jermaine crew. First of all, they were the competition, when it came down to the drug trade on the estate and its surrounding areas. They were the biggest threat to his dominance when he reigned supreme over the estate and the gang that took over all of his territory, once he became incarcerated in prison.

All Jeremy really wanted, was his territory back. His trial of the good and honest road seemed to lead to nowhere but failure and abject misery. It was a road that he knew was coming to an end for him, in a short while, by his own hand, one way or the other.

The whole pretext of looking for information about Jermaine's clandestine activities was to give himself a shot at regaining what he thought was rightfully his. Of course, to the DI's, the thought of Jeremy returning to his crime lord days,was not a serious consideration. Definitely not, with the threat of a rather long jail sentence awaiting him, if it was ever found out. No intelligent man, under as much scrutiny as Jeremy was, would even consider taking such a risk.

That perception is what gave Jeremy the confidence, that he might be able to achieve his plan, by simply not being on the radar of possibilities. Combined with DIs Patterson and Johnson, obsessive desire to get Jermaine, he hoped to be able to undermine the effectiveness of his erstwhile rival's operation, while re-establishing his.

It had been two weeks since he had told the DI's that he had information about Jermaine's managing of the Grahame Park's biggest illegal activities enterprise, while under supposed tight surveillance. That had been the easiest thing to find out about for a man of his connections. Getting the exact information, or rather the precise location to link Jermaine was rather hard to come by.

After all, while the police considered him relatively harmless, the rest of the criminal establishment on the estate didn't trust him, and he knew Jermaine had been successful at hiding his activities, by using a highly disciplined inner circle.It was highly unlikely that he would ever be able to penetrate that circle. The only way Jeremy could implicate Jermaine in engaging in criminal activity would be to draw him into intervening in something, just like the leader of a gang or organization would be expected to do, in event of a problem or issue.But what would Jermaine be bothered enough about, to try to intervene in? If he found that out, then he had a shot at succeeding in his quest…

It was Friday again, and as usual, he made his way to the Job Centre, early again as usual, but then, once again, directed to the little room, that was quite packed this time. A lady, probably in her fifties, brought along her grand-daughter or soit looked. Why anyone would bring children to such an environment of such mental and emotional desolation was beyond Jeremy.

To make things worse, she was the unusually chatty type, a symptom that would normally identify someone that had been coming so frequently, that they were completely relaxed in such an environment. Five minutes into Jeremy's wait, she decided to make a loud declaration, directed at her granddaughter, but loud enough for everyone in the room and beyond, to hear.

"This is what happens, Mandy, when you don't go to school. You end up here,like some sort of deadbeat."

"No" said Jeremy, "People end up here sometimes, for being chatty, airheaded idiots, such as you."

With that Jeremy got up and left the building, jobseekers' allowance and its attachments be damned, vowing never to return. He was so annoyed that he decided to walk the rest of the way home, taking the long 204 bus route, for good measure.

At the junction of Edgware Road and Burnt Oak Broadway, he thought he recognized the Audi waiting at the traffic lights. Looking from a distance, he could see Jermaine and that new friend of his, with the Star Wars sounding first name, sitting in the front. The lady sitting at the back looked eerily familiar and Jeremy wondered why. Then he smiled, he had just found his shot…

CHAPTER FIFTEEN

Eating out is a luxury that I rarely indulged in, especially over the last two years.But, when I had just cause to eat out, I made it count. My favorites were Nigerian and Oriental restaurants.

In Nigerian restaurants my favorite dishes were of a wide variety, depending on what I had eaten recently or anything that I had a sudden hankering for, I could cook the staple rice and chicken stew and could prepare my favorite soup, which was Okra. But with my expertise being that limited and my choices being much wider (and on occasions, my appetite too), I rather enjoyed the opportunity to ear whatever variation of dish that I might prefer at any given time, from moimoi to goat's head soup to pepper soup. These visits were with Jermaine, who had eaten Nigerian food and instantly liked it.

For a date, I usually liked to go the Chinese route. It was safe, because most people liked Chinese/Oriental food. Everyone also had their particular favorite,from the vast menu that was generally enough to keep everyone, vegetarian or otherwise, happy. My favorite was chicken in black bean sauce, served with any variation of rice, and was my invariable choice for any date.

As Jermaine, Delia and I, sat round the table at the Weng Wah Buffet Restaurant in Edgware, I already knew what I was going to order, as the menu was passed around, all I needed to look at, were the prices of the various dishes, especially if I was going to be bothered with any of the starters, an extra I usually avoided if I could help it.

Luckily, today wasn't one of those dates, where I needed to impress. Delia and I had been going steady for three months now and today's meal was basically a "getting to know you" opportunity, that I had fashioned/setup for Jermaine and Delia, my best friend and my girlfriend, to get to know one another.

Delia decided to go for a starter soup, which of course meant that we all had to go on a starter, as we were definitely not going to let her eat by herself, while we sat around watching. Jermaine who knew my eating habits, or more specifically,my pocketbook spending habits, caught my eye and smiled, as he decided to follow Delia's lead and order some soup. Smiling back furtively, I followed suit. This was one of those special days, when I put aside my frugal standards. Every occasion that I got to spend with Delia, was special. Besides, I was only covering the part of the bill that was spent by Delia and me. Jermaine had earlier indicated his willingness to cover the whole bill, it being that he was practically loaded, but with this being my arrangement, I wanted to take responsibility for a part of the expense, at least.

The restaurant was situated on the busy Station Road in Edgware, and as we got in, Jermaine asked that we take a table a bit towards the interior of restaurant and took a seat that overlooked/faced the door.

I knew somehow, that despite the lack of any discernible activity around the Colindale house, or at least anything that I could observe, that he was still involved in illegal activity, but had asked no questions, as it was none of my business.
Besides, Jermaine and his family had been very good to me, over the past two years, and he knew how to look after himself and hadn't confided in me, anyway.

But I had observed the display of wealth, as quiet as it had been done, the new large flat screen TV, the expensive new kitchen fittings and design, among others.I knew how much Mary's business brought in on a monthly basis, and with the expenses/salaries that had to be paid, they couldn't afford what they were buying,with the cash amounts that I observed. This was no credit card splurge.

Jermaine wasn't working as far as I could tell either, which only reinforced my opinion, but left me a little puzzled, as to how he had managed to organize, what had looked to me from the outside, like a gang of kids who just distributed drugs on the estate, and even more puzzled that, the police hadn't been asking any questions about any of this, as far as I could tell.

I had noticed the police presence though, as subtle as it was, as was quite certain that Jermaine had, as well, which only left me amused and astonished, as to the brazen way, in my opinion, in which he displayed his ability to procure expensive things.

"So, you are the famous Jermaine" said Delia, as we waited for the chicken soup to arrive. “I’ve heard a lot of nice things about you from Obi, and it’s good to finally meet you.”

“Don’t believe everything you hear.” Replied Jermaine, smiling. “Some people might even call me the infamous Jermaine” he said, laughing. “But it’s also really good to meet you, too. I wanted to meet the lady, who has been keeping Obi really hard to find, these days.” This said with a playful jab to my shoulder, “And, I think that I totally understand those late-night tendencies. He hasn’t said too much about you, until recently, but the absences and the smile on his face whenever he gets back, speaks volumes.

There was laughter around the table now, as the soup arrives, and an air of familiarity settled around our table. There had not been a lot of conversation, on the ride to the restaurant, after Jermaine had picked us up at Colindale station.

This was the first time that Delia had come up to my part of London. I wanted her to be comfortable and get used to being around there. The first step to that process, was introducing her to Jermaine’s family, the closest thing I had to familyin the UK.

As Jermaine had playfully asserted, I spent a decreasing amount of time at the house in Colindale, sometimes, even whole weekends. This also meant that Delia was spending an ever-increasing amount of her time with me, instead of working to pay-off whatever agreement/contract that she had with the agencies or persons,who put her up, in the apartment in Paddington.

I knew that equation was not going to work out in her favor in the long term, and while she never said anything about it to me, I thought that somehow, it must bother her too. I had slyly asked her a couple of times, within the last few weeks, if everything was going okay in Paddington, if she needed me to get some shopping or anything else, to which she smiled and said that everything was okay. I didn’t press because of the agreement that we made, before we agreed to become a couple. As time passed though, she gradually let me into her world. The rent that had to be paid on the apartment in Paddington, the phone calls that had to be made to arrange her daily schedules, and the cut of the money paid, for the services that she rendered. I never stayed around when she had to work, saying she could look after herself, but she always wanted me around her, which helped to dissipate any feelings of guilt that I felt for taking her time. I knew how much, she wanted to get out of this arrangement, down to the last hour and minute.

This was how desensitized I was to Delia's work. It's like it was a part of her life,but a part that had nothing to do with the Delia that I had fallen in love with.

By her calculation, she only had a few more months to go, by which time, she would have paid off her debt, and at the same time, be able to sustain herself without having to work, the way she did, at least for a while until she thought of what to do next.

This is what she always thought about, the day she couldn't wait for to arrive. It was also the day that I dreamt of. When I didn't need to hide the truth about what Delia did for a living. While I had no problems, at least none that made me want to stop seeing or loving her, I didn't think there was any need for anyone else to know.

I was thinking about the long-term possibilities of Delia and me, moving in together. Staying in Paddington wasn't a feasible option, with the high rent that was paid in the area. Neither was staying in Colindale, in Jermaine's house, at least not for any length of time.

While this was a getting-to-know-you lunch date for my girlfriend and best friend, it was also for me to sow the seeds for Delia coming regularly to the house and for Jermaine and his family to get used to the prospect of me moving away out permanently to live with Delia. I also wanted to get Delia away from Paddington and any lingering memories and influences.

The rest of lunch was fun and after it was over, we went back to the house to meet Mary, Salma and Isabelle for drinks and complete the getting-to-know-you "day session". I could tell that they warmed to Delia after a while. Maybe, it was because she was with me, but I'd like to think that her nice, enthusiastic demeanor,made her quite likable.

Delia was invited to come and stay over anytime and also to do the shopping thing that the ladies liked to do together, which made me glad, as it was one of the things that I abhorred doing.

The thought of strolling around the shops for hours on end, got me tired even before we got round to actually leaving the house and doing it!

This was a new stage in my life, and it was starting to look like I was out from underneath the dark cloud that seemed to have been following me for a couple of years now. I had a long-term girlfriend, a family that it seemed that I belonged in and felt absolutely comfortable living with, that acted like my surrogate family inthe UK, with the absence of my real family back home in Nigeria.

I basically had what looked like a support system again, something that I could lean on, in the hard times, when I needed some type of support. I could actually look forward to the future and plan, for the first time in two years.

CHAPTER SIXTEEN

Earl's Court was one of the busiest locations in central London, being one of those seemed to have transport access to everywhere else, either by train/underground or, by just simply walking down the road in any direction.

The area looked like a blend of old and new London. While everywhere looked clean and well maintained, as you walked down the street, you saw houses that looked like they had been built decades ago, and then when you crossed over to the next street, the buildings looked modern in design, fitted with intercoms in some cases, which suggested that you were looking at an apartment block, even if it appeared from its front view, to look like a family home.

This blend of transport accessibility and well planned, aesthetic residential areas, which provided a good measure of privacy, made it a plum area for the "pleasure" trade. There were no adverts stating anything of the kind in the local paper, neither would you see any sign which might detract you from your first impression that Earl's Court was a beautiful corner of central London, which in fact, it was. Only people in the know about, where to find the relevant info/contacts, were given the appointment and specific directions, to go to the right addresses.

Jeremy came out of the busy Earl's Court underground station, which served both the District and Piccadilly lines, at about 11 in the morning. He used to come over,later in the day, when he first started coming to the area about six months ago. He quickly realized that when he wanted to leave, usually about four in the afternoon that he was running into "rush hour" travel time that affected the London Underground, between 4pm and 7pm, from Monday to Friday.

While Jeremy was living with the mother of his son, he had during his crime lord days, been accustomed to having the most beautiful and desirable women, at his beck and call and, he loved his women. Caucasian, Black, Asian/Oriental, it didn't matter. He loved variety both in terms of numbers and distinct composition.

This morning, Jeremy was seeing Gina, a half Italian, half Ghanaian stunner, with a wonderfully tanned complexion and tall model-like features. He went to see her as many times as he could afford in a month, even though he technically was in no position to meet her £400 an hour visitation price. But he did have a medium-sized amount of cash which had been holding onto secretly, a bonus from his illegal activities of yesteryear. Of course, this bounty was carefully hidden from his partner, to keep her demands in check. As far as she was concerned, they were solely relying on state benefits for their day-to-day expenses.

He turned right, at the station exit and walked down Earl's Court road, which almost always seemed to have lots of people walking in either direction, either straight along the road, or turning into the labyrinth of streets on either side. The house itself was in a square at the end of a street off Earl's Court road, beautifully laid out with a mini garden/sitting area in the middle, surrounded by four streets of houses.

He stopped outside door No. 17 for a moment, a smile starting to play on his lips,as he thought of the ever-satisfying thought of Gina meeting him at the door of the house, and then gradually and gracefully leading him up the stairs to her own room. He pressed the intercom button for apartment 6 once and then waited. She hated repeated pushing of her apartment's buzzer and you never really wanted Gina in a bad mood.

She called back about 10 seconds later in that throaty voice of hers, heavily laden with an Italian accent,

"Who is it?" She asked.

"It's Jeremy. I'm supposed to see you at 1130?"

"Of course, you are, Jeremy. The door is open, come inside. I'll meet you at the top of the stairs."

"That's a little unusual" thought Jeremy, pushing the door as a buzzer sound disabled the door- lock mechanism. Maybe there was a new occupant or occupants in the house, and she was being careful. He was well aware that there would normally be other "ladies of pleasure" occupying the other apartments in the house, as they usually liked to stay together, partly for security and convenience and partly to share the cost of the exorbitant rent prices that had to be paid in and around central London.

That arrangement though, was one that could only be made if you had lived in London a while or worked with an agency that housed its ladies together, meaning you could make friends and develop a social circle of similarly minded ladies.

For someone who had newly arrived and was independent like Gina, such networking was a luxury that was not readily available. She had only arrived six and half months ago and had to setup herself quickly. Jeremy was her first client, a testament to the enduring legacy of his underworld contacts that he still had from the time when he helped supply illegal drugs for the same East European gangs that now brought girls into the UK.

As Jeremy reached the midway point of the first flight of stairs, he spotted Gina on the top step, one hand on hip, in an all-white bikini ensemble that contrasted nicely with her tanned skin and matching 4-inch white heels. She rarely smiled, choosing to put on an air of indifference and supreme self-confidence, albeit with the necessary show of respect towards her clients. She smiled this time though, asher eyes met Jeremy's, and when he had almost climbed to the top of the stairs, she turned and walked back towards her room slowly down the corridor, had four doors each leading to individual rooms with hers being the last one down the corridor.

She turned around as she got to her door, to see Jeremy right behind, his eyes clasped to where her derriere had been just a moment ago, taking in deep breaths with a hazy look in his eyes. She looked down towards his crotch area and smiled at the effect her little walk along the corridor had on him, just as she knew would on any full-blooded man.

Jeremy followed Gina into the room as she pushed open the door. He half- glanced around the increasingly familiar trappings of the apartment, just to see if there was anything new or out of place from the last time he had visited. There wasn't. It still had two chairs, a bed and a medium sized drawer compartment bythe side of the wardrobe with the full-size mirror in front of it. He had only planned to stay for an hour, but as she sat cross-legged on one of the chairs waiting for him to say what he wanted, he realized how aroused he was (which was probably the reason she was smiling a lot more than usual, while giving him the slow up and down look enquiring look) and that he hadn't seen her for a while...and she looked so damn beautiful...

He had a pressing matter to attend to later that would greatly impact on his future prospects with regard to business but decided that the pressure that was building upin him at that very moment, was best relieved quickly and thoroughly in his own interest. He thought it best to stay an extra half hour, then.

After all, neither Jermaine nor Delia was going anywhere, anytime soon.

***

When Jeremy saw Delia in Jermaine's car, that fateful afternoon along with Obi, he was certain that he remembered who she was. The question for him was what exactly was she doing in that car? Was she romantically linked to Jermaine, whom he knew was in a long-term relationship with a lady he knew about? Or was she with that perennial scrounger Obi, or rather, getting it on with both, the thought of that last scenario bringing a wistful smile to his lips, and a longing from deep inside him. Ah Gina, he thought, as he mentally replayed the steamy afternoon, he had just spent with her, which was just never enough.

"Till next time, and very soon" Jeremy promised himself, as he exited Edgware Road Station, looking around to see if anything had changed since he was last there, a while ago.

For two weeks, following that sighting, Jeremy made it his mission to find out all he could about Jermaine, Obi and the girl whose name he came to recall as Delia.

Five months earlier, Jeremy had gone to Paddington for a "date" with a girl that had been arranged by one of his friends, with whom he had mutual business interests back in the day. Even though he could no longer pull his weight, at the moment when it came to matters of criminal enterprise, he had always been well liked and respected by his partners, for his ability to deliver and most had kept their ties with him even after his trial and subsequent incarceration.

One of the people that had kept such ties was Eric Kalinsky, a former KGB agent who had left the spy agency as the old Soviet Union had collapsed. He retired to his family home in St

Petersburg for a few months, weighing his options while maintaining his old contacts, to see what he could do for himself in the new Russia, with the money and resources he had managed to hide away for himself over the few years he had been an agent. After all, even though he was only twenty-three at the time, he had been identified as having a sharp mind, and on his way to great things, by his superiors.

He had gotten involved in the human trafficking trade purely by luck/happenstance. A friend of his, on learning that he had returned to St Petersburg, had asked Eric if it was possible to get documents, travel documents,for him and his girlfriend, as things in Russia had entered a period of uncertainty,with the transition from a socialist state to a free market economy.

One of the many skills of secret agents/spies was the ability to cross borders, moving from one country to another, indiscriminately. To do that, they had to have the ability to forge documents or at least know where to get them. After Eric had forged the British passports for the couple, the UK being their preferred destination, he began to wonder if there wasn't a market for people wanting to travel abroad from Russia, and how he could make a business out of it.

First, he decided to travel to Europe to consolidate contacts across the continent and then find out which areas would be more conducive to his business. He went to the UK, France, Spain and a lot of the countries from the former Eastern Bloc. It was while he was visiting those Eastern European countries, he realized that there was a huge potential market of people looking to head off to the UK, France and Spain, as well as the United States and the Caribbean, and especially among women.

That was the way his business was born, providing to people who could pay for the documents with which to travel, and for the others who didn't have the means, they had to pledge to pay off their debts. This payment was worked out in dollar amounts, for a period of time in which some kind of work/service was done. For men, the work ranged from laboring jobs like gardening or cooking in restaurants, to personal security or enforcers for some of Eric's contacts.

For the women, the jobs that were done to repay the debts ranged from cheap hotel labor, cleaning or Au Pair jobs. But the biggest paying jobs and the most in-demand were for ladies to work in Nightclubs as dancers or to join the illicit sex trade.

Eric had finally decided to move to London full time in the early 2000, s, when he realized that there was even more money to be made from the travelling ladies.

Apart from travel documents, they needed places in which to stay or to operate from, and in a lot of cases, both. So, with his newly acquired wealth, he bought property across Europe, providing apartments for the women to stay, and then charging them huge amounts to cover the costs of the travel documents and accommodation, because he knew that they could and would cover the amount eventually. He didn't do the accommodation thing with men, as, apart from a small minority, they were highly unlikely to be able to afford the rent expense.

This was how he met Jeremy, he needed to find apartments for women, where there was potential for business. Grahame Park had a reputation for being a haven for "women of the night", but because it was mainly a council estate area, flats and apartments were difficult to come by, as with cheap affordable housing, came high demand. Jeremy took care of that, for a fee of course, but also directed clients to those specific apartments. Most of those clients were the regular customers of his drug operation, looking for "extra activities".

When Jeremy lost his hold on Grahame Park, Eric still kept contact with him, as an old friend would, providing money and girls for Jeremy occasionally, when he could. His experiences in the past had thought Eric never to discard old relationships. You never knew when they might become relevant, again.

That was how Jeremy had first met Delia. His two-week enquiry, had finally confirmed that the girl he saw in the car, was in fact Obi's girlfriend and not Jermaine's. But it was on his next visit to Central London, following that sighting that he subsequently remembered where he had seen her before, and his meeting today at Eric's apartment on Old Marylebone Road, was to find out a way to use her as leverage against Jermaine. The fact that she was romantically linked to his best friend was unquantifiable bonus.

Jeremy was quite certain that Eric still "owned" Delia, and

all he could think about was what to do to her, to force Jermaine into a catastrophic mistake.

CHAPTER SEVENTEEN

As the last wafts of Tchaikovsky's Swan Lake echoed through the third-floor apartment, Eric cast a satisfied eye around the elaborately decorated living room.He thought of himself as a mini-Czar, with the power he wielded on the streets ofthe major cities around Europe and the wealth such influence brought, and he thought he should have all the trappings that befitted such a status.

From the beautifully crafted chandelier suspended from the center of the living room ceiling, the wonderfully expressive oil paintings on the walls, to the replica Faberge eggs strategically placed for effect around the room, Eric Kalinsky drove the point home to visitors, that in the world in which he operated, he was king anda very successful one too.

The man sitting down comfortably on one side of the living room wasn't a first- time visitor though, in fact, he probably had stopped being thought of as a visitor along time ago, considering the sheer number of times he found himself at this address, and the huge amount of time he spent at this address, every week.

Ben Clarke, a British national of West Indian Descent, was Eric's "Consiglieri" here in the UK. When Eric had started to put a structure in place, to run his human trafficking ring in England, one of the first non-Russian contacts he had, was Ben,a guy who could get almost anything you wanted on the black market, from guns to hi-tech devices that were only available to certain "qualified" people.

Eric realized that he had a better chance of setting up his operation successfully, if there wasn't too much involvement of Russian ex-KGB men, who formed a majority of his European contacts, or anyone who had been involved with him in his former life, working as a spy, as these people were known or suspended individuals by British authorities. If it had become known that there were large groups of such individuals involved in something, every effort would be made by law enforcement to find out exactly what it was that they were up to. That kind of attention was not a formula for success for any criminal outfit.

That was why, after due diligence of looking into Ben's background and after a string of successful business transactions between the two of them, Eric took Ben into confidence about the type of operation that he was trying to establish in the UK. He allowed Ben to use some of his own people/contacts to form the organizational chain that would run the British part of his operation.

Eric knew that Ben did not have a criminal record, wasn't known in the spy circles and so it would be highly unlikely if not impossible, for any connection to be made between them, alerting law enforcement to his outfit's activities, especially in its incubation stage.

He made sure Ben also brought in "clean" people who had no previous run-ins with the law, just to give his organization this best possible footing. Eric gave the instructions and pulled the strings from the sidelines, and watched his business grow from strength to strength under Ben's guidance. The money generated was laundered through a small chain of phone and computer repair and accessories shops, which was a perfect fit for Ben's underground hi-tech business that was ultimately run by Eric and his associates.

Ben came over to Eric's apartment at least three times a week, so that they could go through the day-to-day workings of the human trafficking business. Weekly payments were made by Eric's clients in the UK, these clients being those who were in the country courtesy of Eric's ring of contacts who arranged for travel and guaranteed accommodation, in exchange for an agreed fee usually in excess of what those clients could afford. Arrangements were therefore made by Eric for regular payments of the remaining balance of payment, to be deposited through Ben, as soon as they had arrived and settled into work. The clients were largely girls in the prostitution/massage parlor trade, and so returns came back quickly.

They paid the money to Ben and his associates who fronted as the landlords of the building where Eric's clients lived, and he in turn kept records and paid the money to Eric's electronics repair business, which came into the apartments regularly, to "fix" some "damaged" appliances/devices of some sort or the other.

The paperwork is what brought Ben over to Eric's apartment, to sort through the details of "who owned what" and "who was keeping up with payments", with the action that needed to be taken. Today, the request to meet had come from Eric himself, and unusually, he had requested the records and observations of one person, Delia Vasileva...

***

Delia left her Paddington apartment at about midday of Paul Ferry, the man who was ever present in her apartment building, staying in "that" room, the first door from the staircase on the third and highest floor. Paul, who went by the title "building supervisor", would be better recognized by the universally acknowledged term, "Pimp". It was to his apartment, that the money made by the girls, from their clients, went. Once in there, Paul recorded the various amounts of money brought in by the girls, and at the end of the day, the girls received their cut, according to any arrangement that had previously been agreed to.

Paul was Eric and Ben's point man in the building, and there was always at least one "building supervisor", in every building that housed the ladies working for Eric, paying off debts that they owed to him. It was unusual for the ladies to see any of them at this time of the day; when the frenetic activity that was the "body massage" business was starting to pick up; outside of their area of responsibility,at the risk of losing money or not recording the correct amount.

Delia knew this. She had not met Eric on a one-to-one basis, since the first time she met him on her first day in the apartment block. She had been preparing for a 1230 appointment; when Paul came down to deliver a personal message from Eric. Normally messages were delivered via phone or text message. The fact that this one came in such a manner and without any warning or fallout from preceding events, gave Delia a cause for concern. That and the fact that she had to be ready to go and arrive at Eric's within an hour.

"Is everything alright?" She had asked Paul, after he had given her the message in her room. "Oh yeah, sure, everything is okay, at least with regards to your time here in the apartment. I was just asked to get you to the Old Marylebone Rd apartment." He replied, declining to mention that he was told to be as casual as possible, but that it was important that Delia got to Eric's apartment before 1pm, and for him to see to it personally. And, as almost an afterthought, that she didn't need to undress or anything, in order to make the arrival time as quick as possible. This made sense to Paul, as he was certain that Delia had been preparing for a 1230 appointment, which had a special outfit request for her to welcome her client in.

Paul relayed the message to Delia in the best way he saw fit, asking her to throw on a jacket over the short outfit he saw her wearing, and get herself ready for the short drive to Old Marylebone Road, which would take considerably longer, because of the road work construction in the area, and its accompanying road diversions. Paul was just a little surprised that Eric was willing to forgo the accuracy of recording business transaction, for such a trivial matter as described by Ben, as "small business talk". Delia was a pretty expensive lady, and the loss of an hour or more, from a pre-booked client visit, would cost at least £300, and that was only if the pre-booked period wasn't extended, as was the case quite often with Delia.

As she left her room to meet Paul, Delia did something that she hadn't done before. She sent a text message to Obi, telling him where she was going and her concerns. Then, thinking that Obi wouldn't quite understand what she was trying to say, she called his number.

"Delia? I was just reading your text message. Is everything alright?" asked Obi, as he picked the call, right away." I was about to ring you, just now".

"Don't worry, baby. Nothing bad has happened, at least not yet. It's just that, the boss Eric who controls everything as far as I know, requested an impromptu meeting with me, and that has never happened before, with me, and none of the girls I know have ever been to his apartment. I just had this feeling that somethingwas not quite right and wanted to talk to you before I left the apartment".

"Well, that's okay" said Obi, "Actually it's great. I know, I know, it's not the best time to say that, but this is the first time you have confided in me, about any internal stuff going on in your working life" he said, laughing.

"But don't worry, I'll ring you every half hour, just to check up on you and see if you are alright, And, I know we didn't plan to meet tonight, but I will be at your place as soon as I finish up here, hopefully about 9, if it's okay with you?"

"That will be fine" replied Delia smiling, "I feel better already. I'll be waiting for you in something really sexy, so don't dare be late."

"Yes madam. I'll be there by 9 am, sharp. I can't wait to see you. Kisses Love you".

"Love you too, Obi. See you later.

Kisses."

With that Delia skipped down the stairs to the waiting car of Paul.

***

The lift that took Delia and Paul up towards Eric's apartment seemed towards Eric's apartment, seemed to take forever to get there, even if it was only a few floors up. There had been very little conversation in the car on the way to Old Marylebone Road, apart from the perfunctory talk about the weather and traffic,and there was absolutely none on the slow ride upwards on the elevator, and thisgave rise to even more tension and anxiety in Delia, with every passing minute spent on the way to meet Eric.

True to his word though, Obi had called every half hour, with just a few sentences spoken to see how Delia was holding up, the last one coming, to Delia's relief, in the elevator.

"Hey Delia, half an hour seems to take forever".

"That's because you are constantly looking at your watch, silly" replied Delia, laughing and drawing a cursory look from Paul. "Maybe you should double it, so that you can relax a little" she continued, looking furtively at Paul, wondering what he might have been making of the half hourly conversations.

"It's okay, baby. Just checking to make sure you're safe. It's no problem at all.Will call you back in another half hour, okay?"

"Okay baby, as long as it doesn't disrupt your day. Love you."

This last bit of conversation drew a cursory look from Paul followed by a slight frown. It was his business to know about any close acquaintances of the girls in his building, and to monitor the relationships. After all, the business model Eric and Ben developed, was rooted in the premise of the girls not being able to financially sustain themselves and having no one to depend on, hence for the ladies involved, the crucial importance "safety net service" provided by Eric.

The longer the girls needed "Eric's service", the longer they stayed in the "personal massage" business, the more money Eric and his associates made. Some girls, long after they has paid off the debt that they owed Eric, decided to stay on in the business, where they would now work on better percentages than they were on before, still pay rent to Eric and for the most part, still presented themselves asbeing under Eric's portfolio of girls. They did this, mostly because it was still the only "family" they felt comfortable being with.

Hence, the need to keep an eye on any relationships the girls developed while working. That way, you weren't surprised when the girls decided to pay you off and move on, ultimately allowing you to keep your "stable" of girls in good shape.

This wasn't the right time to be inquisitive or anything of the sort, thought Paul,but he made a mental note of it, as he led Delia through the open elevator doors,towards Eric's apartment.

CHAPTER EIGHTEEN

The Maida Vale apartment was sparsely furnished. It consisted of two bedrooms, a living room with a dining table for two at one end and a black leather settee at the other end. A twenty-inch flat screen TV graced the wall next to the settee, giving the room at least a semblance of a comfortable occupancy.

As Delia sat on the settee watching CNN, she couldn't help thinking that she had seen quite a few apartments that looked almost a carbon copy of the one she sat in presently. The only difference was that, unlike now, she had never before been a guest in any of them. She was usually the one doing the hosting, and under normal circumstances she would have been glad about the role reversal, after all, it would mean that she was under no obligation to perform any tasks or fulfil any request that she did not care for, but as Delia nursed the glass of orange juice she had beenoffered by Jeremy, and thought about the scene that had played out, a while ago in Eric Kalinsky's apartment, she felt a pang of discomfort.

"Hello Delia" said Eric, as he made his way into the living room where Ben, Paul and a black man whom Delia thought looked familiar, sat. Paul and Delia had gotten into the apartment just about five minutes earlier. The door was opened by Ben, whom Delia knew as a top boss, and greeted him accordingly, after he had exchanged pleasantries with Paul. She shook hands with the black man politely when he stood up to say hi, but as no one stepped forward to introduce him, she kept quiet after returning felicitations, and sat down on a chair that Ben offered.

"Well, it would seem that we have a full house today" said Eric to no one in particular, shaking hands across the room, as if he didn't implicitly invite every single person in that living room.

"Hello Delia, long time. How have you been?" asked Eric, when he got round to her, offering her a glass of red wine from a bottle that had just been opened by Ben.

"I've been doing okay" replied Delia, accepting a large glass of wine from Ben,"Paul has been looking after us quite well, haven't you Paul?"

"Well, what can I say?" said Paul, settling himself back into his chair, after accepting a bottle of Strongbow, at his request, from Ben "I do my very best,Eric."

"Having known you all this time" said Eric, "I expect nothing less, eh Ben?" His head turning towards Ben, who was now pouring a drink for the black man, who kept stealing admiring glances towards Delia, with a furtive, leering smile on his face.

"Absolutely, Eric" replied Ben, as he came forward to pour a drink for Eric. "Paulis a stand-up guy and has always been".

"Talking of stand up, guys" said Eric, as he settled himself into his favorite chair, a magnificent looking black colored, and bear skin piece, closest to the 50-inch wall to wall flat screen TV, and a step away from the corridor leading to the inner rooms. Everyone knew not to sit on that chair, instinctively. Only one visitor had ever sat in that chair...

"I would like you to meet Jeremy" Eric continued, gesturing towards the black man seated to Delia's left. "A really good friend of mine and both of us go a long way back. Jeremy, this is Delia. Delia, meet Jeremy".

As Delia extended her hand to Jeremy, Ben gestured to Paul that they move to the inner rooms, and as they stood to go inside, Ben said to Eric.

"We need to finalize some plans, Paul and I, as we discussed earlier".

"Sure Ben. Go ahead; I'll catch up with you in a bit." Then turning back towards Delia and Jeremy, he continued.

"Now that the two of you have been formally introduced, I can get down to the reason you're here, Delia. Jeremy, like I said is someone that I've known for a long time personally, and in terms of business, he is one of our most valued customers. He requested to see one of our very best for tonight, and based on the physical qualities that he described, it was thought that you were the best lady around. I don't know what you're plans are for tonight and I hope I'm not being presumptuous".

Delia, while listening to Eric, had casually taken a look at Jeremy. She had sensed his intent eyes, boring holes in her body,

but until that moment, had resisted the urge to look back. He was in his early 50's, with medium build and height, and she had noticed the Caribbean accent when they had exchanged pleasantries, earlier.
The rest she figured; she would find out in good time.

"Well, I was supposed to meet someone at 1230pm, but I guess" she said, glancing at her watch "That it's not going to be possible to meet up with that appointment now. So, Jeremy" she continued, turning towards her prospective customer." What did you have in mind?"

"Well then" said Eric, while getting up from his chair. "I'll leave the two of you it, while I go and attend to business with Ben and Paul, inside. It was nice seeing you again, Delia, always a pleasure. Jeremy, I guess we'll see again tomorrow or some other time. In the meantime, you two have the privacy of this room to yourselves". With that, he disappeared inside.

***

"How was the juice?" asked Jeremy, as he came back into the living room, minus his jacket and shirt. All he had on was his inner white vest and his jeans, which was literally hanging onto his hips, as the belt was undone. "If you need more, I can go get another bottle from downstairs. I've tried it before and found its pure natural taste; which you can hardly get these days with everything being genetically engineered or recreated with substitutes; unbeatable."

"No, thank you. Don't bother yourself. I did really enjoy it though, but I think I better get changed inside, and get ready. Yes?"

"Sure. No problem." He replied while reaching for some orange juice "You do that, while I polish off the remaining juice".

Delia smiled as she walked into the inner reaches of the apartment. There was a little kitchen to one side, a bathroom or rather a shower with a toilet to her left, and finally, at the end of the corridor on the right, a medium sized bedroom with a double bed, a small dressing table with a closet and small TV to one side.

She set down the small bag that she had brought with her when Jeremy had gotten a cab from Eric's apartment, that would take them back to Delia's place enroute to the Maida Vale apartment.

As she started to unpack her "special" lingerie and high heels from the bag, she thought about the conversation that had ensued between her and Jeremy, once Eric had left the living room of his apartment, so that they could talk privately.

"So, Jeremy, I guess you and Eric have talked. The only person that is still, how would you say it, little in the dark? Yes? So, tell me what you want me to do for you."

Delia said all this with her trademark sexy smile, but inside, she was quite worried. All of her premonition about the unusual nature of her meeting with Ericseemed to be manifesting itself. She had a certain urge to call Obi immediately, but resisted it, thinking to herself that after all, this was business, and besides, what could Obi realistically do, other than get himself worked up? So, she steeled herself, kept on her smile and waited for him to reveal his intentions.

"I was the guy that you were supposed to meet at 1230 today. I wanted to make sure you had the particular outfit I was looking for."

"So why didn't you just keep the original appointment and extend it for however long you wanted to." Asked Delia, relieved but still not totally at ease.

"You'll see why when we go to the apartment."

"What apartment? What's so special about it and what's going to happen there?"

"Don't be alarmed" said Jeremy, seeing the look on her face "Nothing crazy. It goes like this. I want you...."

***

"JEREMYYY!" Delia called out from the bedroom "I'm ready".

Jeremy who had been quietly waiting for ten minutes downed the last of the orange juice, set down his glass while debating whether to turn off the TV, as yet another report of a suicide bombing in Iraq, and was being read by the Al- Jazeera news anchor. Finally, deciding that it would be better to have some sound in the house, he slightly raised the volume and left it on, as he made his way to the bedroom.

As Jeremy walked towards the bedroom, he came face to face with Delia, in the doorway of the room. She was wearing an all-black skimpy outfit; spandex black bra, black skintight jean shorts and four-inch black stilettos. Seeing Jeremy, she turned around and walked slowly back towards the bed.

"You said that you just wanted me to dress and walk around at first, right?" asked Delia.
"Yes" replied Jeremy, looking at his watch "For now. I just want you to pose for me too, just like you would, if you were posing for a racy men's magazine. Of course, I'll have some suggestions" he said smiling.

Delia then proceeded to "ham it up", part walking around, part lap dancing and part posing for what looked like an age and wondering why Jeremy kept looking at his watch intermittently, until a doorbell rang, prompting Jeremy to getup.

"Are we expecting someone else?" asked Delia.

"A little surprise, but I think that you will recognize her" replied Jeremy as heheaded out to the front door.

"Recognize her?" asked Delia to no one in particular.

A minute later, Jeremy came back in with a familiar face, albeit one Delia had not seen for almost a year.

"Erica?" said Delia, in a bit of shock, partly because Erica was the last person that she to see, and also because she noticed that Erica was wearing an almost identical outfit to hers, but also with some relief. At least she knew who Erica was and felt a bit at ease. The surprise could have been much worse...

"Delia, long time" replied Erica "I have to confess that I knew I would be meeting you today, but I was told to keep it a secret.

Apparently, they wanted to surprise you."

Erica was Polish, with chestnut brown hair. She arrived in the UK about the sametime that Delia had, which was why they had roomed together at the time. She had just turned twenty-one, and her nickname was "Neon", to reflect her vivacious personality.

"So, everyone knew, but me?" asked Delia as she exchanged hugs with Erica."What's the plan then?"

"Just go crazy" said Jeremy, while pulling up a chair to the center of the room. "Keep doing the same thing you were doing before. We've only got about half an hour left; I'll step in with suggestions, once in a while".

With that, Erica practically tore off her latex bra, and began cat-walking around the room, pausing intermittently to walk up to Jeremy, step on his chair and lusciously kiss him. At other times, she would stop Delia in her tracks, and do the same to her.

All the while, Jeremy was watching intently, both at the girls and at the camera that had been installed on top of the closet.

The small TV was tuned to one of the music-video channels, with the volume raised close to its loudest, for effect, to resemble a photo shoot environment. Erica had also come into the room with some champagne, which was swigged from the bottle by the two ladies, to keep the mood up.

"Delia, come here and kiss me" said Jeremy, standing up and positioning himself for the optimal camera angle. An unwitting Delia complied with his request.

"Now, tell me you're a whore. A very bad, bad girl", and Delia again complied.

"Erica, come over here" said Jeremy, holding Delia gently within the camera shot until Erica, who was also unaware of the camera, came into the shot. Jeremy had spent his time planning this, just to make sure he would get it right.

"Now, the two of you, kiss and say the same thing again..."

CHAPTER NINETEEN

One of the many consequences of any on-going civil war is the exodus of peoplefrom the country or affected area. Families, both nuclear and extended, are torn apart, due to frequent, sudden and unplanned decisions to vacate a particular area,predicated on the eruption of violence or mass killings in that place.

The people who survive have to keep moving, siblings die, and the others move on. Cousins, uncles, aunts and grandparents become lost and are left behind. The ones who make it out alive together, usually become refugees in neighboring countries, and where conditions aren't favorable, they seek emigration to much better places, further away.

In the case of Eritrea, the indigenous people migrated everywhere, from European countries to the United States, where they settled into migrant communities in different areas. Sometimes, as people arrived at these communities, they discovered relatives they thought had been lost, already living there to great joy and celebration.

But, for young Eritreans like Suli, t lost family members or to keep in touch with relatives, living in different best place to rediscover lost family members or to keep in touch with relatives, living in different countries, no matter how far away they lived, was through social media.

This tech savvy generation of Eritreans kept tabs on each other and multiple other communities on Face book, Twitter, Myspace, YouTube and various other communication friendly, free media.

With cousins, uncles and aunts spread out everywhere from continental Europe tothe United States, and even as far as Australia, Suli absolutely loved his social media accounts. All he needed to be constantly in touch or updated, was to be on his Laptop or have his Android phone, on the ready.

In addition, to the staple social media, video and live feed sharing sites, there were numerous other sites and blogs, that were of either Eritrean or Islamic interest, and then others that had local content, only of real interest to the residents of a locality; workers or mates who lived in that particular environment.

One of such sites was named GPbandcrazies.com, a favorite of the under-thirty crowd in Grahame Park, as well as the criminal element that either lived in, or were just interested in the goings on, in Grahame Park and of course the undercover police. Generally everything you needed to know or almost everything, about Grahame Park, form parties to community events, property lettings to job opportunities.

But there were other things on the site as well, which were of particular interest to the criminal element that operated in and around the estate; suspected police surveillance apartments, newly noticed routes for police foot patrols(beats), and of course, inevitably, there were the adverts for sexual companionship, in theirvarious guises. Even though the police monitored the site, there was always different ways to sniff potential plants out.

Suli, as he tended to do in his spare time, decided to go online and see what was up with the world. As it was a Friday evening, the beginning of the party weekend,he decided to check out the Grahame Park site, for any info on potential parties or events to go to.

While going through the site's various offerings, his eye was caught in the video section, by a particular title "crime family sex tape". Normally, depending on his mood or if he was in a hurry and just taking a "sneak peek "on the site, there was a 50/50 chance that he would ignore it. But, the still image of the uploaded video, showed a face that Suli was absolutely certain, that he had seen before and also disturbingly sure, that it was one he had seen more than a few times before.

So, he immediately opened the video, and as happened sometimes with long video titles, the rest of it came into view, as the video began playing "Crime Family Sex tape of the J Adams' family, featuring ..." and he immediately recognized who he was looking at, or at least one of the two girls that he could see cavorting onscreen. The video itself, had a duration of only two minutes, but that was enough time to see Delia, he could now remember her name, dancing half naked, while kissing another girl, calling herself names, prompted by someone in the room who appeared to be a man, even though his face was digitally blurred and voice, somewhat altered.

In the long video title, also came a declaration that there would be more video excerpts to come on the website, every couple of days.

Suli immediately closed the site and shutdown his laptop. First, he called Moyo, then Riccardo, asking them if they had seen the video, he had just looked at, and ifthey hadn't, to do so and tell him what they thought and that they keep it to themselves, and as the time was 6pm, they agreed to get ready to meet at the Bullion Hill shop at 7pm.

Riccardo got there early by about 6:45, with him being the one in the group with the knack for always being on time. He was also the most cautious one in the group and the one who suggested meeting up at the Bullion Hill shop. At 6:45 in the evening the shop was starting to empty out as the last dog race of the afternoon session had been run, signifying the end of the major racing schedule for the day. So, you had a bit of privacy, with really, only shop staff and maybe a stranger or two in the extra-large customer area. Also, the shop sound system was left on and was usually loud, making it difficult for anyone to attempt to eavesdrop, without making it look obvious.

It was to this environment that Suli and Moyo arrived, and after exchanging pleasantries with the shop staff and the one other guy in the shop, they moved tothe seats that Riccardo had secured for them close to the front door.

"Did you guys see the video?" Suli asked.

"Yes" replied Moyo "It's distinctly Delia; I never forget a pretty face".

"No, you don't" said Riccardo with a smile, and then with his face turning serious once again, he asked "What do we do now? Surely, we have to let Jermaine know, if he doesn't already".

"I doubt, he does" said Suli "First, you know Jermaine is not a big internet guy, and second nobody really knows Delia, apart from Jermaine's family, us, and of course Obi. I wonder how he will take this. But first things first, we need to go to Jermaine's place and tell him quietly. This is no kind of conversation to be had on the phone. Besides, information from the video itself made mention of another segment to be posted online, tomorrow or so."

"Okay" said Moyo "But why do we all have to go and see Jermaine? You saw the video first and get to see Jermaine a lot more than we do. Why don't you go and tell him yourself? This is one thing I don't feel comfortable talking to Jermaine about."

"That's exactly why I want you to come, bro. I don't feel comfortable doing that, either. For some reason, I just felt that, if all three of us went, he would believe us,and not get mad, thinking it was some kind of silly joke."

"Alright, so when do we go to see him?" asked Riccardo.

"Tonight, I'll ring him now and let him know that we'll be coming to see him later on."

"I wonder if I can win anything on the evening dogs, before then" murmured Moyo, to no one in particular.

***

Jermaine cleared up the remains of the takeaway Chinese meal that he had ordered earlier. Mary was with Obi at one of their cleaning sites in East London,making sure that they did a good job in one of their newly acquired client buildings. Salma had gone out to a friend's birthday party, while Isabelle had travelled up north to Leicester to visit her expecting sister.

That left Jermaine alone in the house, for a large part of the evening, which was unusual in recent times. He had been busy enjoying the meal consisting of fried rice with chicken in black bean sauce, when his phone rang with Suli at the other end of the line, asking if he could come over with Riccardo and Moyo, to catch up on some things.

"Sure Suli, no problem. Just come on down here" with a quick look at his watch, "in an hour's time, which should be at about a quarter past eight, according to my watch. That should give you enough time to get some food into that skinny body of yours, because you won't be getting any here. I've about finishing my

Chinese takeaway and no one else, is around."

"Alright" replied Suli, with a chuckle "see you, then".

With all the cleaning done, Jermaine settled onto the living room couch, checking out the TV schedule, to see if there was anything interesting to watch, while waiting for Suli and the others to arrive. One of the sports channels was showing a classic game, involving Arsenal, his favorite football team. It was that brilliant 1999 game, away at Stamford Bridge, to Chelsea. Nwankwo Kanu had just completed his hat trick and the winning goal, the one from the seemingly impossible angle, when he heard the "grandfather chimes" of his front doorbell, followed by Suli's number, flashing his phone.

"How is everything going" asked Jermaine, after he had let them into the livingroom.

"Everything is going fine, generally" replied Suli, "I haven't heard about any problems from our other guys, either. No arrests or problems with customers, or anything like that."

"How about you guys" asked Jermaine, "Moyo and Riccardo, any problems?" To which they both replied in the negative.

"Something, else...? Like what, exactly?"

"Something we thought you should know about." Replied Moyo

"Well, go on then."

"I found this video on the local Grahame Park website." Suli said, hunching forward. "I think we are the only ones that saw the personal connection. It has to do with Obi's girlfriend, Delia..."

CHAPTER TWENTY

Jermaine had a Sunday schedule that he had kept for as long as he could remember, probably for as long as he had the opportunity, to live in his own place.

The morning started with his favorite cereal, Rice Krispies, immediately followed by a trip to the park with the boys, for some Sunday league football. Whilst he always loved playing, he found himself indulging in a bit of coaching in recent times.

By the time he got back, thoroughly exhausted, usually around 1130am, he was ready for his late version of breakfast; the full English version, with the emphasis on "full", six sausages, five beef burgers, three eggs, baked beans and a slice of bacon. Completely full, he could now relax and wait for the Sunday Premiership fixtures to begin. Usually, a few of the guys would show up at his place, creating a mini stadium effect. Of course, they were usually fellow Arsenal fans, even if once in a while, close friends who were supporters of other clubs and who could endure the ribbing, also came around.

Today however, wasn't going to be one those days. He had some Quaker Oats because he needed to have something in his stomach by 7 in the morning. It was going to be a long day. He was still sitting at the table with the half-eaten bowl of cereal, when the 8am kick-off for the Sunday league games passed. He didn't even notice.

When he received a call from Moyo, asking if he was still coming, Jermaine decided that it was best to pass the word that he would be busy all day, just in case anyone was planning on coming to the house later on as usual, in the early afternoon for the televised football matches.

Having been taken out of his long thoughtful reflections by Moyo's call, he started going through the things he had to do today, as he washed the dishes.

First, was his meeting with Obi, whom he hadn't been able to see ever since he found out about the errant video, last Friday night, Obi, having had to stay over at the work site on that Friday evening, had decided to stay over at Delia's place, as they had been planning to be together for most of the weekend anyway, after she had told the agency that she would be unavailable for the weekend.

So, when Jermaine called, asking if they could meet to talk about something important that had just come up, they agreed to meet for "brunch" by 12 noon in Brent Cross Shopping Centre, in a ground floor cafe.

They actually met instead in at the Brent Cross Underground station, where Jermaine waited for Obi after he ascertained via text, that Obi was already one station away, at Golders Green.

They eschewed the No. 210 bus, in favor of a long walk through a side street, leading to the main footpath to the shopping center. As they walked along the path, catching up on their weekend activities, so far, Jermaine decided to gradually let Obi in on what he had been thinking about, for the previous two nights.

"I actually wanted to see you for a particular reason, Obi bro. I thought it best that we met face to face."

Nothing the change in tone, Obi replied "I hope it's nothing serious or bad?"

"It's not about you or me" replied Jermaine, seeking to calm the look of anxiety on Obi's face, at least for now." But there's a video on a local Grahame Park website, that concerned me, and I thought you need to know about it, too."

"What video?" a sudden unexplained dread, starting to creep up in Obi's chest. From Jermaine's previous sentence, whatever was the matter, it wasn't about him.But it obviously concerned him. Since they hardly had any mutual friends, surely,this couldn't be about..."

"It was Delia, in the video. I can't really talk about it. You need to see it for yourself."

Images flashed through Obi's mind, as he looked at the pained expression on Jermaine's face, all he could think about, was how badly damaging the video could be? What exactly was she doing in the video? Having sex with a client? Then, it dawned on him, that no one else knew about Delia's other life, at least none of his friends, not even Jermaine. He had not yet gotten round to telling Jermaine about her. Obi had been hoping for a bit more time, to establish the side of Delia that he wanted people, especially Jermaine and his family, to know about Delia, her kindness, honesty and true love for him.

As he noticed Jermaine studiously looking at an object in the distance, he knew that the time to do that had probably gone. Jermaine was also about to find out that Obi hadn't trusted him enough to tell him about Delia, even if he told no one else. Obi thought also that Jermaine would never look at Delia the same way, again.

"Is your tablet charged" asked Obi, having noticed at the station that Jermaine brought his along.

"Yeah" said Jermaine, handing it over, along with earphones." I've already gottenon the website with the video in question, ready to be played".

They had now reached the bus terminal/bus stop, front area of the shopping center, so they decided to go to the cafe they'd agreed on earlier, which was half empty, the day being Sunday when most people decided to have a lie-in or go to church in the morning hours. They picked a table where they could have some privacy, and then Obi started to watch the video. Jermaine saw the embarrassment, and then a resigned look without any outwardly shown anger, which told him all he wanted to know, but waited for Obi to speak for himself. With the video finished, Obi looked up to see the expectant look on Jermaine's face, but not quite knowing where to start.

"How long have you known about her?" Jermaine asked.

"I've known for quite a while. Actually, it was how I met her... the second time at least."

"The second time...?"

"It's a long story. I'd actually met her the first time, on a train, on my way home from work. But I'm sorry I couldn't tell you right away. I was always waiting for the right time, trying to get you guys to know her well enough, without her other life prejudicing your view of her, first. I just needed time, but it would appear thatI didn't have enough. I just want you to know that she is a really good caring girl,as well as beautiful, and we love each other very much. She really wants to quit that line of work, very soon. The only reason she is still in it, is to pay her debts. I'm absolutely certain; she knows nothing about this video."

"Well," said Jermaine smiling "That was, some testimonial, and I believe that you love her, too. My only worry when I first saw that video was that maybe you didn't know about this side of her, or even worse, that maybe you were doing a bit of pimping, on the side". This last bit, bringing a sudden outburst of laughter, from the two of them, that drew the attention of other customers, but more importantly, broke the tension that had been building up for a while.

"Yeah" continued Jermaine "that had me worried" and with the smile still in place, "You didn't have to keep it from me or be worried about what I would think. Remember my background? I've been there and done that. My only concernis to make sure that you are doing things for the right reasons, and I hope it all ends well. However, right now we have bigger problems. There is another video out now. It's not much worse than the first, but they are being labelled with my name. Soon enough, my mum and the rest of the family will know, and also, it's bringing me back into the public consciousness as a crime lord, something I've tried to avoid. There's the promise of more videos to come, and I've a feeling that the videos will get progressively worse. We need to speak to Delia and find out if there is a way to figure out where this is coming from."

"I'll give her a ring and arrange a get together, ASAP," said Obi.

"You do that, bro. The sooner we figure this out the better for everyone."

With that, they finished the coffee and sandwiches they had ordered, and went off to indulge themselves in a bit of window shopping.

***

Obi and Delia took a cab from her Paddington apartment to

Trafalgar square, where they were to meet up with Jermaine. They would have taken the underground to get there, but Delia was in no state to go on public transport, after Obi had met her in the apartment, about two hours earlier.

Delia didn't have much to do, in terms of clientele that afternoon, and so when Obi called saying that he needed to see her urgently, she asked him to come straight down. After all, they had only parted company that morning, because Obi had to meet up with Jermaine, urgently. Delia enjoyed the time she spent with Obi, it felt like living in an alternate reality. It was the beautiful life that she craved, even if it was temporary. For now, she thought, those temporary moments,were glimpses of the future.

But when Obi got back to her apartment, she sensed that something was not quite right, especially after he gave her a side hug, with a sad look on his face. She had been crying ever since Obi had gotten round to telling her what he knew.

Obi decided then, that he didn't want that meeting with Jermaine, to happen in Colindale or anywhere around there, as had been previously agreed, not knowing who had seen the video, and who hadn't. But instead, he wanted somewhere "neutral", and probably somewhere nice, to lighten the mood.

Jermaine agreed when told, and they gathered at the bottom of the steps of the National Gallery, and then proceeded to walk around the square as they talked,until the benches became free.

"Okay Delia?" asked Jermaine, after they had gotten their rather solemn "hellos" out of the way, to which she shrugged nonchalantly. "I know that this might not be pleasant to remember, or even talk about, but we need to know everything that happened that day. This was obviously a set up, but if we can figure out who is behind this, we might be able to know what they are trying to do."

"I'm really sorry that you had to find out about me this way. But this is me. I can't apologize for what I do. Hopefully, you can understand this?"

"You don't have to worry about me, Delia" said Jermaine, smiling for the first time since they had met up. "I'm not exactly your law abiding, upright citizen, either. I've done a lot worse than you have or could ever know. The important thing for me is that you and Obi..." with a nod to his friend, who hadn't said much, but had a protective arm around his lady, "Love each other. Now, just go through the events of that day, for us."

"It was a weird day, as I remember "said Delia "Things that didn't seem right or unusual came up. I even told Obi, to keep ringing me every half hour or so, just in case something happened". Jermaine smiled again as she spoke, not because anything she said was funny, but because she subconsciously or consciously, snuggled closer to Obi, as if for extra protection and warmth.

"I've found out more about them in the last five hours, than in all our previous meetings combined, and they look good for each other too" thought Jermaine.

Delia continued to describe the events of that day, from the time Paul his message, to their trip to see Eric where she eventually met the client, who then took her to the place where the video was made.

"So, who was at the apartment that day, and who is Eric?" Jermaine asked.

"Well. Eric is the big boss; Ben is kind of his deputy and of course, I came withPaul, who is the caretaker of my apartment building."

"I don't know any of them and can't see any connection there. Who was the client?"

"It was a black guy, Caribbean like you and I think I've seen him before. His name was Jeremy..."

***

"Jeremy" thought Jermaine, as he took the train home to Colindale. Everything became a little clearer now, but there were still some unanswered questions. What did he have to gain from embarrassing Delia? Even if a connection could be made back to him, why go through all this trouble, just to embarrass him?

He got out of the train station and took the short work home, still pondering Jeremy's motives. When he eventually got home, everyone was there; Mary, Salma and Isabelle; debating whether to make Rice and Peas or go out and get some chicken from that brilliant chicken shop near the Burnt Oak Broadway Station on Watling Avenue, Dixy Chicken. Jermaine sided with the majority, who wanted some Dixy chicken. The ladies all decided to gout together, and get the chicken meals, whilst getting some fresh air and a bit of the night life, leaving Jermaine, to his designs, in the meantime...

Monday morning felt very good. Whilst the video was still out there, online, at least for the first time in three nights, he could enjoy his sleep. He now knew what he needed to do and whom he needed to tackle. No more shadowy figures to think about, there was now a face to put to the distant silhouette. All he could think about now was how to confront Jeremy, and how to figure out what his angle was.

He was still deep in thought, when his phone rang. Looking at it, he saw that it was an unrecognized number. Usually, he would have ignored the call; he never answered calls from unknown numbers. From past experience, such calls only usually brought about undesirable and unhelpful distractions, but this had been a weird weekend that had just gone by, with plenty of unexpected happenings, andjust because of that, he picked the call, something inside him prompting him to, afeeling that he might want to take this one.

"Hello, who is this?"

"Hold on" a voice he didn't recognize, asked, then with a bit of noise in the background, a familiar voice, came on.

"It's me, Obi."

"Obi...?

Why are you ringing me with this number" Jermaine felt a rising dread?There was something about the call he was receiving that felt very familiar, and that sound in Obi's voice."

Is everything alright?"

But he thought he already knew the answer to that question.... He thought he heard some incoherent babbling, which he couldn't make out.

"C'mon Obi, I can't hear you, bro. What's up?"

"Delia....It's about her She's dead."

The line went dead, too.

CHAPTER TWENTY-ONE

NOTHING LASTS

Obi and Delia left Trafalgar Square about 15 minutes after Jermaine had gone home. They left in much better spirits than they had arrived in. For Obi, there was a palpable feeling of relief. He had been planning and waiting for the perfect opportunity to tell Jermaine about Delia's secret life. That problem was no longer an issue. He actually felt that somehow, this whole episode had raised the stock of Delia in Jermaine's eyes. Had noticed the smile and look of respect on Jermaine's face, and thought that maybe, some sort of kindred spirit had been forged between the two of them. Maybe, it had something to do with the fact that both Delia and Jermaine, had to make a living outside the lines of legality to survive, build up their lives and realize their dreams, and were not afraid to do so.

Besides, Jermaine had promised that Delia had nothing to fear from the rest of his family, and would be as welcome to their home, as ever. His family members had all been engaged in some form of vice or another, or had grown up surrounded by one, and he thought that, they wouldn't have any problems accepting her, especially if they were convinced, the way Obi was, about how strong and special the relationship was.

For Delia, it was an unburdening of the soul. She had always felt embarrassed, when she would come over to Jermaine's house in Colindale, knowing that there was a part of her that she couldn't tell them about. When they asked what she didfor a living, she would say that she was an Au-pair and that she also did some bartending at night to explain her long and late hours. When they would go shopping; she, together with Mary, Salma and Isabelle, she offered little in the way of her experiences, when everyone would talk about how their day or week, had been.

This was the first time that anyone outside of the people she worked with, or anyone that she was in any type of personal relationship, knew about her "other" life, and it made her feel accepted, whole, and judging from the look she saw on Jermaine's face as she recalled the events of that strange day, respected.

Delia and Obi both felt particularly happy, and they decided that instead of taking the underground train from Charing Cross Station, next to the square, they would instead take the scenic route that consisted of walking through a series of winding streets and paths to Leicester Square, especially as daylight was fading into the nighttime, the streets filled with revelers and tourists alike. They lingered in the square for a short while, hands linked together, walking round the cinemas, theatres, clubs and restaurants in the area, taking in the atmosphere of the square, as if it for was the first time.

Finally, they walked into the Leicester Square Station and took the connecting trains to Paddington, heading home to Delia's apartment. After Obi had told her about the internet video earlier, she had asked the agency, not to book her for the rest of the day, telling them that she didn't feel well. That meant that, for the rest of the night and the following morning, she was free enough to have Obi spend the night. In all of the day's frenetic activity, they had forgotten to get any lunch and were quite famished, so Obi decided to pick up some Shish Kebab and chips from the Turkish place, that was close to the apartment, while Delia had a sudden desirefor fine wine, and went down too, to pick up a bottle from the local all-night shop.

They had to quickly quiet themselves, as they got back into Delia's apartment, laughing hard and loud as they were, at one of Obi's impromptu jokes, which while not particularly funny, as Obi would later remember, but, in the spirit of the evening, it was the reflection of their happiness of the good times to come, and less secrets to keep.

Obi and Jermaine had agreed with Delia, in spite of her initial protestations basedon personal pride, to raise the money needed to pay off what was left of her debt to Eric Kalinsky and his cohorts, the very next week. They said nothing to Delia, after a brief aside, in order not to alarm her, but they wondered if her personal safety had been compromised.

All that planning though, was for the future. However, for that night, as Delia and Obi enjoyed the brilliantly prepared kebab, with the wine Delia had purchased, nothing else mattered aside from enjoying precious time spent together. After clearing away the takeaway dishes, they sat up late, fooling around, with Delia doing what she always tried doing, teaching him to speak her language, this time with the variation of teaching him to sing a song, with predictably hilarious results.

They eventually slept off late in the night, utterly exhausted from the exhilarating events of the day, leaving the Lionel Richie songs they loved, playing at low volume.

In the haze of the sleeping gas being steadily pumped into the room, Delia's last thoughts were decidedly happy ones....

***

"I never even got the chance to tell her goodbye." Said Obi in a voice barely audible to Jermaine as they sat together in one of the consultation rooms, reserved for defendants/plaintiffs in the courthouse.

Obi's lawyer had asked him to go in there, so that they could go through their trial defense once more, and Obi had requested that Jermaine come in there with them. Jermaine had barely had any contact with Obi since that extraordinary morning phone call, three months ago, after the police had apparently burst through the door to Delia's apartment, to find the bloody body of Delia on the bed,alongside a suddenly woken Obi, with a blood-stained knife in his hand…

"How are you holding up?" asked Jermaine, while taking in the sad sight of his good friend; an empty look in eyes that were bloodshot from what must have been frequent bouts of crying, and also the stunning, but understandable appearance of a dash of grey, in the beard of the normally young looking and clean shaven, Obi.

"I don't know what to do. All I can think about whenever I close my eyes is her,and the way we were so happy that last night, and then I can't remember anything else, no matter how hard I try" replied Obi, as tears began to well up in his eyes. "Then, I remember the interrogation by the police officers, telling me horrible things about Delia's body….and Delia's face…I keep having nightmares."

“Surely, you have to remember something?” asked Kathy Benedict, Obi’s lawyer.She was the best lawyer that Jermaine could afford, whom he brought in to represent Obi, within days of receiving that early morning shock from Obi. She was in her mid-forties and of Afro Caribbean heritage, by way of Barbados, and had the reputation of being a good, tough defense lawyer.

“All that I can remember” answered Obi, “is seeing the blood-stained sheets. Theofficers never let me have a look at her. They just hustled me to one end of the room, read me my rights and then led me out of the room in handcuffs. I remember shouting, as I saw what looked like a body, under the blood-stained sheets, and someone taking pictures. That’s all I remember.” Then, turning to Jermaine, he continued, “You’ve got to help me. Everything, kind of looks quite bleak, right now. I’ve got no real defense to counter the charges. There is a blood- stained knife with my fingerprints, all over it. I was in the room when the body was discovered, too. I can’t even mourn; the love of my life that I will never see again, without thinking of what is to happen to me, should this trial progress to its seemingly obvious conclusion.”

“Someone knows what happened that night” continued Obi, “Someone murdered Delia in that room, maybe more than one person. I just don’t understand how I could be asleep, while all that mayhem was going on.”

“That’s all the more reason why, you should plead guilty right now, at thepre-trial hearing.” said Kathy, who had been watching Obi, during his plea to
Jermaine. “I’m not a miracle worker, especially when the physical evidence, is thisstrong. This isn’t like the O.J. Simpson trial, where there was a lot of circumstantial evidence, and physical evidence which could be undermined, because of one critical difference. You were found at the scene, with the murder weapon in your hand. That crucial fact is undisputable.”

“Just do your best for now, but I think from what Obi is saying, he doesn’t want to plead guilty.” This said with a look towards Obi, who nodded accordingly. “I’ll see what I can do. Something obviously happened that night, something horrible, and someone out there knows exactly what went down, that night. I’ll aim to try and find that person or persons.” the declaration, bringing the first smile of the day from Obi.

"In the meantime, just keep yourself together." Continued Jermaine, "and let the two of us" with a nod to Kathy, "do our very best, and see where that takes us."

With that, he got up to leave "I'm going to leave the two of you to go through thelegal strategy. Don't worry…" said Jermaine, to calm down the look of alarm, which had appeared on Obi's face, "…I've just got to go and get some things done, with regards to what we've just been discussing. I'll be back as soon as I can."

Jermaine closed the door behind him and left through the security barriers of the front entrance to the court building. Jermaine walked to the bus stop deep in thought, got on the waiting bus and made his way to Delia's former apartment building, yet again.

This time, there was no noticeable police presence on the outside, but he had seen someone go inside, from a distance, as he approached. As no one was around, he took his time to study the intercom system and the door lock, furtively taking pictures with his phone, thinking that the knowledge gleaned would be useful when he could come up with a strategy to get inside the building, with a good cover story.

Having got the information, he wanted and was about to leave, he noticed a middle-aged lady approaching the building. Instinctively, he tried adopting the mannerism of the Met officers he had encountered on so many occasions.

"Good afternoon, madam, might you be living in this building? I'm an officer with the London Met, and we are making some enquires in the area."

"Don't you remember me? The lady asked, with a strong East European accent"I'm here to clean the apartment. Remember?

"Oh, that's alright then. You must have spoken to one of my colleagues. We'rejust making sure we haven't missed anyone. You can go in. Have a good day." Jermaine said, stepping aside.

He took a quick peek, as the lady punched in her access code, and left quicklyas soon as she had shut the door behind her. He didn't want to take the chance of running into someone else from the building.

The beginnings of an idea, started to take shape in his mind as he left Paddington via the Underground, making his way back to Colindale. There wasn't much time left, to try and save his best friend's life…

CHAPTER TWENTY-TWO

The mood in Eric Kalinsky's apartment was quite tense, in complete contrast withthe opulent and relaxed décor of the room. This contrast was a direct result of the presence of one man, Jeremy. He had arrived at the apartment only ten minutes earlier. This visit was one that he had expected to make about three months ago, but had been seemingly rebuffed at every opportunity, with one excuse or another.

Jeremy's vision, prior to the death of Delia, about the way, the last three months was supposed to have gone, was a total 180° from what actually went down. All the difference could be directly attributable to one major event, one that was not of his making. Even if the chain of events that culminated in Delia's death, was kick started by his nefarious video scheme, the final outcome wasn't in the plan.

The proposed strategy behind his plan, was supposed to be the gradual, but steady, embarrassment of Jermaine, his friends and family, and also pushing him back under the radar of law enforcement, bringing unwanted attention and exposure to a man who, was supposed to be under strict, criminal court-enforced, community service.

Jeremy knew that upon investigation, Jermaine would trace the video back to him., and if he was recalcitrant enough, he could force Jermaine into doing something silly enough to violate the terms of his community service, which was where DI's Johnson and Patterson came in, and take him off the Grahame Park criminal hierarchy, leaving the door wide open for him to walk in and assume control.

What he'd now had to deal with, in the aftermath of the murder, was now less personally beneficial. The entire criminal community of Grahame Park thoughtthat he had been behind the killing, and virtually every one of them, had swiftly shifted away or cut links and personal contact with him. No one wanted to be caught up in the middle, or the wrong side of the expected backlash from Jermaine.

Jermaine's former stepdad had not received any implicit or explicit threats but had taken a gauge of the charged atmosphere in the council estate, and sent off his girlfriend and child, to stay with his aunt in Watford. He kept a few of his most trusted people around his apartment while he tried to think of his next move.

In the living room with Jeremy that evening was, the ever-present Ben, Paul, a slightly hefty man named Vlad, who was almost certainly a muscle man for Eric;whom he was informed after being let into the apartment by Vlad, was taking a bath.

Jeremy didn't mind. In fact, he didn't mind if Eric took the rest of the night to take his bath, just as long as, whenever he decided that he had enough, Jeremywould get to see him.

"How have you been?" Ben asked Jeremy "It's been quite a while."

"That's kind of why I'm here." Jeremy replied, "There are a few things that need straightening out."

"Oh" said Ben, in a non-committal sort of voice, excusing himself "I'll go get Eric, then. I think he'd got some business that came up suddenly, but I'm sure he'll be down shortly." With that he disappeared into the inner recesses of the apartment.

He emerged a short while later with Eric, who appeared to be in a jovial mood, orat least as it would appear, by his facial expression, a sharp contrast to that of Jeremy, whose temper had gradually built up with every passing minute he spent in the apartment, even as he outwardly tried to project a cool and detached look.

"What? No drinks for Jeremy?" Eric asked, as he moved to shake Jeremy's hand.

"Ben did offer me a drink, but I said no. I didn't feel like one, at least not now."Jeremy said, as he sat back down on the cushion chair.

"So, how have you been, and what have you been up to, in the last few weeks?" Eric asked, from the mini bar, as he poured himself a half glass of Vodka and ice.

"Well," replied Jeremy, with some sarcasm in his voice, "For one, I've been trying to arrange a meeting with you, especially over the last few months, as you so succinctly noticed".

This drew looks from Ben, Paul and a quiet smile from Eric. Everyone was aware of the real reason this meeting was taking place, but no one, it seemed, wanted to be the first to broach that topic, so as not to show what they knew, or didn't know.This was especially true for Eric and his crew, but Jeremy hadn't gotten to where he was, by coy or subtle. Besides, he didn't have the time to be patient, either. It had taken so long to get this meeting to happen. His earlier insinuation about his inability to get this meeting to hold earlier was an effort to get the meeting to the important issues at hand, as quickly as possible.

"It's been a bit of a busy period for us in the last few months. It's just one of those periods when there is so much demand for our expertise." Eric said, with a movement of his open hand in the direction of Ben, Paul and Vlad. "So" he continued "It's not like I've been trying to avoid you or anything of the sort, as youare trying to imply, I'm sure."

"I'm not implying anything, Eric. As one friend to another and as a person that I've worked with, for years now, all of a sudden, I couldn't make any contact with you at a time when it was most needed. Not even an e-mail or calls to your cell phone, seemed to get through. You're trying to tell me that you couldn't send an e-mail, for three bloody months!"

"All this coming right after the incident involving the lady, we had talked about." This last sentence by Jeremy, said with a cursory look around the room, like he was looking for a hidden surveillance device in the room. After all, the incident he was referring to, was a murder that the police had no reason to suspect that, anyone else apart from Obi Udo, knew anything about. He dared not even mention her name here, at least not till the coming murder trial and possible conviction of Obi, was concluded.

Ben had watched Jeremy's not so subtle look around the room, barely suppressing a smile, as he knew what Jeremy was thinking about, and that he obviously didn't know that the apartment was swept for hidden surveillance devices daily.

As a former KGB operative, Eric had this practice installed and strictly adhered to, and like other former operatives, especially those who were still actively involved in one enterprise or the other, criminal or otherwise, such a practice was like second nature, as straightforward as sleeping at night and waking up in the morning.

"Would you be referring to the incident that happened at one of Eric's apartment building, about three months ago?" Ben asked, a smile playing on his lips.

Eric, who had missed Jeremy's furtive look around the room, while on his way tohis favorite sitting position, added his voice to the conversation.

"The Delia incident in Paddington…? About three months ago? Eric asked, as a rejoinder to Ben's question, and wondering why Ben had a bemused smile on his face, only to follow Ben's gaze to Jeremy's momentary confused look around,at the four other people in the room, and then immediately understood the source of Ben's amusement.

"It was really unfortunate, what happened on that night to that pretty girl" Eric continued "Hopefully, justice will be done, and her killer brought to book."

"She was a really nice girl, too" Paul said, speaking up for the first time "All her friends were quite upset about the whole thing. One of those things, that you neverquite see coming, I guess."

"It cost me money as well" Eric said "As, the girls were so traumatized and scared to work. I had to put in new security measures at all my apartments, before the ladies could feel safe and confident to work again, and that took a few weeks."

"So, you can see why Eric and the rest of us were quite busy over the last few months, since we last met." Eric added, "It was a difficult situation that had to be taken care of promptly."

"Not to mention, having to deal with the police." Eric said. "It was quite difficult at first, especially with the kind of operation we ran there. Luckily, Paul did a great job of not getting me involved." This said with a smile and nod towards Paul,"As, he took responsibility for the ownership of the building. The other girls there also left me out of it too, when they were questioned. As the news started filtering into us that morning, about what had happened, the atmosphere around here became tense, but I think our fears were unfounded, as the police already had the perpetrator of the crime, who just happened to be her boyfriend."

"It still was an unpleasant experience, nonetheless" Ben said. "I believe the trial will be happening sometime soon, from what I've gathered, and I guess justice, will be done."

Jeremy had sat down through all this conversation. Very quietly observing the other four men in the room, trying to see if he could pick up any signals being silently passed around as, Eric, Ben and Paul talked. He knew now that the men seated around him, were either telling the absolute truth, or that the room had been thoroughly swept for "bugs". Jeremy thought the later scenario, was more plausible.

Eric Kalinsky & Co didn't have a monopoly of the information on what happened that night, in the Paddington apartment. Rumors tend to spread fast, especially when they had something to do with anyone from Grahame Park, in thiscase Jermaine and Jeremy.

According to the version of events that Jeremy had heard from multiple sources, the police had caught Obi in bed with the slain Delia, in the wee hours of the morning, which meant that, someone had informed the police about the murder. It wasn't like it had been discovered by someone accidently, or that anyone had been alerted by some strange noise or altercation. Someone, knew what had taken place before the hapless Obi himself, did. The question was, who?

The answer to that question, Jeremy thought, lay in this living room. He was absolutely certain that Eric, Ben and Paul, in spite of the seeming drama of innocence and self-pity they had just played out, knew the true version of events that took place that night, and talking of the people in the room, Jeremy had watched with fascination, the demeanor of the other man in the room, the only person who hadn't said anything. He had wondered why Vlad hadn't been asked to leave the room, when they had started talking about the Delia incident.
Information about such sensitive subjects was unusually limited to an inner circle, unless of course, Vlad was a part of that inner circle of people who knew what had happened that night.

Even as the information of the incident kept filtering through, the question on the lips of those with knowledge of the crime on the street had been that if Obi hadn't done it, how on earth could it have been pulled off? In Jeremy's mind, more than one person had to be there, to be able to move Obi around, in the way that the physical evidence seemed to show.

While Eric, as a former KGB man, might have been at home with such a phenomenon; creating a crime scene would be child's play, he wouldn't have been physically involved, because he had too much to lose. Neither in fact, would have been Ben, his right-hand man.

Jeremy guessed that Paul would have had to be involved, as he was the one in charge of Delia's building, but he definitely didn't have the size to have performed such a demandingly physical task. With the dastardly nature of the crime, in order to keep its antecedents secret, the set up would have to be small in manpower.
Based on his observations that day, Jeremy thought that Vlad was definitely physically involved, as well.

"Well," said Jeremy, getting up to leave, "If that was how everything went down, and is your reason for the lack of communication, then, no worries. I'll accept that.But we are friends after all; let's not make the past few months a habit, all right?"

"I'll try my best" replied Eric, as he led Jeremy towards the door." Hope your family is doing well?"

"As well as can be helped" Jeremy said, as they walked along the corridor." What about yours?"

"It's all good. We'll catch up again, soon" Eric said, as Jeremy stepped through the elevator doors "Good night."

As Eric walked back down the well-lit, easy décor corridor towards his apartment door, he turned to Ben, who had accompanied him in seeing off Jeremy.

"I'm not entirely convinced that Jeremy bought our story. No loose ends. For now, just have him followed."

Ben nodded, as he followed Eric through the door to the apartment, momentarily wondering about, and then settling on the man who he thought was best suited for the job…

CHAPTER TWENTY-THREE

"We are almost done." Thought Jermaine, as he left Delia's old apartment building, for what he thought might be the final time in a spate of clandestine visits in the past couple of weeks.

It had all taken a while to set up, the idea that had come into his head on that afternoon following his encounter with the apartment cleaner for Delia's old building.

Jermaine had wanted to take a look inside the apartment, and Delia's former apartment in particular. He had told Obi about the plan he had in mind, the next time he had a chance to visit Obi, following the pre-trial hearing. He, Gina and Salma, took turns to visit Obi, whenever it was visitation time. The family had taken as their duty to make sure that Obi was alright, at this critical juncture in hislife, especially as his family was so far away. Obi had kept up communication with his parents as much as he could. Jermaine and his family, who had gotten to know Obi's people over time, as Obi had intimated his family about the way Jermaine and his family had really taken care of him. Jermaine's family had given Obi their word, that they wouldn't let word of the current goings-on in Obi's life, reach his parents.

Obi had a lot to worry about, without the added burden of thinking of the way his parents, and especially his mother, would react to the news that he was currently incarcerated on a murder charge. At the age his parents were, there was a high possibility of high blood pressure, a stroke and all kinds of health complications arising, as an adverse reaction to such calamitous news. So, Jermaine and his family, in spite of their initial disagreement, especially from Mary, acquiesced to that request. All they could do, was try their best to keep his spirits up, whomever it was among them, that turned up to visit him.

Jermaine decided to come today, to intimate Obi about his plan, and also to try and get some information from him.

"How are you doing today, bro?" Jermaine asked, as he pulled his chair closer to Obi, taking a good at his friend, having not seen him since that pre-trial hearing, where Obi had, just like he said he would, plead "not guilty". It seemed that everytime they had met since Delia's murder, a few extra grey hairs would be visible in Obi's unruly stubble.

"Doing alright, I guess..." Obi replied ...In the circumstances, having to do without some things and forget completely about others. For example, can you believe that they don't have chicken in black bean sauce with rice, on the menuhere? It's killing me."

That brought the first laugh of the day for the two of them and deep down, Jermaine was happy that there was still some of the old Obi spirit, in that worn out body of his. He would need all of it, if he was to recover his old self, when this was all over.

"Remember when I left you with the lawyer, in the courthouse consultation room,the last time we met?" Jermaine asked "Well, I just came up with a plan, after a visit to Delia's old apartment building."

"You got in, how?" Obi asked to which Jermaine briefed him on his encounter with the building cleaner, and his subsequent acquisition of access to the building.

"I just need to know a few things, to make the most of this opportunity". Jermaine said,
"What opportunity are we talking about, exactly? "O b I asked, with a quizzicallook on his face.

"We both know that what everyone thinks happened that night, while plausible, is totally impossible. There's no way, you did what they are accusing you of doing, but the evidence is so overwhelming. If you are going to come out of this, pronounced innocent, we need even out the odds, somehow. That the evidence is so contrary to what we know happened, means that someone else, probably more than one person, was involved. We need to know how and why, and the answers to those questions I think, can only be found in that apartment."

"So, what exactly are you going to do, now that you've got access to the building?"

"I need to know her apartment room number, and the names of the ladies that she might have been particularly close to?"

“Her apartment number is 7, and her best friend in the building was Helena, a blond girl from Budapest, Hungary. We were introduced, just once, so I can’t give you any real insight as to how close they might have been. But I have to warn you not to expect any cooperation from Helena, or any other girls you might encounterin the house. It is in their self-interest that nothing bad happen to Eric. It might be logical to think that they, the ladies, would be happy to see the back of the man, to whom they owe money, but you would have to remember that a lot of their livelihood and shelter conditions are dependent on him. Not to mention the ones who still need false documents to stay in the country. So, with self-preservation factored in, assume that you will get virtually no cooperation, and that if they alert Eric, or his people, about what you are doing, it could be dangerous for you.”

“Got it Obi, but it’s our only shot or least, the only one I can see right now. It’seither that or we let things take the course that circumstances are charting us toward, at the moment.”

A smile gradually spread across Obi’s face, in contrast to the sad look in his eyes,a contrast that Jermaine had come to notice ever since Delia’s murder ordeal had begun.

“I know, Jermaine, You are the only one I’ve got, who can be of help to me, right now. But I’m thinking of Mary and Salma, and if anything happened to you on account of your helping me, the guilt would be all mine. I don’t want anything to happen to you. I already feel that Delia’s death had something to do with me, evenif I didn’t strike the fatal blow.”

“Don’t worry about me, Obi. You and Delia would be doing exactly the same thing, if the tables were turned. That poor girl can’t have just died for nothing, andin such a brutal, horrible way. I didn’t know her, as well or for as long as you did,but in spite of the life she lived, there was something good and beautiful in her, that the life choice she made and lived couldn’t kill, no matter how tough her life was. That’s something that I could identify with, and I want to find out who thought that they had the right to do that to her, what all the bad circumstances in the world, couldn’t? I’m doing this for her, just about as much as I am doing this for you, Obi…”

The tacit approval of Obi gotten, Jermaine now swung into action the following day, armed with the entry code to Delia’s apartment building, and a plan.

First, assuming the persona, that got him his entry chance to the building, being that of a policeman, he watched for the work patterns of the apartment cleaner. She came around in the morning that day, and on seeing him told him she was about to begin, and in the brief side chat they had, he learned that she came in either early in the morning or around midday, when the building was, “less busy”.

With Helga, that was the apartment cleaner’s name, thinking of him as a police officer, and thus, now a trusted and familiar face, he wanted to get into the building whenever she was around. He thought it would give him some cover to move around the building, at those times, knowing that she would be chatting with her fellow East Europeans, talking about “that police officer checking out the room where that poor girl was murdered”.

He located Helena in Apartment 12. She had actually lived in Apartment 8, but had moved to, the then empty, Apartment 12 after Delia’s murder, because she couldn’t sleep there anymore, not with the story she had heard about what had happened to her best friend, in the very next apartment, that fateful night.

Jermaine casually asked her if she knew anything or had heard anything that night, or had any second-hand information about it, to which she replied in the negative.

Acting on a hunch, he discreetly broke into the now empty Apartment 8, to see if there were any connections to Apartment 7. He found the expected hidden camera,located in an unlit corner of the ceiling, directly over the bed, and sparse furniturein the room.

Jermaine had the conviction that in order to do what was done to Delia, and to get Obi’s physical complicity in the crime, some kind of noise been made in that room, that could have attracted attention of the people in the adjoining rooms. He wondered if the reason that no commotion was heard was because the murder hadbeen done in a perfectly noiseless manner, or if the perpetrators had taken precautions against any slip-up on their part. Jermaine was hoping for the latter.

Testing the side of the wall, bordering Apartment 7 from

Helena's former apartment, checking for thinness or otherwise, Jermaine noticed almost by accident, the presence of two small holes at the base of the wall. The holes didn't look like anything mice might have made, and the electrical, television cabling, as well as the phone line sockets, were at the other end of the room.

Jermaine had avoided an in-depth search of Delia's old apartment, knowing that the police would have picked up any evidence they thought might be relevant to their investigation. The room had an eerie feeling that Jermaine absolutely abhorred. He called it the "stench of death", stench he remembers from going toa Grahame Park flat of a family friend that had just been murdered quite gruesomely, when he was in his early teens. Then, just like now, he had tried to spend as little time in the room as possible.

Apartment 8 however, was another matter entirely. Jermaine was almost certain that the police hadn't been into that apartment. After all, nothing happened there. Both the victim and the alleged murderer had been found in the other room, along with the murder weapon. The only thing that had probably been done in 8, would have been to interview Helena, just to further collaborate the evidence,asking if she had heard any unusual sounds during that ill-fated night. She had given them the same answer she had given Jermaine, when he had asked her the same question, absolutely nothing.

As Jermaine opened the door to head out of Helena's former apartment, he began to wonder if the fact that Helena hadn't heard anything that night, actually made perfect sense. This time, as he re-entered Apartment 7, and disregarding that uncomfortable feeling he felt on entry, he started to make a more detailed search, beginning of course at the base of the wall bordering Apartment 8, where he found the other end of the two holes he had discovered in the other room. Again, just like in 8, there was no practical reason for the openings. There were also no other such openings, at the end of the room bordering the opposite apartment, which perturbed Jermaine. He had a theory about what could have happened that night, but the non-emergence of any other holes, especially along the base of the wall bordering Apartment 6, left a substantial gap in his theory.

"Please Jesus, let me find something." Jermaine thought "I know I'm missing something here."

With that thought, he intensified his diligent search, this time even checking for the long shot of a hidden camera undiscovered somewhere. There were none in thewardrobe, or in any part of the room from what he could see. The sound of hoovering from the floor above, signaled that the cleaner was rounding up her work there, and Jermaine used that as his cue to leave, as he didn't want to be seengoing through the various apartments, regardless of the fact that she thought of him as law enforcement, he didn't need to draw much attention to himself. After all, he was the only "police officer" that was currently visible in the building; months after the murder had taken place.

So, he made his way downstairs and out the building, deep in thought all the way home to Colindale. Jermaine was pretty sure that both Obi and Delia were unconscious that night. The discovery of the holes in the base of the wall adjoining apartments 7 and 8 bolstered that theory, but his failure to find an adjoining one to 6, meant that his theory couldn't hold water.

Jermaine had taken time to study the 1st floor and the apartments on it. Apartments 6, 7 and 8 were the only ones on that floor. He suspected that, with Obi's total lack of memory of the events of that night, after he and Delia went to sleep, was because something had been administered to them through food, liquid,or probably by inhaling some type of gas. With Jermaine clearly remembering that they had bought some takeaway food, and had some wine to go with it, and that it had been properly sealed, and so it was highly unlikely that, any potentially nefarious substance would have been slipped in through whichever medium. That left the gas possibility, which Jermaine thought would have had to be pumped intothe apartment from somewhere. He didn't think that whoever the murderers were,they would take the chance of waking up the sleeping couple, while attempting a break-in.

Helena was barely 19, if that, and Jermaine studied her closely, during the conversations that he had with her. He thought he was a pretty good judge of character, and he thought he saw an innocent girl in a woman's body. Jermaine couldn't fathom her agreeing to or being inducted into being an instrument to another human being's death, never mind her best friend. So that ruled her room out as being the possible launching point for the presumed gas, for the samereasons, as the risk of trying to break into Delia's room, while she and Obi were semi-conscious.

That left Apartment 6, an apartment whose occupant(s) was a mystery to Helena.Sometimes when there were a lot of customers booked by the agency, especially on weekends and bank holidays, it was used as an overflow room where ladies could attend to the gentlemen. At other times, when new ladies came into the country, that was the room that they would stay in. Lately though, a tall chestnut-haired lady had been seen entering and exiting the room, by Helena. She didn't look like most of the other girls. In Helena's eyes, she seemed to have a level of sophistication, or at least perceived herself as better than the other ladies.

Jermaine smiled as he remembered the disdainful look on Helena's face, as she described the mystery lady from Apartment 6. It took little things sometimes, for ladies to dislike another lady. A perceived arrogance was one of those little things,and in an environment such as the one the girls lived in, where self-pride was in precious little supply, arrogance was scarcely tolerated.
Still, it didn't matter who or what, was in Apartment 6, if there wasn't some kind of entry point between it and 7. All through the next day, while dealing with his own affairs, he thought about the chasm in his theory, going over the layout of the apartments, over and over again, in his mind.

That day, he needed to be on the estate, to meet up with Suli, Moyo and the rest of the gang. With the seemingly more visible police presence around his home, ever since Jeremy's return to prominence had manifested itself, it had been no longer safe for his lieutenants to casually stop by his home and brief him on "business matters". An alternative meeting place had been scouted out on the Grahame Park estate. It was a flat of a low-level member of his gang, who lived with his girlfriend, who was a friend of Salma, and their two-year-old son. The flat's location was considered ideal not just because of Jermaine's relationship with its occupants, but also because all the flats around it, were also occupied byfriends of Jermaine's family and families of his gang members, or people who Jermaine knew had a lot of reasons, never to trust law enforcement.

Riccardo was accompanying Jermaine to one of those meetings, having run into him on his way there, from his girlfriend's Middlesex University hostel, which was right round the corner from Grahame Park. Jermaine, still deep in thought about Obi's situation, had barely seen Riccardo jogging up to meet him, but was glad for the company. Together, they strolled through the back paths of the estate, exchanging gossip on the latest happenings on the estate. As they got close to Kofi and Tricia's apartment, the conversation switched to security and which path to take to their scheduled rendezvous. For safety purposes, they always took a circuitous route to the apartment, to make sure they weren't being followed.

That route took them past a hauntingly familiar apartment to Jermaine, but one he would rather forget. He made the sign of the cross as they went past the apartment,and Riccardo noticed.

"Oh, I've heard about what went down there, some years ago. It teaches you that you can never be too careful, or ever have enough security. They apparently got to him, by breaking into his neighbor's apartment and then climbing in through the ceiling, didn't they?"

A small bomb seemed to go off in Jermaine's head, as his mind snapped back to Delia's former apartment. He had been so preoccupied with searching for the holes he had first seen in Apartment 8, that he hadn't bothered or been diligent enough to look for other possibilities. He kept cursing himself, silently, all throughthe meeting, almost absent-mindedly going through the motions of conducting the meeting, while his mind was fervently re-mapping the ceiling of Apartment 7.

The next morning, he left for Paddington hoping to catch the cleaner on an earlystart, which would normally commence around 7am, but after waiting outside the apartment for fifteen minutes and seeing no one, he realized that the day was actually going to be one of her mid-day starts. So instead, he made his way into the apartment, having known since the previous day, since he had the epiphany about the apartment ceiling that he wanted to get to the building as early as possible, in order to get as much time to do a thorough search of the apartment.

Unlike the previous times he had been in the building, he didn't run into a client of the girls, either on their way into, or exiting the apartment of one lady or the other. This time, he ran into a man whom he didn't recognize, but whose demeanor betrayed the fact that he was no client. The men that Jermaine ran into either in the hallway or the stairs, walking in or out the doorway, entering or exiting the building, generally tried their utmost to avoid eye contact, or any kind of contact in fact, in their haste to leave “the scene of the crime”.

This man walked down the stairs, looking at Jermaine the way a homeowner would, if he came down the stairs to meet someone he hadn’t invited to his home,inside his hallway. Jermaine knew instantly that the man was probably Paul, the caretaker for both the building and the ladies plying their sex trade inside, as described to him by Obi.

“Who might you be, Sir?” asked Paul “I don’t know that any of the girls are expecting any one at this time?”

“I’m not here to meet any of the girls. I’m DC Pennant from the London Met.”Replied Jermaine, as he showed his ID, inwardly thankful and congratulating himself for thinking ahead, about exactly this type of situation, and thanking hisfriend Andre, for faking a really good one.

“Oh” said Paul, taking a peek at the ID as they met at the bottom of the stairs “You must be the officer Helga talked about, who’s been around in the last fewdays or so. Why is that, if I may ask? I thought the police had concluded their investigation of the murder scene in Apartment 7.”

“That might be true …Sorry Sir, but what’s your name?” asked Jermaine.

“It’s Paul. I’m the supervisor of the building, a caretaker for the owners.”

“Nice to meet you then, Paul” said Jermaine, as he took Paul’s extended hand in acurt handshake. “Just as I was saying, a minute ago, it might be true that the crime scene investigation is over, but until the trial itself is concluded, the prosecutors, and probably even more extensively, the defense lawyers, would like to make sure that the apartment is preserved, just in case there is a need to go back to check something.”

“Ok Officer, I don’t know investigation procedure and protocol, but the owners of the building, asked me to extend my cooperation to the relevant authorities, concerning Delia’s murder.

She was a nice girl, and we want that guy, the murderer, behind bars for the rest of his life."

"Well, I don't know about putting the guy behind bars. That's the work of the Crown Prosecution Service, and the judge of course, when the trial is over."

"But you've seen the evidence, detective. Surely, there is no doubt?"

Behind the seemingly mild mannered and polite enquiry, which could have passed as the interest in the case from a concerned neighbor or housemate, Jermaine noticed the hawk-like look in the eyes of the man in front of him and realized that he was being pumped for information.

"I'm not really in a position to make a judgment on that. Like I said, that's a job for the CPS. If you don't mind though, I'll make my way upstairs and give the room a once over, before going off to do other things. You'll be at the trial, I takeit?"

"No, at least I haven't been informed otherwise. Some of the girls in the building might be called to provide some evidence about Delia and that guy, but not me."

"That's alright then" said Jermaine as he quietly breathed a sigh of relief, thinking that he wouldn't have to worry about running into Paul at Obi's trial." I better get cracking, have a good day." as he started to move past him, to go up the stairs.

"No problem, Constable. If you need any help with anything, you can find me in Apartment 13. See you later."

As he went up the stairs towards Delia's old apartment, Jermaine felt, that now more than ever, there was something to be discovered, about the night Delia died. He got to the apartment and unlike the last time, wasn't pre-occupied with a thorough search of the entire living room. Instead, he focused all his attention on the ceiling of the room, as soon as he had secured the door behind him. The ceiling was a nice design, pearl white with intermittent circular indents all through its surface. The ceiling was 10ft high from the floor, and so Jermaine couldn't reach it unless he jumped up, and even then, just barely and ineffectively.

He looked around for something that might allow him to get close enough to the ceiling, to investigate it thoroughly and comfortably. The stool in front of the dresser, looked like it might suffice, but he took off his shoes before climbing on the leather cushioned top, to test if it would carry his weight. Assured, as to its suitability, he mounted the stool to begin the task at hand, not sure exactly what tolook for, as he surveyed the ceiling from close quarters.

Jermaine decided to start his search from the wall bordering Apartment 6. Using his hands and fingers, he started checking every square inch of the ceiling bordering 6. He poked at every partition and every single one of the indents that he encountered, as he made his way from one end of the wall to the other. As he got to the middle area, one of the circular indents started to flip inwards under the upward pressure of his finger. Standing on tiptoes, he put his eye as close to the gap as he could and peered into the void. He was hardly able to contain his excitement, as his eye made out what looked like a rubber-like pipe, tailing off into the dark distance. Jermaine got down from the stool, as he realized that his calves and feet were aching, from standing on tiptoe for a while, as well as the nervous energy coursing through him at that moment.

It was while he was down on the floor, massaging his calves and feet, after taking off his shoes, that he realized that in all his excitement, hadn't fully grasped the full extent of what his eyes had seen. He quickly climbed back up the stool, to peer once more through the crevice in the ceiling. When he had first spotted the rubber pipe, he had followed its length, down in the direction of the border wall of Apartment 6, but as he turned in the other direction, his eyes confirmed what his mind's eye had shown him, that the pipe also snaked its way back across the ceiling, towards the partition wall to Apartment 8.

Taking out his Smartphone, Jermaine proceeded to take pictures of his find, forthe record, and also deciding not to take chances on being able to see his discovery, a second time. He then came down from the stool, a second time, to move the stool he had been standing on, towards the end of the room which bordered Apartment 8. Having followed the path of the pipe, in an imaginary line,according to the trajectory his eye had made out, he stopped right next to the wall,placed down the stool and alighted. Jermaine then started gently, but firmly, prodding that section of the ceiling, just as he had done with the opposite side, but unlike his discovery on the other end, none of the ceiling sections moved, and neither did any of the circular indents. He tried his technique on the areas bordering his search arc, but without any success.

Jermaine knew that the "travelling pipe" had to come out somewhere, so if it didn't come out where he stood, then it definitely would come out in the next room. Casting a perplexed eye on the twin holes that he had discovered on his previous visit, just in the vicinity of his feet, after he had come off the stool, he made his way to the door of Delia's former apartment. He put his ear to the door, listening for any sounds of passers-by or loitering in the corridor, and on hearing none, made his way out of the apartment, enroute to 8. He made his way directly to the twin holes on that side of the wall, which would make a reasonable connection with his trajectory of the rubber pipe from the next apartment.

Looking around, he found a similar type of stool to the one that had been of great use to him in the other apartment, to solve the same problem that had arisen, right where he was. This time as he prodded the ceiling with his hands and fingers, one of the circular indents showed signs of not being structurally secured, but unlike in the neighboring apartment, the indent section wouldn't flip inwards. After several efforts failed to bear any fruitful resolution, Jermaine resorted to the handy pen knife that he had always carried with him, for as long as he could remember. He then tried gently prying with the blade, at the circular lip of the indent, or what heconstrued to be the lid of the hidden crevice. Under pressure from his gentle probe, the circular lip moved outward slightly, with one end acting as a fulcrum.

With excitement building inside him, he used his fingers to slowly pull open the circular lip, until he was certain that it wouldn't move out any further.

Unlike in the previous apartment that he had been in, he didn't need to peer into the dark void on tiptoe. Protruding out of the opening left by the circular indent, was the seeming end, of the rubber hose that he had seen minutes earlier in Delia's former apartment. While the part of the pipe that he saw from the hidden opening in Apartment 7 had two parts; the one with the open end, which was positioned just above the opening, and another section which continued on, and which had alerted him to the fact that the pipe had continued on to the next apartment; this end of the pipe had just the single part, based on what he could initially see.

Using his trusted pen knife once again, he stuck the blade into the pipe's opening,pushing it upwards and then backwards, attempting to get a better look inside the ceiling crevice. After he thought he had pushed it back inside enough, he once again got on his tiptoe and peered inside. Checking to see the continued progress of the rubber pipe or lack thereof, he wasn't surprised to see there wasn't any length of pipe going past the opening, and into the next room, which, if Jermaine'ssense of direction had badly degenerated in the last few minutes, led to a cleaning closet from which Helga usually retrieved her cleaning materials, further bolstering the burgeoning theory that Jermaine had about the true sequence of events, on the night that Delia died.

Jermaine could barely just suppress belting out a celebratory whoop of success, ashe descended from the stool, barely noticing the slight tightening of his calves, yet again. As he sat down on the floor, and then on second thought, lying down gently on the polished wood flooring, he thought that there was just piece of the puzzle left to find. The rubber pipe didn't have its origins in Delia's old apartment,and neither were its beginnings to be found in this apartment. Rather, it seemed that the "trail" seemed to end here, in Helena's old apartment. All of which begged the question of where the pipe had been installed from.

The answer to that question, Jermaine suspected, was also the key to solving thewhole mystery, or at least the mystery in the minds of Obi, Jermaine and his family, surrounding the upcoming murder trial of Obi Udo. The only way to get the answer to that initial and all-important question, the key to solving the puzzle of the events of that night of horror, was literally also the key to finding an entry to Apartment 6, the only other apartment on this floor, and the only one that Jermaine hadn't gained access to. He was still pondering how to get into the onlyapartment on the floor that still had active occupancy, when he heard the door to the cleaning closet, which was right next to Helena's old apartment, being opened, signaling that Helga had arrived for the start of her day's work.

The beginnings of an idea, started to crystallize in Jermaine's mind, just as it also started to dawn on him that this chance, might be the last for him to be of real use to his friend, in changing current course of destiny and life path of Obi Udo, in this closing, shortening window of opportunity. Jermaine didn't think that he would be coming back to this building anymore, after this visit. He kept that thought in mind, as he got himself together and walked towards the door, his plan of action already clear. There could be no going back, not now. In poker terms, he was all in, trying to call the bluff of the invisible hands of dark mystery and brutal, senseless violence threatening to shroud the future of his friend, and in the act of trying to blind the eyes and pervert the course of lady justice.

"Good morning, Helga. I guess I got up earlier than you, this morning, yes?" Jermaine said as he casually strolled out the Apartment 8 doorway, walking towards the building cleaner, who was busy trying sort out which her bottles of cleaning liquid still had sufficient content to do the job right.

"Yes, you did." Helga replied, as she put the useful bottles on the floor in front of the closet, and the empty, not so useful ones, in the plastic bin liner that she held inher left hand. "I went with some friends to have fun at a hen night, yesterday. We stayed at the bar until the early part of today. I knew that I had to work in the morning, but I thought I should enjoy myself, for once." She said with a sheepish smile. "It was my first one since coming over to this country, and it was very good.How about you? Did you have a good night, yesterday?"

"My night was very quiet, just one of the normal variety. Was the bride-to-be from your country, or was she British?"

"Neither. She is Spanish. We know each other from another building that I used to clean with a group of others. Maria has been here longer than me, and she's getting married to a British guy, which is nice. She will soon get to the stage, when she wouldn't be able to have children, so this is a happy time for her, and we wanted to all have a good time, yesterday."

"It sounds like it was fun. Good for you. Are you sure you will be able to work today, without falling asleep?" Jermaine said, with a laugh.

"Have no fear, officer. I am a true Polish lady. I can hold my drink, very well. Maybe one day, I will invite you for a night out and we will see who can hold their drink better, yes?"

"That's fighting talk, lady." Jermaine replied laughing. "I'll hold you to that challenge someday soon. For the record, I know I'll win though."

"I'll wait for you, then." Helga said, laughing. "So, are you finished for today?"

"I'm almost done. I just need to check something in another apartment, but I'mnot sure if there is anyone in there."

"Which apartment is that? There is no one living in Apartments 7 and 8, as far as I know?"

Jermaine's chest tightened as the realization that Helga had just seen him emergefrom Apartment 8, something that he had assiduously tried to prevent from happening. This was part of the "all in" game plan, thought Jermaine. No going back.

"Something came up when I was looking through Apartment 7, so I had to check the other apartment, just to make sure. But I haven't gotten into that apartment",His arm, pointing in the direction of Apartment 6, a little way down the corridor. "I need to check something in there, before my report is completed. But I know that someone has been living there, unlike the other two apartments. So, I'm not sure what to do."

"Well, you are lucky today. I saw the lady, who lives in that apartment, leaving just as I came in. She was with the caretaker, Paul, but I don't think he left with her. He has the keys to the different apartments, so if you ask him, I think you will be able to gain access to the apartment."

"Result", thought Jermaine. He had no intention of asking Paul for the keys to the apartment, but thanks to his impromptu, but patient enquiry, he had found the opportunity that he had craved for. He knew, right after he had confirmed the beginnings of the route for the rubber pipe, while on top of that cushioned stool in Helena's old apartment, that it was essential that he see the inside of Apartment 6.His only worry was, for someone to be in the apartment, either when he would be attempting a break-in, or for someone to bust in on him while he was rummaging through the apartment. Now, all he had to worry about was completing his search in the window of opportunity that had been afforded him, by the absence of the room's sole occupant, a window of opportunity with a certainly limited, but also perilously unknown time frame. He was still vulnerable to being caught in the act,but it was a risk that he had to take and take right now.

"Thanks Helga. You're a star. I'll go and finish up with Apartment 7, and then I'llgo and ask Paul for the keys to the 6th apartment. Hopefully, I'll see you before I leave."

"No problem, Mister Policeman. By the way, I was just thinking that I don't know your name."

"It's John, Helga. John Pennant."

"Ok John" Helga said, as she gathered up her cleaning chemicals and started maneuvering her Hoover into position, "I need to start cleaning now, so hopefullywe'll catch up before you leave." and, as she moved past Jermaine towards the stairs, as, she usually started her cleaning from the top floor. "I won't forget aboutour little challenge, just in case you think I will." This last sentence, said with a wink and a cheeky smile in Jermaine's direction, as she disappeared round the corner and up the stairs.

"Don't you worry, Helga I won't be forgetting either, you can count on it." Jermaine called after her, to the sound of her slowly ascending feet, and to which he heard the ringing sound of her laughter, in response.

As he waited for Helga to get all her equipment and supplies, to the top floor,he wondered if she actually was giving him the green light to make an approach of the romantic type. She looked nice, even if she was a little older. It might have actually been worth exploring, he thought, but he knew that almost certainly, he would not be returning here, to the building after today, and that meant that he wouldn't even have the chance of having that drinking battle with her, on a nightout, and the pleasure of adding her to his list of vanquished drinking foes.

The sound of Helga, starting up her Hoover, was the signal Jermaine had been anxiously, but patiently, waiting for. Taking a quick look up and down the stairs, to see if anyone was approaching in either direction, satisfied that he had at least two minutes to do what needed to be done, Jermaine turned his attention to the lock on the door of Apartment 6. It was exactly the same one as the ones on the doors of the other two apartments on the floor, apartments that he had brokeninto earlier, under the assumption; especially with Apartment 7; that as the police officer that he was thought to be, would be assumed to have the keys that were initially provided to the London Met.

"I have a lot to answer for, if I am caught right now." Thought Jermaine as broke into the apartment, without much fuss or fanfare. As he closed the door behind him, the first thing that he noticed was the difference between the apartment and the previous two that he had been in. This apartment showed definite signs of recent habitation, and of the activities that transpired there. There was a used bathing towel, still damp to touch, slung across the bed, right next to a pair of pink wool ornamented handcuffs on the untidy looking bed sheets. On the floor next to the bed, were pairs of high heel shoes, slip-ons and slippers, some neatly arranged and others, lumped together in pairs. Either she was an untidy person normally,

Jermaine thought, or the state of chaos that the room was in, was indicative of a rather hasty exit.

As Jermaine went about the now familiar ritual, of looking for the foot stool that would enable him to pursue his sleuthing desires, and the affirmation of his potentially life-saving theory for the exculpation of Obi Udo, he tried to ignore therising sense of panic that he felt, about the scene that would play out, on the circumstance of his potential discovery…any minute now, he thought…

CHAPTER TWENTY-FOUR

Adrianna stepped off the carriage of the underground tube service of the Central line at Sheppard's Bush and followed the throng of people walking up through thewinding, interconnecting exits from the station to the ground floor level. The crowd moving in a discernible line as wide as the tunnels would allow, were made of all sorts of people. Parents, trying to keep up with their rapidly moving children, and the others grouped together with their infant children pushing the baby buggies and holding their other kids, who could walk, by the hand. Various nationalities of people from far and wide, mostly clutching cameras and either capturing or filming whatever catches their fancy. From the Far East and South Asia, the rest of Europe, as well as the Middle East, to the ever-present Americans, immediately recognizable by their large frames and boisterous personalities. Young lovers, arms linked to each other's arms and shoulders, totally engrossed in their own company and oblivious to the ruckus around them, their eyes only taking the time out of their blissful delirium to see the obstacles that might lie on their path forward.

They all came to enjoy the frenetic but enjoyable experience of shopping at the massive Sheppard's Bush Shopping Center. From Next to River Island, Timberland to Adidas and Nike, Marks and Spencer, Karl Lagerfeld and Yves Saint Laurent, every spectrum of the shopping experience; exclusive and high-end fashion, good value quality and bargain value; were catered for. Everyone wantedthat experience, whether it be to actually buy something, or to enjoy the sights of the things that they would love to buy, when the finances and priorities allowed; the much practiced, window shopping. Even the opportunity of wanting to enjoy the cinematic experience somewhere else, was dismissed with the presence of a multiplex, in-house cinema, with all the latest releases and the 3D experience, fully guaranteed. In fact, every conceivable form of outdoor entertainment was catered for, with the obvious but unstated intention of keeping potential customers, and their ever-helpful credit and debit cards, in the vicinity of the various shops in the sprawling complex.

It was into this fray of commercial, social and visual exuberance that Adrianna arrived at, in the late morning hours of a mid-week Thursday. She had been thinking of this outing all night and early that morning, even as she had entertained her well-paying overnight customer Andrew, a regular of hers over the past couple of months who had generally the same requests, wishes and expectations. A successful city banker in London's magnificently built financial market, and born into an even more successful wealthy family, he could easily afford her expensive rates, and as one of the few that she knew could be relied on to consistently visit on a thrice-weekly basis, she welcomed his excesses and patronage, even if she didn't care for the man himself. She had only been in London for a few months, didn't know that many people and was happy whenever she could generate customer loyalty from her clients.

She understood that there were worse things than extreme or unusual client habits, and one of those things, especially for a young, foreign, single lady, living in a big city, in a country far away from home, was not having money and a roof above her head. The only thing that fully guaranteed her the aforementioned staples of big city life was the service that she provided to her clients.

It was the price, that a girl born to middle class Russian parents, had to pay for a young life that seemed only dedicated to finding the very edge of acceptability and possibility, and then driving recklessly past those limits in the proverbial brand new, red Ferrari, with its young lady driver having consumed enough alcohol to inebriate two people and a few wraps of cocaine to be found on the backseat, thrown in for good measure.

Adrianna dropped out of school by the time she had turned fifteen, had been arrested countless times but was always let off with stern warnings, on account ofher father's influence, as a city official for St Petersburg. After a while, the police stopped bothering to arrest the young rebel and her fellow aristocratic cohorts, settling for just herding the unruly bunch from the scene of their latest communal shunt, into the available police transport vehicles to the illustrious dwellings of their embarrassed parents and guardians.

It was a miracle that she had never gotten pregnant, a miracle her renowned pianist mum, attributed to her constant prayers to God, to protect her outrageous young progeny, who reminded her of her ill-fated elder sister, an equally rebellious young lady who didn't make it past sixteen, the victim of the excesses of cheap cigars and an unknown, rare heart condition.

The teenage, former church choir soprano didn't care for her mother's fervent prayers, or the past history of her long dead aunt. She just wanted to experience everything, the boys, the alcohol and drugs, the teenage party scene, and most especially the adult, city nightlife scene. That spirit of curiosity had always been present in her for as long as she could remember, and the older she got, the morecurious she became. Her father secretly wondered if his only daughter had simply inherited his own feral instincts, his weekly rendezvous with the vivacious Anna, his only holdover from his own colorful days of youth, especially during his armydays, in the far away outpost of Kazakhstan.

It was that adult, city nightlife scene that first brought her in contact with Eric Kalinsky, a known fixture in the darker recesses of the St Petersburg society,for reasons that she didn't quite know in the beginning. She however saw the way he was received at the entrances of the various clubs that she went to, and eventually, after a few months, her ubiquitous wild child curiosity overpowering her ladylike pride, and having found out through mutual acquaintances on the nightlife scene of the particular establishments that were his favorites and the ones that he particularly frequented, she "accidently" ran into him, and as the beautiful young Russian beauty that she was, caught his fancy and thus, started a complicated relationship that had been on and off for its two year duration.

After she had dropped out of school and effectively and irretrievably sunk all of her parents hopes that she might one day, in the near future, aspire to their level of societal relevance; which of course led to a parting of ways between the two factions of the Chekov family, with life in the household proving to be untenable for Adrianna; the irrepressible teen made her way to London, with Eric's help of course, to be closer to her newfound love and confidant.

Eric, for his part, loved her brazenness and her zest for life, quality of hers that helped neutralize the awkwardness of the twenty-year gap in age between them. While Eric was a boss, a king in a world and society of his creation, he was also generally a bit of an introvert. He had been attracted and excited by her fearlessness, right from the off, loved her for it, but had lived long enough to see other people of a similar character ilk to hers, be gradually engulfed in a personal inferno of their own making and didn't want to see her go down a similar path.

So, in a twist of faith, Adrianna again found herself in the situation that she had left in St Petersburg, in the gloomy spires of autumn London, and repeated her virtuoso act of teenage rebellion, to discourage the progress of what she thought ofas the path leading to Eric's attempted takeover of her life choices. The first salvo thrown, was her decision to begin entertaining clients in an apartment that she had noticed as being unused in one Eric's many properties, to Eric's fury and embarrassment. However, he was wise enough in the ways of the modern teen rebellion, to prevent himself from making the same mistake that the Chekhov's made, and being a bit of a voyeur himself, allowed her to continue her enterprise, under strict conditions, to which she happily acquiesced.

It was this environment, a carefully monitored truce between the clandestine lovers in Adrianna's mind, and temporary compromise arrangement in Eric's, that she decided to enjoy a little fresh air and some sightseeing on the side in the shopping center at Sheppard's Bush.

Truth be told, she didn't really enjoy what she was doing. After the first few weeks of encounters, the novelty of her experiences wore off. She had never been all-out crazy for the art of love making, but she did like the power that she held over the men that she came across. It was the reason that why she had settled for being a Dominatrix. She loved the sight of men, all of them older than she was, begging and clinging to her every command, doing exactly as they were asked to. That, and the independence that she got from being able to earn her own money to buy whatever she pleased, without having to ask Eric for everything, was what kept her going.

But every once in a while, she wished she could be truly free and independent.Even now, in her late teens, she realized that she was not truly free. Yes, she no longer had to shoulder the burden of her parent's expectations or heed their direction, but now she earned her "independence" by doing what other men wanted her to do, and lived in a house that wasn't truly hers, an arrangement that would come to an end whenever she decided to leave Eric.

As was the case, whenever she felt those pangs of independence, she made her way to one of the many outdoor attractions of

London. Something about seeing kids her age, walking around having fun, gave her some hope that her own time to feel free and "fly" was at hand. She wasn't in too much of a hurry to get attached to one of these "foreign English boys", though. She had heard of the gruesome murder of the girl who lived in the apartment next to hers in Paddington.
Apparently, her boyfriend had come over to spend the night, and for reasons bestknown to him, decided to brutally murder her. Maybe, he wasn't quite pleased with the love-making that had gone on that night mused Adrianna, as she browsed through the perfume section in the Boots store. She was in no hurry to join Delia in the land of the dead, and quietly beat back the advances of the boys and men that came her way, until she felt the time had come when she could better understand the way of life of the British male.

She also didn't want to entangle herself with those pesky British police. She had ample experience with the police in her home city of St Petersburg, but she thought that the police in the UK seemed to take their investigations to a seemingly longer and even unnecessary level.

The murder of Delia had been done over three months ago, a trial had been set, the main suspect was in police custody along with the murder weapon, and yet still, the police were still coming into the apartment. The officer that she had noticed, a black detective whom she studiously avoided coming in contact with, had been going back into Delia's old apartment for a while now, and also according to the gossip that she had picked up last night while out on a drink-up with some of the girls from the apartment, on an off night, had actually been into some of the other apartments in the building, an action that Adrianna did not quite understand the rationale for. What else could they possibly be looking for, in the building?

The thought of him searching through her own apartment made her uneasy, and as the only one in the building that had extensive, if not enforced, knowledge and experience on legal issues, she didn't buy the explanation that had been bandied about during the riotous drinking session, that the reason for the prolonged police enforcement visitations, was to preserve the evidence that was "still in the room".

She resolved, as she finally had her fill of window shopping, to tell Eric about the situation and get some clarification from him on what she thought, could possibly be her lack of knowledge about the British legal enforcement scene. She made her way down the escalators, from the topmost level, down to the ground level, all the while eliciting admiring glances from males of all ages; from the young teens,the single men out on the prowl, and even the men walking along with their wivesand partners, slyly stealing glances at lithe long legs in the thigh length mini, and then up into the mischievous look in the eyes of that beautiful, angular teen face of Adrianna, who kept the smile off her face, in order not to further aggravate the terse look that their partners would usually give her as they passed by.

Adrianna quickly moved down the station escalators to catch a train back towards Central London, on her way to meet up with Eric at his Old Marylebone Road apartment for their regular rendezvous. They both looked forward to these encounters. For all their differences about the activities that Adrianna was engaged in , all was usually forgotten once they were in close proximity to one another. The passion between them was the main reason that she had left St Petersburg, in orderto be able to see him whenever she wanted and not be encumbered by the limitations of a long-distance relationship. Sometimes she tried to surprise him in his apartment, arriving unannounced knowing that he loved to be taken aback once in a while, especially after he had sent her home the first time, she had tried it after arriving in London, only to walk into an important meeting that he was having with business partners. Afterwards; and after much pleading for her understanding, when he found out what she had been wearing under full length leather jacket that she had worn that morning, information that she had casually dropped in during their conversation; he made a point of letting her know that he actually liked being pleasantly surprised, and looked forward to and actually encouraged her visits, secretly hoping that she would replicate the hidden ensemble that she had worn, on the very first occasion, but so far she hadn't and he suspected she was knowingly making him still pay for his first indiscretion. Joao, the building concierge, smiled broadly as she sauntered into the lobby of Eric's apartment building, excited eyes shielded by the Prada sunglasses she wore, as she had walked in the midday sun, from the underground station.

"How are you today, Miss Chekov Joao asked.

"I'm alright Joao. How is your family back home?"

"Everyone in Brazil is doing okay. Thanks for asking. Should I let Mr. Kalinskyknow that you are on your way up? Or is this a surprise visit like the last time?" The last question asked with a harmless smile from the affable Brazilian.

"No Joao. Don't ring him. I think that I'll surprise him, again." This said,knowing that he would still inform Eric of her imminent arrival, as per the strict security instructions and procedures that were a pre-requisite of a man in his position. I'll see you later, if you are still on duty, then?"

"I'll finish my shift in two hours, and Paulo will take over. If I don't see you later,have a good day, Miss Chekov."

"You too Joao, take care." Adrianna said, as she walked round the corner and pushed the elevator door button.

The smile on her face became more prominent as the elevator climbed up the floors to Eric's top floor apartment. This now ritual trip to Eric's was usually the highlight of her day, or at least one of them. She knew that ever since Eric had made the mistake of turning her away from his apartment, the first time she tried one of her surprise visits, he had been genuinely sorry, especially after she let him in on what he missed out on. Truth be told, she had secretly understood why he had to send her away that day, she had never known him to have his "business meetings" that early. But, after she left the building and had calmed down, knowing that an apology would eventually be forthcoming, she sensed an opportunity, and like a lot of women, used the incident as a valuable bargaining chip in the subsequent period of their relationship.

Walking down the corridor towards Eric's apartment door, she quietly let out a little laugh. She knew how much Eric wanted to see the ensemble she wore on that day, again. She was saving that trump card for a special occasion, one in which the effect of her effort would be felt and appreciated to the maximum and rememberedfor perpetuity.

The door was opened, almost immediately after she knocked, by Vlad the heavy- set tough guy from Sochi, Eric's personal bodyguard, confirming her theory that Joao, in spite of his assertions to the contrary and good willed intentions, always would call ahead to let Eric know that she was around, just like he was supposed todo with all visitors.

"Hello Vlad. How are you doing?"

"I'm alright, Miss Chekov. It's nice to see you again. How has your day been so far?"

"It's been alright." She replied as she walked past him into the living room, and deposited herself into Eric's favorite chair, much to Vlad's amusement, as he closed the door and walked to his normal seating position at the mini bar stool. He knew how much Eric disliked anyone, taking up his seating position.

"Where's Eric?" Adrianna asked, once he was seated down.

"He went inside for a quick shower. He just came in from the gym. He asked that you wait here, he said something about having a surprise for you."

"A surprise…? Very nice, I'll wait." A curious but excited expression on her face;she grabbed the remote control and tuned the Sky decoder to MTV Clubland, to check out the very latest from the Euro club music scene. Because of the sensitivities involved, at the location that she currently called home, she hadn't been able to have her own personal Sky dish, installed.

"There you are." Eric called out to her, as he appeared out from the inner rooms of his apartment. "You look stunning, as always." A compliment that she never seemed to have enough of, bringing out a broad foxy smile form Adrianna, as she stood up to plant a lingering kiss on Eric's lips. As she went to sit down on the living room couch, gently pulling Eric along with her, he gave Vlad an eye signal,which prompted him to get up from his place at the mini bar, grab his coat and head for the door.

"Are you leaving, Vlad?" Adrianna asked, more out of politeness than anything else.

"Yes, Miss Chekov. I have to go out and get something. See you later, Boss."

"Alright Vlad, get me some Pistachio nuts when you get back

later." Eric said.

"Yes Boss." Replied Vlad, as he closed and locked the door behind him.

"Right, so where were we? Eric asked, as he pulled Adrianna closer to him. "I missed you, my angel."

"It's only been twenty-four hours, or even less than that." Adrianna replied as she gently and playfully pulled away from him, re-crossing her supermodel legs, which were prominently displayed in her short skirt, and then letting out a playful squeal as Eric tried to grab her supple thighs. "Is this the surprise that you were talking about, Eh?" The stern, almost reproachful look on her face betrayed, by thelaughter in her pretty eyes.

"No, my love...." Eric replied, as he once again tried to grab at her thigh, andthen settling for the pleasure of gently stroking them. "I had something much better planned." He said, with a mischievous smile, playing on his lips.

"Dream on, Mister. Not today. She countered in a playful voice. "What makes you so confident that it was going to happen? Or is that why you sent Vlad away, so that you could persuade me, strongly?" Then drawing closer to him, so that she could feel his strong breathing, which told her that he badly wanted her, she gently asked him in a sing-song voice. "Are you going to be forcefully with me? Should Imake you beg me? How..."

The rest of whatever it was, that she was going to say, was muffled up in hot kisses, first on her mouth and then everywhere else, as a fully aroused Eric, succumbed to the spell of the bewitching seductress, at his side...

***

"Czar..." Adrianna cooed from the bed as Eric returned from the bathroom to rejoin her, knowing how much Eric liked to think of himself as one, with the vast array of people and contacts, as well as wealth, at his disposal.

"Princess Anna" Eric replied, as he pulled the sheets back, to reveal the unclothe and desperately ravishing body of the young tigress that it had embraced momentarily and got in to bed to reclaim the embrace of the lively jewel of St Petersburg for his jealous, selfish and exclusive possession. "You are magic. Everything you are, is the greatest and most magnificent magic, my Anna. Surely,you know that." With that declaration of wide ranging, unending commitment of admiration and affection, he proceeded to demonstrate the depths of his passion for finding the boundaries of her seemingly interminable wanton sexual energy.

"Oh Eric, I almost forgot." Whispered Adrianna, from beneath the multitude of kisses that he was bestowing on her willing bosom, and gently pulling his head upwards half-willingly but resolutely, as she felt that this was something that was important, a question in her mind that once remembered, needed answering.

"All right, Anna." Eric said, a bit grumpily as he realized that Adrianna was serious about suspending his frenetic attempt at lovemaking. "What do you haveon your mind?"

"It's about the apartment".

"What about it? You don't like it anymore? Is anyone bothering you over there?

"No Eric" replied Adrianna, caressing his cheek lovingly at the protective tone hisvoice had assumed. It always made her happy, whenever she could get Eric to rally to her side. He was after all, the closest thing to family that she had in the country, in addition to being her lover. "It's all about the never-ending police investigation in the apartment building over the death of Delia, in the neighboring apartment to mine."

"What investigation are you talking about?" Eric said, suddenly sitting up straight and attentive, all thoughts of sensual foreplay disappearing from his mind.

"There's this officer, who keeps coming into the building to look at the dead girl's apartment. He says, according to the girls that know that he's checking to make sure that all the evidence, remaining in the room is preserved. But I thought that they had collected all the evidence almost immediately after the murder was discovered about three months ago. I was just wondering if the police here in Britain, were a bit fussier with their investigations than others. Besides, he apparently has also been checking the apartments next to Delia's, which includes mine and that freaks me out a little. Just the other day, I had the feeling that someone had been in my apartment, don't know if that actually happened,but the whole thing is making me uncomfortable, and I'm just trying to get my head around it."

Eric had been quiet all through Adrianna's long monologue, barely making any physical movement while his mind was at Mach 2 speed, furiously processing theinformation and its ramifications. Something was very wrong, he thought, but that was a little beside the point. His main worry, in that highly organized mind of his,was why no one had told him what he was being told right now by his girlfriend? What was Paul doing, that he hadn't noticed the activities of this "policeman", whom Eric seriously doubted was actually law enforcement, as well as its potentially disastrous consequences for the organization? He slowly got up from the bed gently pulling Adrianna along, and moved to the living room mini bar, to pour himself some Vodka.

"I think we are dealing with an overzealous policeman, Anna. I will send someone over there to make sure that everything is being handled in the right way.In fact, I'll send someone there right away, just so that you have nothing to be afraid of, whenever you get back there. Now, get back in there, my queen." Eric continued, pointing in the direction of the master bedroom, "We haven't quite finished yet, you know."

A giggling and relieved Adrianna sashayed lustily back inside to the comforts ofthe bed. As soon as she was out of earshot, Eric, the relaxed smile of a few moments ago now vanished, grabbed his android.

"Vlad, get to my building in Paddington. Something's going on in there that doesn't make any sense. When you get there let me know. I'll have Paul there waiting for your arrival." As he started to cut the call off, he suddenly thought ofsomething else." Vlad, Vlad, can you hear me?"

"Yes Boss?"

"Grab a few men with you, as well. You might need them when you get there.Paul will brief you or what to do when you get there, got it?"

"Yes Boss, I will there as quickly as possible, with the others."

Eric then cut the call off and went through his phone directory, for the nextimportant call that needed to be made.
"Paul…"

***

Jermaine left Adrianna's apartment shortly after one in the afternoon, only noticing the time for the first time since he had encountered Helga in the corridor.He lingered for a moment in that corridor, straining his ears to try and locate her current position. The soft sound of voices in the distance, including that of Helga, gave Jermaine an idea of her current location, engaged in the telltale sounds of gossip. "Hope it isn't about me" thought Jermaine as he moved stealthily and quickly down the stairs, happy that he didn't have to talk to Helga again, to make phantom plans for a meeting. The light afternoon sunlight hit his face, bathing him in a glow of refreshment. He felt like he had just emerged from a prison, albeit one that concealed within its confines, the true nature of man's brutality and propensity for evil.

The feel of the fresh breeze on his face and the reassuring weight of the phone in his right hand, with all the evidence that it concealed in its photo memory, brought back the hope to his soul that the clandestine activities of that dark night a few months ago and the resultant horror, would be as visible to everyone concerned, as the afternoon sun high up in the sky.

As he turned right, off Old Marylebone Road on his way to the Edgware Road underground station, he noticed Paul standing at the bus stop on the opposite side of the road, watching the corner that he had just emerged from. Jermaine pretended that he hadn't really seen him and continued on his way down the street.Years of living in one of the more dangerous parts of London, had sharpened his awareness skills on the study of his surroundings. It made the difference between being caught red-handed on a drug bust, and noticing just before the police net was sprung, that there were a few strangers in places where there weren't usually any, or at least not anyone unknown to the people of the area. It was that heightened observatory awareness, which ensured that he, spotted Paul in the firstplace, and then thereafter, a cursory survey as he walked, checking to see if he might spot anything out of the ordinary from his previous walkthroughs.

Marylebone Road was always busy, being a major West London thoroughfare,with cars, buses and pedestrians buzzing up and the road, and the numerous bus stops teeming with people, especially at that time of day.

Jermaine took a measure of his surroundings as he walked up the road, passing Paul who seemed preoccupied with an approaching bus. He kept on walking, only to pause at the next street corner to see if anyone had either peeled off from the general direction that they had been walking in to follow him, or if anyone who had been waiting at the bus stops, was suddenly following. Having observed neither and seen that Paul had indeed gotten on that bus heading in the opposite direction from him, he continued up the side street towards the station, smiling briefly at the lady trying to sell him some new brand of international phone cards but declining to purchase any, murmuring that he had quite a few already at home.

He passed through the entrance happy at the day's discovery, a smile on his face while thinking of the future prospects of his best friend, a marked difference from the brooding nature of his countenance as he passed through the same entrance earlier that morning.

As he made his way down the escalator to his platform, he didn't notice the heavy-set man and the three other men with him, following at a discreet distance,their eyes firmly fixed on the Caribbean man in front of them…

CHAPTER TWENTY-FIVE

Jeremy had a fixed smile on his face as the train pulled out from Earl's Court Station. It was the smile of a man who had either hit the jackpot at the local betting shop, or maybe cleaned out his opponents at a game of high stakes poker. His carriage was unusually bare of commuters as he looked round, enabling him to spread out his arms to the seats on either side of him, and point his bended knees inthe same direction as his arms, then bring them back towards him continuously in a fan- like kind of motion, drawing the attention of an elderly couple on the far side of the carriage, who after taking a look at the blissful indifference on the face of their fellow commuter coupled with that unsettling, faraway horizon, smile, tut-tooted disapprovingly, resolving to ignore the lack of manners and self-awareness of the man; probably high from one drug or the other, of the type that was so common these days; and enjoy the rest of the journey on their way to see their grandchildren.

This was no drug-fueled, inhibitions dropping, out of body trip experience that Jeremy was under, no, he had just experienced something much more profound. An experience that, in his mind at least, had no comparable substitute, and one heseemingly couldn't get enough of.

Gina. That girl is going to bankrupt me, he thought, as the train entered the tunnelsection, an apt metaphor for his obsession with the half-Italian lady of pleasure. It just seemed that his time and resources developed a tunnel vision leading straight to Earl's Court, whenever thoughts of her surfaced in his head.

"I have to get a hold of this", said Jeremy to no one in particular, as the picture of Gina in his head, gradually faded; as it always seemed to do, only after he had spent all the time and money that he could afford, and then left her general area; to be replaced by a picture of his bank statement, albeit one that did not belong to any bank, but one that reflected the hidden resources that he kept for himself, a dwindling stockpile that had only recently been gradually replenished due to the uptick in his clandestine criminal activities. Still…

"This is the second time this week, at £400 a pop. Damn man." Thought Jeremy as he navigated his way towards the entrance to the Northern line entrance/exit at Kings Cross Station, where he had disembarked, to continue on his way home to Colindale. The station was of course, teeming with people, which was the norm atthis station which served both underground and over land train services. In the swarm of commuters, various languages could be heard, combined with the sight of people of all races and nationalities, in this most cosmopolitan of London rail stations, especially as it also served as a take-off point for the Euro tunnel rail services to and from France.

The point of entry to the Northern line trains was also actually a multiple entry point that served other London Underground lines, such as the Piccadilly and Circle lines. He made sure to press his Oyster Card firmly against the sensor andwatch the sensory light to see if it turned green in acknowledgment of the commuter's journey. The last time he hadn't taken his time to make sure, he had only found out about the acknowledgement failure when his card was given a "double charge" penalty, thereby taking a lot more money out of the card before the start of his next journey and leaving him embarrassingly stranded at a faraway station with family in tow.

"The bad old times", Jeremy thought as beeping sound of the sensor gave rise to the green light of acknowledgement, as he passed the barriers and headed down towards the northbound platform of the Northern line, without bothering to look at the directions. He had been down this route so many times; he could practically walk blindfolded, through the route all the way home. "Yet another consequence of his regular trysts with Delia", he thought as the train pulled into his platform.

At one thirty in the afternoon, commuter traffic was fairly busy with the school crowd and Rush hour, still to come. This being the case, the carriage he was seated in, had quite a few people on it and was quite warm inside. With the Northern line trains devoid of effective air-conditioning, running in tight tunnelsand slow to boot, Jeremy couldn't wait to get off the train, and only then remembered that he hadn't checked to see if the train was headed to High Barnetor his actual destination branch, which was Edgware.

"They always mix them up anyway" he thought, hoping that there wouldn't be any delays, especially the type which the Northern line was seemingly infamous for.

As the train moved off the platform from Euston station, the next station northbound on the line from King's Cross, the train driver made an announcement.

"This train is headed High Barnet. All passengers wishing to go onwards to the Edgware branch should switch at the next station which is Camden. Thank you."

On hearing the announcement, Jeremy got up from his seat and moved towards the carriage door closest to him, in order to beat the traffic of people that would be seeking to get on and off the train, as Camden was the last or first chance to change tracks on the line, depending on which direction you were headed in, and was usually filled with commuters, with it being a bit of a tourist destination itself.

A lot of the Rock music artistes and bands in London could claim their birthplace/origins from this eclectic corner of North London. A walk through the streets of Camden seemed to put you in the midst of the people returning from the last Woodstock music Festival. There were people who were obviously musicians, springing out virtually from every corner, and every street seemed to harbor an elder statesmanlike looking pub advertising some type of musical show/performance from one band or the other, most of whom sounded unfamiliar. Even the corner shops had people in black leather and eyeliner, strolling in and out of the premises. This trend continued, but to a gradually lesser extent, as you journeyed northwards, up towards and past Kentish Town, and southwards through and past Mornington Crescent.

Also, there were copious Ink or Tattoo shops in the area, as well as a vibrant Artscene, filled with painters, sculptors and various other innovative and obscure talent on display throughout Camden Town, and nowhere more especially so, than in the historic Camden market. All these features brought tourists in their droves, adding to the commuter footprint at Camden Town Underground Station.

The train had stopped at the Charring Cross branch of the Northern Line and with Jermaine needing to be on the Edgware branch of the line, he made his way through the interconnecting tunnels, towards the track he needed to be on. As he emerged onto his platform, he noticed that there were quite a few people there already. The exit that he had come out from, lead him towards an end of the platform, giving him a clear view of the entire platform and everyone on it.

The train arrival/departure display located near the middle of the platform, came up with the information that everyone there was waiting for, that the next train going towards Edgware was arriving in five minutes. Meanwhile, Jermaine could hear the sounds of other trains pulling into the different platforms of Camden Town, and with those sounds came more commuters, arriving onto the platform, swelling the number of waiting people already there.

There were three tunnels that lead to the platform, one at either end of the platform, one of which Jeremy stood beside. But the one that came into the middleof the platform was the main one, and the one that most people came through. It was from this platform that Jeremy saw Jermaine emerge from, stand at first and then look at the Departure display hanging over the track in the middle portion of the platform, and then thankfully for Jeremy who didn't want to endure any awkwardness, moved along towards the other end of the platform.

Jeremy heaved a sigh of relief as he moved to find cover beside one of the waiting passengers on the platform, while keeping an eye on his former stepson. He watched Jermaine stroll on almost to the other exit point on the platform and then stand facing up to the tracks. While he was observing Jermaine's actions, something grabbed the attention of the corner of his eye, pulling him instantly away from his observations of his erstwhile Grahame Park adversary. He trained his eye on one of a group of people that had just emerged from the same tunnel exit that Jermaine had come from, just a minute before.

The heavyset man, who to Jeremy's experienced eye, seemed to be leading the other three men around him, reminded him of someone. He kept his eyes on them,completely forgetting about Jermaine for a moment, and then being drawn to where their eyes seemed to be going furtively, only to find his attention drawn back to the figure of the man he had battled for a time, for the control of the biggest council estate in Europe. Now, his curiosity was truly piqued, why were they so obviously following Jermaine? What exactly had Jermaine gotten himself mixed up in?

It was as he was pondering the answers to those questions, that he suddenly realized where he knew the heavyset man from, and felt his blood grow cold, as he realized exactly what was going on.

The man in the midst of the shadowy figures, who were on the trail of Jermaine,was finally recognized by Jeremy as the toughie he had encountered at Eric Kalinsky's apartment, the last time he had been there. Even then, Jeremy knew that this would be the type of guy that Eric would use to do the truly unpleasant stuff, not Ben or Paul. He had his suspicions about Delia's murder, and the circumstances surrounding Obi alleged complicity and had wondered if someone like Vlad didn't have a hand in the execution of that onerous task. As sound of the Edgware train, pulling into the platform got louder, those suspicions gained more traction in his mind, and he resolved that his first instinct, which would have been to let Jermaine handle whatever it was that was about to happen, would be a missed opportunity and a mistake, because ever since the murder of that beautiful Romanian lady, he had felt a personal weight in his mind of what he thought of as his own culpability. Besides, all the blowback from the incident had affected both his business and relationships within the Grahame Park community, undermining the latter while disrupting the transactions of the former and this was one of the times when he could truthfully claim to have no inkling of the events of that tragicnight.

However, everyone knew that he was the one that had put the videotape online, which was the first that all lot of the Grahame Park community knew of Obi's love, and so the trail of evidence in the court of public opinion, lead right to the doorstep of Jeremy, and not to, as Jeremy believed it should have, Eric's own. Getting to the bottom of the Delia mystery was important, but the general picture of Jeremy's world, not as important as making sure that Eric's men had nothing to do with any unnatural misfortune that might befall Jermaine. Delia's murder was bad enough, but if anything happened to Jermaine only a few months after, there might be unpleasant consequences for whoever was thought to be responsible, andwith Jeremy already in pole position as the fall guy, Jermaine's loyalists, of which there were quite a few from personal relationships going back decades, would make it untenable for Jeremy to stay, never mind operate, in Grahame Park.

It was this last thought, coupled with the picture of his

girlfriend and child, that occupied Jeremy's mind as he started to move toward the other end of the platform, as the train pulled in, hiding as he walked behind the passengers disembarking and boarding the train, as he wanted neither Jermaine nor his stalkers to recognize him, spoiling the observatory role that he wanted to play, for the time being.

Vlad, and his associates, were walking in the opposite direction towards an oblivious Jermaine, who Jeremy could see; based on the fact that Vlad and his cohorts, were not necessarily concerned that Jermaine might see them; did not know who Vlad was. They all got into the last carriage, seated at different positions, while Jeremy got into the penultimate one, seated at a spot close to thecarriage interchange doors, so as to get a good look at anything going on in Jermaine's carriage.

The train started on its journey northwards, after the driver made one last announcement concerning the destination of the train, prompting a few people to quickly disembark from the train before the carriage doors closed, after realizing that they were on the wrong train. From his vantage position, Jeremy could see that Jermaine was seated at the farthest of the three sections of his carriage, with Vlad and another, of whom Jeremy now thought of as Eric's men, sat in the middle section while the other two sat in the section closest to Jeremy's carriage.

Jermaine was concentrating intently on something from his phone and was almosttotally uninterested on anything happening down the aisle, in Jeremy's direction, for which the latter was grateful. For even if Jermaine had wanted to, he would have found it extremely difficult to spot his erstwhile stepdad, due to the length of the carriage and its undulating movement which made a clear view of people in the other carriage rather hard, for which Jeremy was grateful, as he didn't need to hide himself to watch the proceedings, quietly thanking his genes for the excellent vision he had always possessed, cat-like eyes his wary mum had always called them, eyes that gotten him out of a tight spot or two, in his life's journey.

Vlad and his cohorts were also not very much interested in things going on in Jeremy's direction, but as the train stopped at each of the approaching stations; Chalk Farm, Belsize Park and Hampstead; the ones who were farthest away from Jermaine, moved down to take any seats that were vacated by passengers getting off at their destination, getting ever closer to Jermaine. Jeremy wasn't bothered by that development, knowing that nobody would be silly enough, to try anything onboard the train, which was laden with CCTV cameras, in every carriage.

However, the body language that Jermaine's clandestine pursuers exhibited, lead Jeremy to believe that something would happen to Jermaine, while not inside the train, but somewhere else, and Jeremy didn't like Jermaine's odds of pulling through a violent altercation against those four toughies.

Jeremy thought of his options, on what to do in case things came to a head, all while an incredulous voice inside his head kept asking him what the hell he was doing? He didn't want to get his boys involved because he knew they would be asking the same question that persistent voice in his head was asking him, and that there might be consequences for his business, if his own gang thought that he might have lost his edge.

Contacting Jermaine's own gang was also not an option, as they might also think that he might have something to do with whatever fallout there was for Jermaine, getting him into the exact kind of situation that he had got on this train to prevent.

There was only one option left open to Jeremy, and it was a high-risk, low-reward option for both he and Jermaine, and that was only if the people he needed to contact, would want to get involved anyway, and not leave him high and dry.

"There's only one way to find out" Jeremy said quietly to himself, as he got out his phone to make the call, only to realize where he was. The Northern line had one of the longest stretches of underground track, if not the longest, on the London Underground network. The stretch of track that Jeremy and the others had been on, running from Camden Town to where they were, having just past Hampstead, was all underground, and so phone services were compromised, as all networks were rendered useless at the depths that the train was travelling at. So, Jeremy put his phone down, waiting for the train to reach the next station, which was Golders Green and above ground.

As the train came to a stop outside the affluent and largely Jewish corner of North London, Jeremy began to make a call that every old instinct in his body screamed at him not to make. The only reason he was making that call, was the sake of an old love and a face that he had never quite forgotten...

"Hello. It's me.... I need to ask your opinion on something..."

***

Eric and Ben arrived at his Paddington apartment building about thirty minutes after Jermaine had left, along with a few of his men. Paul was just inside the door,waiting for the appearance of his boss. The atmosphere in the building had radically changed within the last hour; right after Paul had received a terse phone call from Eric. All appointments that the ladies had booked for that afternoon and beyond, were hurriedly cancelled or rebooked with girls from other buildings that Eric owned in the vicinity of Central London, while any clients that were already in the building, had been waited out. The last one had actually just left ten minutes before Eric arrived.

As the two men strolled through the front door, Paul felt himself physically wilt under the glare of the look on Eric's face. He felt like the biggest idiot in the world, as he had absorbed what Eric had talked about on the phone earlier. He had never cared much for the police, and while he had never been in any major trouble with law enforcement, he had as a general rule, kept his distance. This waswhy he had allowed all that latitude to the man, who after Eric had checked up with his contacts, was found to have been impersonating a police officer. It was only now, after the fact, that he realized the potential damage and danger, that his negligence might have put a lot of people, including Eric, in.

Eric passed Paul with nary a word, barely acknowledging the latter's greeting,and along with his right- hand man, Ben, climbed silently up the stairs, the posse of men that had come along with him after he had hastily assembled themat his Old Marylebone Road residence, mostly former acquaintances of his from his past life as an intelligence operative, following swiftly behind. The resident ladies all were out in their various corridors, having been informed that their benefactor boss was going to be about and needing to see everyone.

The visiting group that Eric led made their way to the topmost floor, all the while exchanging pleasantries with the girls. Even though this was a visit borne from troubling circumstances, Eric did not allow those circumstances to becloud his vision on the future of his business enterprise, and the ladies in his different apartment buildings were a huge part of that enterprise. Besides, until he knew exactly everything about the goings-on in the last few weeks, he didn't know if he might end up needing their help, in a legal sense, so he thought that in spite of the tense uncertainty pervading the day, it was best to ensure that all the ladies were happy and secure.

After all the ladies had been seen, the group proceeded to the much-visited Apartment 7. Every inch of the apartment was searched for surveillance equipment first, before anything was said in the room. After Eric had been satisfied that the room was "clean", he then asked for a briefing from Ben, being the one who had come up with most of the surveillance gadgetry on short notice.

"Well, we know there aren't any bugs in the apartment, but the place has obviously been searched thoroughly and most importantly from our perspective,the ceiling partition has been discovered." Said Eric's second in command.

"Was anything taken?" Eric asked.

"No. The rubber hose is still as it was installed. But it has definitely been seen and so we can't discount the probability that photos might have been taken."

"What about the cylinder or canister that was used?"

"We can't see it from here. It most likely would have been in another room, which Paul or Vlad would have been aware of." This reply prompted a turning ofheads by the assembled group, towards the still figure of the building supervisor.

"In what apartment, was the canister installed in?" Eric asked Paul, in a dispassionate tone."

"It was installed in Adrianna's apartment, Boss." Paul answered.

"Why exactly in that particular apartment?" Eric asked Paul, as the group of men, started making their way out of the Apartment of the slain Delia and towards the apartment of Eric's girlfriend, whom Eric had made to stay back in his Old Marylebone Road apartment.

"We did it for convenience, as we knew what times she would be out, especially to yours" Interjected Ben, "But whatever happens, nothing will come back to her.That, I can assure you, Boss."

"It better not, guys. Let's make sure that we can contain any fallout from this thing." Eric said, as the door to Adrianna's apartment was opened by Paul, and everyone then followed him inside.

The first thing Eric saw, were the pair of exotic shoes, leather outfits and exotic paraphernalia, lying around his girlfriend's room. He even saw the outfit that she had worn to visit him the very first time, hanging in front of the wardrobe in the same vivid detail that she had described it. Under normal circumstances, he wouldhave been pleased, as it would mean that she was planning on wearing in the near future, but as his eyes scanned the rest if the room; quickly absorbing every detail in the room, as his team went to work on a comprehensive search of the apartment; all he wanted was to find the evidence or lack thereof, to dispel the rising tide of panic, well hidden from the rest, that something based on the goings-on in this building in the last few weeks, could potentially unravel the organization that he had painstakingly built up over the last decade.

All eyes then switched to Fyodor, one of the men that Eric had brought down from his apartment, as under the direction of Paul, now positioned a stool at a corner of the apartment bordering the one that they had just exited.

"You need to push that corner of the ceiling section." Paul told Fyodor, as thelatter motioned upwards towards the ceiling.

"I could already see that from here." Fyodor replied, "There is a little gap that Ican see in the ceiling. It looks like a demarcation between two sections of the ceiling."

This observation from the Crimean-born Ukrainian brought the rest of the group much closer to the section of ceiling that he was pointing at and a feeling of coldness to Eric's chest.

"That means that he's been here, for sure, now." Ben said, stating the obvious. "That gap was not visible the last time we came here, just before the police had started their investigation, about three months ago, and I doubt anyone would have touched it since. Especially no one, that knew that the gap existed." The last sentence was accompanied with a look in Paul's direction.

"No. I haven't been here either and neither has Vlad to the best of my knowledge. He would only have access if he got a key from me." Paul said.

"Well then, let's check to see what other surprises we have in store for us this afternoon." Eric opined in a sarcastic voice, and an equally scathing look in Paul's direction, and who was himself wishing that this was some sort of nightmare he was going to wake to from, and hoping that, in addition to possibly losing his place in Eric's organization, he didn't end up putting his own life in jeopardy. There would be ramifications for him and others, if the police had any reason to suspect that there was a different reason, for the murder of Delia, than the one they had already accepted as fact.

Fyodor pushed the corner of the ceiling were the tiny gap, could be observed. The ceiling section flipped inwards, in an inside out motion, revealing a small cylinder attached to the other side of the ceiling section, with a hose attached to it,which then wouldn't allow the section to align properly with the rest of the ceiling as before.

"Well, well." Eric said, still in the sarcastic tone of voice, "At least the gas cylinder is still there. Our first bit of good news, so far."

"What do we do now, Boss? Ben asked.

"Isn't it obvious? Eric answered. "We need to know everything that our fake police officer knows, and fast. Using our police contacts wouldn't necessarily helpour cause, because if he is smart and bold, which we know now that he is," This said with another scathing look towards the hapless Paul. "He will be certain that we don't want to get the authorities involved, legally. Especially, with the evidence he has. No, we need to take care of this problem in a very basic, but effective way, so we can be sure that we don't need to worry or think any more about this mess, ever again. Now, is there anything else we need to check for in this building?"

"No Boss." Ben answered," I think we know all that we need to know about whatwent on here. Now we have to solve the arising issues."

"All right then, let's all gets out of here." Eric said, and as everyone started filing out of the apartment, he motioned to Ben. "Get Vlad on the phone immediately".

The entire group had a crestfallen air, as they descended the stairs leading to the front door, with Paul peeling off from the building's departing visitors; to meet thegirls and let them know that things would return to normal in about two hours, andso to get themselves ready.

"Boss…" Ben called to Eric as they left the front door of the apartment building."What's the matter, Ben?"
"I've been trying to get through to Vlad on the phone, but no joy yet."

"It must be those damned Northern line tunnels. The last message that I got fromVlad was that they were at Golders Green, heading northwards. Keep trying; the tunnels can't go on forever. I wonder where they are, right now though."

***

Jermaine studied the pictures on his phone like he was preparing for an exam.The only thing that might convince a casual observer that there might be an alternative reason for his intense concentration was the wide, giddy, and enormously self-satisfied smile on his face.

As the train sped through the last bit of tunnel on the line, which lay between Hendon Central and Colindale, Jermaine looked up finally from the images that promised an earth-shattering change to the status quo of his incarcerated friend. He had almost fallen off the stool when the ceiling section flipped around in Adrianna's apartment. The sight of the cylinder attached to reverse side of that section, left him stunned momentarily, so much so that he almost forgot about taking pictures, he just stood there looking at it, wondering why sure effort and stealth planning was put into the murder of a simple girl like Delia.

Even his elaborate hypothesis, about what really happened on that fateful night, would never have propounded the extent of planning, and thought that would have gone into such a criminal undertaking.

This had been no crime of impulse, or rash reaction to something, with Obi beingin the wrong place and at the wrong time, ending up being used as evidence bait for the police to pick. This scheme had taken time and planning and did exactly what it wanted to do. There had been no mistakes, until now.

A phone rang, further down in the carriage, just as they exited the tunnel leading up to Colindale Station, breaking him out of his deep reflection of the day's events.He turned to look at the source of the sound and found himself looking at the face of a heavy-set, East European looking man. Jermaine turned away but not before the thought registered in his mind that he had seen that face somewhere before. He turned back to look at the man who was carrying on a conversation on the phone in a foreign language he didn't recognize.

Intuition and facial recognition, honed during a life of living dangerously on the edge, jogged his memory to remind him that had he seen the man seated a few carriage chairs from him on another train that day. It wasn't something unusual, chance encounters like that happened every day on the busy London Underground.It was the look of the man, which pricked something in Jermaine's consciousness. It was the look that people engaged in certain fields knew when they would run into one another, outside their areas of operation; Men with calloused hands, shaking each other at a ceremony, recognizing by touch of hands,of a man who made his living in a field of physical exertion; Fellow accountants ata business convention concession stand, arguing with the sales attendant over the increase by a few cents, of their favorite doughnuts; Strangers meeting the victim of an automobile accident unbeknownst to either of them, but asking her questions with strikingly similar legal parameters. Whatever it was that pricked Jermaine's consciousness, it was not physical or anything in of the five senses would pick up, but he knew there was something there, and he had long since learned to trust or pay attention to the beckoning of instincts gone awry.

Jermaine put away his phone and kept a side eye on the man, who along with him was the only two in the carriage, as the train pulled into Colindale Station. He walked towards the carriage doors and waited for them to open. The man stayed on his seat as the doors opened, after which Jermaine stepped off the train and casually strolled to one the benches on the platform. Some other passengers from the other carriages got off the train, but not the heavy-set man that had been in thesame carriage as him.

The train continued on with the rest of its commuters, towards Edgware and to the relief of Jermaine. He started walking towards the station's stairway which took commuters to and from the ground level, when he noticed someone walking directly towards him. He stopped abruptly to take a better look at the man, his radaractive again. He didn't see, nor hear the footsteps, drowned by the sound of the departing train, of the two men moving quickly behind him, and after he felt a pin prick in his arm, along with the feel of arms reaching up under his, he wasn't aware of much else either.

CHAPTER TWENTY-SIX

The BMW X5 SUV rolled up the Station Road from Colindale up towards Edgware Road, turning left at the junction where the impressively large ASDA megastore located in Colindale, stood. The vehicle continued at a brisk, but legal pace along Edgware Road, past the Colindale high street with its parade of shops,the high court, and the medium sized Sainsbury's next to it. Jermaine started to come to, as the SUV started to approach West Hendon, with distinctively visible Mediterranean/Middle Eastern/East African population, especially around its High Street, largely influenced by the presence of the council housing and estates in the around that area. Jermaine recognized the area even in his partially conscious state. He had enjoyed his share of parties and dalliances there, enough memories to last a lifetime.

He didn't have much time to reminisce about it as the vehicle kept up its steady pace, prompting Jermaine to wonder for the first time, what he was doing inside the vehicle. He tried to turn around to take a better look at his surroundings but found that his movement was a little restricted. A look downwards enlightened him to the fact that his arms were bound to his sides. He turned his head to either side of him, to see two Caucasian men, none of whom he recognized.

"He's awake, Boss." The man to his right said to someone in front, to which the man in the passenger seat, then turned around, and Jermaine instantly recognized him as the man who had aroused his suspicions, on the train. He was still trying to get his head around why he couldn't remember how he made it from the train to this place, when the man in front addressed him.

"Mr. Jermaine Adams, I presume. Don't bother answering. I took the time to go through your pockets, while you were still asleep earlier. It's nice to finally meet you, sir. By the way, my name is Vlad."

"Where exactly are you taking me to? And why?" Jermaine asked, even though the sinking feeling in his stomach, pretty much underscored the fact that he had strong suspicions about the why.

"Well, it would seem that you've been visiting us quite regularly, and have gotten to know us quite well, and we really appreciate your efforts. So, just like the good people that we are, we, my boss and the rest of us, decided that it would be nice to bring you in and find out about you, so that we can know each other better, and on equal terms. Which is only fair, I think?" Vlad replied, after which the other three men in the car, joined him in gentle laughter.

All the while the SUV sped on, past Staples Corner with its myriad of roundabouts, turn-offs, and the flyover. They had to stop at it for a bit, to obey the various traffic signals that guided drivers to their various destinations; taking the left turn would lead you to Brent Cross Shopping Center, as well the cinema and the huge PC World megastore: the right turn went towards the magnificent Wembley Stadium. But they continued straight on towards Cricklewood and its multicultural and multiethnic High Street, the lovely hotel on left, just after the junction leading off towards Harlesden and Willesden, which was probably the only sign of any Englishness along that High Street, and then the myriad of multiethnic fast-food outlets and restaurants; Oriental, Mediterranean especiallyTurkish, Indian and West Indian, along with the representative population to patronize them.

On through and past Kilburn, which was largely West Indian and African and quite busy on its High street, with the Over ground and Underground stations bringing in people by their thousands to patronize the numerous shopping outlets on the street, both large and small, as well as the cuisine of the area and its brand name fast food competition. After Kilburn, the buildings on either side of the roadstarted their accent to upscale status as their location changed from North London middle class neighborhoods to West London's wealthier addresses.

Finally, they turned right as they got to Maida Vale, an area outside Jermaine's social and business circuit, but having rolled past the area numerous times in thepast; especially during his teen, all weekend-clubbing days; on the No. 32 from Edgware, he knew exactly where he was. The high-rise buildings that housed the high-priced apartments, dominated the skyline of the area, a theme that became more accentuated as you moved further in towards the heart of London from its Western periphery.

"We are almost there" Vlad said, breaking Jermaine out of his observational reverie. "There will be no sudden moves from you, once we get out of the car. Beunder no illusions that the consequences of any such intransigence from you, will be met with a permanent discomfort, that we will be quite happy to administer to you."

With that the vehicle came to a halt outside a high rise, which Jermaine assumed to be an apartment complex, as so many in the area were. As per instruction, he got out of the car as directed and moved towards the front of the building, not that he could do anything else, anyway. The residual effects of whatever it had been, that was injected into his system, still left him weakened and barely able to walk unaided. As the two men beside him, gently commandeered him into the lobby area of the apartment complex, having already removed the bonds that had held him, before they exited the car, all Jermaine could do was look around his surroundings. He noticed a small corner shop across from their building with a stack of bottles of orange juice, homemade as was advertised, and turned to the man on his right.

"Is there any chance that I could have some of the orange juice over there?" Jermaine asked. "It looks good, and it would be nice to have some to drink, toquench the thirst."

"I think you have bigger problems to worry about, my friend." The man answered, as he tightened his grip on Jermaine's arm and quickened their pace asthey moved into the lobby.

"Don't worry though; I think that they intend to look after you, very well."

The party, led by Vlad, moved swiftly through the lobby without any fear that they might be discovered by anyone, prompting Jermaine to wonder if the building wasn't another one of Eric's properties. Two men came down to meet them just outside the elevator door, whispered something to Vlad who nodded in acknowledgement, and then stayed down as original four men who brought Jermaine, guided him into the lift and then they started upwards. Nothing more was said to Jermaine on the ride up. There wasn't anything that needed saying really. Jermaine might have been flippant, minutes earlier outside the building, but it was an outward show of bravado. He knew now, especially after regaining his full cognitive abilities that he had truly stepped into it this time, and he couldn't think of a way out of this one. The silence in the elevator left him contemplating his fate, and cursing what he thought of as his carelessness, wondering if he had survived so many tight spots only to be flummoxed by one that he was in, not for personal gain or business, but as a big favor for a good man who was he's best friend.

"Sod's law, I guess" he thought to himself, as the elevator doors opened to reveala well-furnished corridor, which they started to stroll down. They stopped outside the door marked Twenty-Eight and after three knocks, it was opened, to reveal a sparsely furnished apartment, which Jermaine observed was in sharp contrast to the rather expensive furnishings that he had seen in the rest of the building that hehad seen, so far, which lead him to postulate that this apartment was rarely used, and that unlike Eric's other buildings, this one was probably not used for the any clandestine activities.

As they stood in the middle of the living room, where three men already sat, clearly waiting for them to arrive, Jermaine had an eerie feeling that he had seen the layout of the apartment before. He couldn't explain why, but he was sure that he could recognize some of the furnishings from somewhere but was absolutely sure that he had not been here before. He was still processing this puzzling turn of events, when one of the men, in front of whom they now assembled standing, spoke.

"Good day, Mr. Adams. My name is Mr. Kalinsky. I wish we could be meeting in different circumstances, but this unfortunate turn of events is largely of your own making. It has come to my attention that you have been regularly paying us visits, under the false pretense of being an officer of the Law. I had you brought here, so that you could tell me why exactly. We both know that the police are not going to be informed about this, but I still want to hear your own side of the story, on why you decided to do this and for who, because I am absolutely certain that our paths have not crossed before."

Jermaine took his time to study the man who was addressing him as if giving a lecture to a rather petulant ward of his, who had gone a step too far this time, and was going to have to suffer a significant retribution for his actions but was going to be given a chance to explain his actions, nonetheless.

So, this was the infamous Eric, he thought. Physically he was an impressive specimen, six foot tall, with blond hair and intelligent-looking eyes. There was also an unmistakable aura of authority about him, and from the tension that could be felt reverberating through the room, he was feared, and since he was certain that from the look of the men in the room that they had seen their share of violence,that fear, at least at the moment, was justified.

"Now" Eric continued with a motion towards the men standing next to Jermaine,"I would like to see your phone and anything else of mine that you might have in your possession."

"I didn't realize" Jermaine countered, as the men began to search him "That my phone, was also yours?"

A quick punch to his face from Vlad, who had been standing quietly to the side,while the others began conducting a thorough body search, drew both blood and Jermaine's attention to his erstwhile travel companion.

"It would seem that you've forgotten my earlier warning, while on our way here Mr.Adams."

"Actually, I didn't. It's just that I was stunned that you could use such big word,as intransigence that I missed the rest of what you said."

"That will be alright" Eric said, as Vlad made a move towards Jermaine, stopping him from doing further damage to Jermaine. The men had also now, finished their search, and brought the phones that they had found in Jermaine's pockets to Eric, who motioned them to give their find to the black man seated to his right.

"Take a look at them, Ben." Eric asked, "I want you to thoroughly check all the photos and videos on those phones. Now Mr. Adams, why have you been snooping around my property?"

Jermaine almost didn't hear Eric's question. He had been thinking, as his phone was handed over to Eric, about Delia and Obi. He was thinking how much of a shame it would be, that the true perpetuators of the murder of Obi's girlfriend would be going scot-free, leaving his friend to carry the can; when he suddenly realized why he thought that he recognized the apartment, or the living room at least. It was the memory of Delia, which brought back the vivid images of that infamous video, the actual circumstance that had brought them even closer together, as friends and survivors…

"I have a question for you, as well." Jermaine said, and quickly added as one of the other men, took a step towards him, "How do you know Jeremy?"

There was an immediate silence in the room, as Vlad waved the other man to back down and all eyes moved towards Eric who had a dark expression on hisface.

"So, you are with Jeremy." Eric finally said. "I didn't expect this from him. A bad move, I assure you. So, tell me, how do you know him, and what did he ask you to do, at my apartment building?"
"He never asked me to do anything" Jermaine stated, enjoying the momentary look of confusion on the faces of the other people in the room.

"But you know who he is?" Ben asked, punctuating the moment of silence in the room.

"Of course, I know who he is. The reason I asked, is that I recognize this apartment from a video he made portraying a lady I know, in a bad light."

"Ah" Eric sighed. "You must be talking about the video that Jeremy made, some months ago. But you still haven't told me why it concerns you and what it has to do with snooping around my apartment building."

"The lady in that video died in your apartment." Jermaine said.

"What has that got to do with you? Were you a client of hers?" Eric asked, the latter question generating a ripple of laughter around the room.

"Her name was Delia, and she was murdered in her apartment, in your building,three months ago".

"I believe that the man accused of her murder is currently under police custody and awaiting trial." Eric said.

“I don’t believe they have the right man…” Jermaine stated, and then pointing atthe phone that Eric was holding in his hands, “…and I think we both know that’sthe truth, which I am sure the law enforcement authorities will be very interested in knowing.”

“You still haven’t said how and why it really concerns you, Mr. Adams.” Eric stated.

“The man that you and your acolytes framed for the murder of Delia, Mr. Udo, is my closest friend and a man totally incapable of perpetuating the horror that he has been accused of, and I will not rest until the true villains are brought to book.”

“Unfortunately for you Mr. Adams and I don’t see how you plan on accomplishing such a feat. The photographic contents of your phone will never be seen by anyone else, after today. I only came here to find out for myself, who you actually worked for. Now that I am satisfied that you don’t work for ant rival syndicates or anyone in the relevant law enforcement authorities, I can assure youthat the last few hours that you will spend on this planet, will impress on you the magnitude of your ineptitude, in dealing with matters, and powers, above your station.”

“You seem comfortably convinced that no one else will be able to see the evidence that exists on my phone.” Jermaine said, as the men standing next to him,now turned in his direction, obviously waiting for further directives from Eric or Vlad, concerning the state of his wellbeing. “I can assure you that it will be a big mistake.”
“He sent some pictures to someone named Kathy Benedict.” Ben said to Eric, pointing at the phone that was in the hands of his boss. “The message wasn’t very specific , even though it did mention something about “a case”. But, without corresponding pictures of the outside of the building, I think that situation is salvageable.”

“So… Mr. Adams.” Eric said, with a wide grin spreading across his face. “You can see that my organization, has very little to fear from someone such as yourself.All your effort, was all for nothing, but the consequences for yourself, I can assure…” His facial expression, now morphing into a grim mask, “…will be dire.”

With that, he motioned the two men next to him, towards the door, and then turned towards Vlad.

"This idiot has cost me some of my precious time and energy, not to mention anxiety. Please make sure that he is handsomely rewarded, before setting him free."

The three men immediately started on Jermaine, leaving him doubled up on the floor, with blood running from his mouth and nose, while Eric, Ben and Vlad moved towards the door.

"He is not to leave this room alive." Eric quietly instructed Vlad, "See to it." To which Vlad nodded and turned back towards ruckus in the middle of the living room.

Jermaine knew that there was little chance of his leaving this apartment alive. His only regret was that he didn't have more time, to make sure that the case against Eric and his acolytes was airtight. As the blows rained down on his head and neck,he didn't hear Ben open the front door, or the gasp of horror that escaped from his lips at the sight before him.

"I think that will be enough, gentlemen." DI Patterson announced as he pushed the stunned Ben and Eric out of his path, making his way, followed by DI Johnson, Jeremy and five officers, to the prostrate form of the man on the floor, surrounded by the suddenly paralyzed toughies standing around him.

He then turned towards Eric with a broadening smile on his face, "I think have a lot of explaining to do, mate."

"Delia...It's alright, if I call you by your real name?" The man who sat across from her, on her apartment bed, asked.

Emerald green eyes shot out of a face that instantly became the very picture of alarm and alert distrust.

"Who are you really?" Delia asked, "I take it that your name is not really Barry,then? What do you want with me and how do you know my name?

"That's a lot of questions, Miss. But I'll answer them because maybe, we could help each other. My name is DI Johnson." And with the alarm her eyes gave away,he quickly added, "Don't worry, I'm not here to arrest you or anything of the sort, I just came to see if we be of use to one another and exchange favors. You, bringing me information, and I, helping you get out of the mess that you are in."

"Why me, if I may ask? Why are you sure that I can, or will help you? And what do you mean, about getting me out of a mess?"

"You know this man?" DI Johnson brought out a photo and handed it to her.

"Yes" Delia answered tentatively "But you already knew that."

"Well done, Madam. Yes, I did, but I had to know if I could trust you. By the way, you may call me Derrick." He got up from the bed, but not before extending his hand and shaking Delia's, who was still wary of the handsome,early thirties looking Caucasian man, standing across from her who had yet toshow her any identification, he could be a spy sent by Eric, to check up on her trustworthiness…

The man seemed to read her mind, though. "This is my ID, Delia" Derrick said as he handed her his badge. "Those can be faked, you know. We are under no illusions about the danger we could be putting you in, but we think you might be getting in too deep for your own good, and we can offer you a way out of the life you are living entirely, if you can help us."

"You still haven't told me why I should help you, or trust you for that matter"Delia said, thinking that she might as well string this out and find out what this was all about, after all she could always claim to have been digging for information, if things went sideways. And besides she had dealt with a few gentlemen of law enforcement in her time, and there had been something odd about him, compared to her usual clientele, which she had been unable to put afinger on, and he might just yet still be telling the truth. Still, there was no rush…Best to make sure.

"This is why we thought you would be interested in helping us, Delia." DI Johnson had moved from his position next to the bed, towards where his belongings had been carefully placed, which Delia had noticed at the time, and brought back Smart Pad. As he sat back down across from her on the bed, he placed the device into Delia's hands. "I think you would want to see this video."

Delia changed to a more relaxed position and proceeded to see what the fuss about. Derrick watched her closely as the video played, noting the gradual look of horror that spread across her face and then feeling surprised at the feeling of pity that he felt for her. It seemed to prompt him to pull out a clean handkerchief, even before she had finally pulled her face away from the images before her,turning towards him with tear-filled eyes, as he had noticed the slow heaving of her upper body.

"Where did you find this?" She asked, as soon as she had gotten her voice under control. "Is it everywhere?

"No, Miss Vasileva, it isn't. We noticed it in the Grahame Park area. The man whose picture I just showed you, his name is Jeremy." She nodded in agreement.

"I know." Delia said, "They all called him by that name."

"They…?" DI Johnson interjected. "Anyway, we'll get to that in no time. Like I was saying the man in that picture, works for us, in a way, but we don't trust him one hundred percent, or maybe not at all. We have kept tabs on him, on occasion, and we noticed him with you, sometime ago. When this video surfaced in our areaof operation, it came to our attention that you were the girlfriend of an associate ofsomeone on our watch list."

"Has he seen this video?"

"Whom are we talking about, here?" DI Johnson asked.

"My boyfriend… Obi…." "I can't be sure, Miss Vasileva. But, if it remains in circulation, where it is, it will only be a matter of time before he does, if he hasn't already, Delia, and there's nothing we can do about it."

That brought about a renewed bout of muffled sobbing. Derrick looking at his watch and knowing that he had about half an hour, to do the job he was sent here for, before the time for his scheduled visit ran out, gently tugged at her folded arms.

"I think there's a lot more that you should be worried about, than your boyfriend finding out about your activities. Does he still not know what you do for a living?"

"He does, but not like this" Delia said, whilst pointing at the images of the still running video.

"Well, I'm sorry, but hope it doesn't ruin the relationship that the two of you already have, but like I said, you still have bigger things to worry about. We feltthat the video was some type of move to roil Jermaine, and the only person capable of gaining anything from that scenario, would be our pal, Jeremy. We then tried to track you down and linked the two of you from our surveillance photos. We now know of your connection with Eric, whom we know from his previous dalliances with the criminal establishment of Grahame Park. He melted away some time ago, before we had a chance to take him on, and this is the first that we have known of his whereabouts and activities, since then."

"You still haven't told me what you want from me?" Delia observed.

"This is our preposition, Delia. We would very much like to apprehend your boyfriend's best friend, Jermaine. He has given us a bit of a headache in Colindale, which is where I am actually based. But, based on what we know about him previously, Eric is involved in human trafficking. Back in the day, we only knew of the Grahame Park angle, which was only a small part of the area's crime puzzle, and so we concentrated our efforts on the drug trade which was massively affecting the life of the residents of the area, young and old.

But now, thanks to your video, we have found him again and seen the true size of his organization, and we think that he just might be the single largest organizer of human trafficking in the UK, and that is a significantly larger pot to seize in crime fighting parlance, than our mutual friend, Jermaine, especially in light of the efforts around the world to combat slavery and human trafficking. So, we would like you to help us bring him down, and in exchange for your help, we give you a new life, a clean one, were you can live whatever life, as long as it isn't crime affiliated. A fresh start Delia, to build a good life for you, and whatever family youwill chose to have in the future. All you have to do is cooperate with us, fully."

"Why should I help you do this, officer? I have a good life here and am treated well. I have never been put in any danger or forced to do anything that I didn't want to. So, Mr. Derrick, tell me why I should risk joining you and risk everything?"

"The only way that Jeremy would have done that video of you, would only be with Eric's consent, which I believe means, that right now you are unprotected, free to be used to do whatever Jeremy needs done with you, and with the face that Jeremy is no longer in control of Grahame Park, I suspect that Eric sees a significant opportunity to have some leverage to move back into the Grahame Park end of the crime business. That turf is currently being run by your friend Jermaine. If they have deduced that you could be a bit of a pawn in the scheme to reclaim that turf as their own, how safe do you think you really are now?"

Delia had listened stoically to Derrick's pitch for the last couple minutes, and then stayed silent for a few more, face moving intermittently between the video playing on the Smart pad and DI Johnson's face. She wished Obi was here, she needed someone that she could trust at that very moment. Derrick seemed to read her mind.

"You can't tell anyone about what I have just told you. For one, we will not look kindly on you, and we will treat you like an accessory to the crime, should we bring Eric down through other means. Second, what you are about to do, if you agree to do it, will be dangerous, and it will be prudent of you to not involve anyone else, especially those you might love, because trust me, you will never forgive yourself if anything should happen to them, because of it."

"Will you give me some time to think about this, it is a bit too much right now, and besides I think your time is almost over. I need a few days, and I'll give you an answer, probably the one you will want, as I know you are telling me the truth now. I just need to prepare myself for what's coming."

"You are right; it's almost time to go." Derrick said getting up from his perch on the side of the bed and moving towards were the rest of his belongings lay. "Just make sure, that you give very good thought to what I've said. Believe me, it's the best choice for you. Take a few days though, if you need to. You can contact me with this number." This said, while extending his hand towards Delia, with a card displayed between his fingers. "You can reach me at any time, if you ring me on any of the numbers shown there. Good evening, Delia. Take care of yourself."

With that he moved towards the door with Delia in close proximity, just as it would have been at the end of normal encounter with a client. She waved him goodbye at the foot of the stairs, as was her custom, and then made her way back upstairs, as Derrick opened and walked through the front door into the street running in front of Delia's Paddington apartment building. After a minute of walking, he pulled out his Smartphone which was now ringing.

"Did she go for it?" The gruff voice of DI Patterson came across the phone to Derrick.

"She needs a few days to make up her mind. I can't say I blame her for doing that, it's quite a bit to take in on one day, really."

"Well, I hope she makes up her mind soon, the earlier the better for us." Jack replied.

"I just hope we haven't put her in any sort of danger, she sounds like a really nice girl." Derrick opined, "…just mixed up in the wrong gang, I think".

"Aren't they all, Derrick? "Not this one, I don't think…"

Meanwhile Delia had gotten back to her apartment and after taking a few minutes to gather herself, picked up the phone.

"Paul, is it ok if I took the rest of the day off and the weekend? I don't really feel well."

"It's your funeral, Delia. Just as long as you know the obligations that we will expect from you when the time comes."

"Yes Paul, I know. I just need some time to myself. It's already Thursday today,I'll make it up, I promise, next week."

She ended the call and then immediately rang the one person that she wanted to speak to the most, right at that moment.

“Obi, can we talk?”

“Sure, my queen, are you alright?”

“Yes, baby, but I would like to see you tonight if possible.”

“I wish I could, babe, but I’ve got to work tonight, just outside London. It’s our first job there and so I’m not sure when I’ll be back. How about, I get there, first thing tomorrow morning?”

“That will be great. I took the rest of the weekend off. So, we can have plenty of time for each other.”

“I’m looking forward to it, my love. Can’t wait...”

“And I neither, my love….Kisses baby”

She dropped the phone, feeling instantly happy, seeming weight dropping from her shoulders. She laid her head back on the giant stuffed animal that she used as a pillow and slept off.

.

In the blissful relief of sleep, she was entirely unaware of the listening devices that had been installed in her room, ever since Jeremy had turned up asking questions about her, claiming that she held the key to regaining Eric’s lost market of Grahame Park…

CHAPTER TWENTY-SEVEN

Obi looked around the restaurant, taking pleasure in observing the décor of the place, as if for the first time. The patrons, sitting comfortably at the dozen or so tables sumptuously arranged around the delicately lit eatery. He had been to the Wazobia restaurant, a Nigerian restaurant just up the road from the Hendon Central underground station, before, but not under the present circumstances. The aroma of freshly prepared Okro soup, filled the air around him, alongside the mouth- watering whiff of the other Nigerian staples; Chicken stew, Banga soup, moimoi, Jollof rice et al. His presence today was by his personal request, and one which was almost immediately granted, as an opening statement of intent of a collective will and responsibility, to try to make things right, as much as it could possibly be done. The start of a long process with a two-fold objective, rectify the injustice done in the life of one person and cherish and correct the memory of another.

"We are truly sorry about Delia, Obi…" The apologetic statement brought Obi's senses back from their culinary sojourn to his immediate environment, the dinner table that he sat at, along with the four other men who only a few days ago, would never have contemplated a scenario where all five men would be seated at the same table in a cozy restaurant, exchanging pleasantries, or trying to…

"…There's no way we would have anticipated what happened, or even the speed at which it was done. If we had known, we would surely have taken steps to prevent it."

"How, could you have prevented what happened, exactly?" Obi asked, without a hint of sarcasm in his voice, DI Johnson. He was seated next to DI Patterson, who in turn sat next to Jeremy, with Jermaine completing the circle unlikely table occupants by seating next to Obi.

Noticing the slightly subdued effect that his question had on

Derrick, he tried to reciprocate the DI's well-intentioned apology. He knew that they, both DIs Derrick Johnson and Jack Patterson, hadn't needed to be here. Their presence was only well-intentioned gesture, to try and somehow, make things right.

"I'm just trying to say, I know you two were only doing your jobs to the best of your ability." Obi, continued. "At least, even if you feel responsible for the death of Delia, then you should also, be equally responsible for saving the life of Jermaine."

Obi's philosophical take on the tragedy of his girlfriend's murder, was not a flippant attempt to mentally forget the horrible memories that he would carry with him almost certainly, for his entire life, but rather the first steps on the journey of healing. He had cried himself to sleep, every day, for almost the entire period of his incarceration, spanning almost four months, thinking of ways to overcome the fact that he would never see the love of his life, ever again.

That, and the fact that he had been in the same room with his ever glamorous and eternal rose, when her life was so gruesomely and callously taken, left him wishing that he could join her in the afterlife of eternal peace and beauty, the only place she could have gone to, with any means possible.

However, Obi, a man of proud Igbo heritage, born into a family of deep Christian faith of an Anglican persuasion, eventually discarded the idea taking his life, or giving it up without a fight. Once the tears had dried up, when the frequent nightmares about Delia's lifeless and battered corpse became less troubling and terrifying, if only because he had seen it so many times, he also remembered how strong a character, his Romanian rose was, and what she would think of him giving up so easily, especially with her murderers still on the loose and not answering for their heinous crime. He thought that she would be ashamed of him, and that was a thought that he could not bear in his heart. So, only a fortnight before, he had started to gather up his mind and body, for the onerous legal task ahead, trying to get in touch with Jermaine, to find out where his investigations had led to, only for the dramatic events of the past week to turn everything on its head, but restore his life's direction to its rightful forward course, and so here he was, in a lovely restaurant, among the most unlikely companionship, preparing to order some freshly cooked Okro soup and Cassava flour meal, and he wasn't even paying for it. It was a mind boggling, but wonderful turn of events, with just one person missing, to complete the picture…

"I'm afraid we can't even take full credit for that, Mr. Udo." DI Patterson replied,while frantically studying the menu guide. "The initiative for that and in fact, the beginnings of the operation that brought the prosecutor's case against you crashingdown, would be Jeremy here."

All eyes briefly went to the face of Jermaine's one time stepdad, everyone wondering how that decision had come to be made, knowing very well that it been a decision that had cost him the chance to become the overlord of Grahame Park, and thinking to themselves that they would never judge anyone based on their past, ever again. Sometimes, the true essence of a man, in spite of his antecedents, was waiting for the right circumstance to present itself.

"Jeremy." Jermaine called, speaking up for the first time. "I just want to say thank you, for saving my life. I've known sketchy details about what truly went down that afternoon, but I have known that you basically made the call that brought the officers over to that building and saved my bacon. I thank you, Mum and Salma thank you, and maybe someday, it would be nice to have you come over for dinner, or maybe play some scrabble, like we once did, a long time ago."

"Look, son." Jeremy replied. "I know that I made some

mistakes in the past, back when you were a kid. I guess it started like some battle to win your respect and obedience, and let you know who the man of the house was, and it took on a life of its own after that. But I would never truly wish the son of the woman, who I loved the most through my life, dead. Even if I once thought I could go through with it, I think I always failed because deep down, I wanted to." Then, stretching his arm out across the table to Jermaine, he continued, "I would like to come over and play scrabble, sometime."

To which, a slightly smiling Jermaine responded by warmly grasping hisoutstretched hand.

"Hear, hear." Bellowed Jack, who was followed by a spontaneous outbreak of back slapping around the table, causing a stir around the restaurant, with the mostly African clientele, taking sideways, amused glances at the rowdy multiracial table of diners, in their midst.

"Now that we can put away our handkerchiefs" Jack continued, to a brief spate of laughter around the table, "Will someone please help me out with this menu? I swear that I've been looking at it since we got here, but I can't seem to find anything recognizable."

"Me, neither" echoed Derrick, which brought about another round of laughter round the table.

"I think…" Obi said, after the laughter had died down, "…that it's best that you have some white rice and chicken stew. It's really nice, and it's as close to anything you'll get in Continental, Oriental, or Indian cuisine. Think of it as, Basmati rice with, Chicken Tikka Masala or Korai with a different but extremely mouth-watering, stew set-up. Same goes for you too, Derrick,"

"I think I've been to quite a few Nigerian restaurants, in the time I've known you,Obi." Jermaine said. "I feel like I have sufficient license to freelance. I'll go for the Jollof rice and some fried chicken."

"You call that freelancing?" Obi asked, derisively. "Wake me up, when you go for the heavy stuff. Why don't you try some Okro soup and some white stuff? You do that and I'll know you're for real!"

"Baby steps, bro, baby steps. This is a restaurant, and you know I've got a weak constitution for new cuisine. I promise I'll try it though, when you're fully settled in your home. Maybe, you could get your girlfriend or something to make some for the two of us."

There was a bit of a quiet silence after that, with everyone immediately remembering that Obi didn't actually have a girlfriend at the present time, and then feeling somewhat guilty, as to being part of the reason why that was, nonemore so than Jeremy.

He politely asked Jermaine if he could exchange seats with him, at least temporarily. Obi's best friend, understanding the poignancy of the moment, especially in light of his indelicate previous statement, acquiesced and quicklyexchanged seats with Jeremy.

"We've not ever really spoken to each other." Jeremy started, pulling his chair slightly in Obi's direction, looking him directly in the eye. "I think the first time that we spoke any words to each other, was on the ride that here from Colindale. Ihave a lot of things to apologize for, Obi. Most of them, I am too ashamed to evenbring up. But I feel I bear the most complicity for her killing. After all, I was the one that brought her to the attention of Eric Kalinsky and Co. I of course, had no reason to think that they would eventually do what they did, or even the manner in which they did it. But it still doesn't change the fact that I inadvertently, and selfishly, put the events into motion, and I will never be able to forgive myself, much less forget, for the actions I took that led to the death of that beautiful, innocent lady,

Delia."

There was now a palpable silence around the table. The brief outbreak of spontaneous back- slapping camaraderie around the table just a few moments ago,had all but disappeared, replaced by a somber ambiance, as the occupants of the table sensed that they were witnessing one of those epochal life-changing, moments.

"I'm getting out of the game." Jeremy continued, as he shifted his posture a bit, and looked around at everyone at the table. "I can't ever be responsible for anything like that, ever again, not even in the slightest way possible. I must not ever be responsible for causing pain or putting people, whom I might know or be somehow connected to, in danger. I won't be able to do that, if I try to relive or re- enact my crime spree ridden glory days. So, I'm leaving Grahame Park, leaving my gang, contacts, and everything. I'm going up the road to Watford, to join my lady and young son. I've got some family in the area and have some cousins who are into the building and home repair business, and I did a bit of that a long time ago, when I was still a wee lad. We'll join up and see how strongly we can get thebusiness to grow, while try my hand at the first legitimate work in decades."

There was a moment of stunned silence around the table, punctuated by the arrival of the ordered dishes. Obi waited for the waiter to serve all the dishes, and everyone to settle in before he turned towards Jeremy.

"Again, just like I told Derrick a few minutes ago, for all your actions, and for whatever things you might blame yourself for, when the time came for you to make the decision to save a life and lose your personal ambition, you made the right call. That decision, is the reason that my best friend Jermaine is alive today, the reason I am not confined to the four walls my cell, and the reason all five of usare sitting at this table, enjoying the fine cuisine and each other's company, right at this very moment."

Everyone around the table nodded their heads approvingly, briefly catching the eye of Jeremy, as they again wondered if they might ever witness or be the recipients of such an unprecedented, volte faced experience of life saving humangenerosity.

"I would be the last person to castigate you for the unjust nature of your past deeds, while failing to recognize the unselfishly righteous road that your present actions hint, at the path your character is embarking on, in its search for the future.The reason I was held in confinement, was because of a previous experience, an unforgettably unpleasant one, that I had with another female, and one for which I paid the price for, of legal ignorance and seemingly misplaced human trust. So, when I was charged with Delia's murder, it was assumed that I could be culpable whether justly or not. One wrong conviction and assumption, lead to another.

I personally know the cost of such a circumstance, and I have intention of replicating such a notion, especially towards a man, who of his own accord and volition, helped save my life and bring the true perpetrators of the murder of mylady, to book. All I can, and will say, is thank you and that we can be friends, as long you continue on the path that you have just talked about."

Obi then stood, raising his glass of malt beverage towards Jeremy, who then stood and clinked glasses with him, and then everyone else stood up as well, clinking glasses and bringing back some of the feeling of camaraderie that had engulfed the table earlier.

"I guess this means that you're the main man in Grahame Park, again" DI Johnson asked, punching a suddenly perturbed Jermaine on the shoulder, who had a pressing question to ask the visibly ebullient law enforcement officer, but decided to make a few pronouncements of his own, first.

"No Derrick, I won't be. Just like Jeremy, I'm getting out,

too." A visibly contrite Jermaine, stated. "My mum and Obi have this cleaning company operation set-up,and I have already spoken to both of them about joining up and expanding its potential reach and capacity. I've been in a few close shaves in my time, but Maida Vale was my tipping point. This time there was nothing I would have been able to do, to get out of that situation. If Jeremy hadn't happened to be where he was, when he was, I don't make it out alive. All I was thinking at the time was that it was the first time that I had a chance to do something good for someone, and that I was going to fail at that. It reminded me of the fact, as my life proceeded to flash right before my eyes, that I hadn't done too much good in it. I want to spend what life that I have left on this earth, trying to correct that discrepancy."

"Wow." DI Patterson exclaimed, without a trace of sarcasm or disbelief. "This is turning out to be quite the night. First Jeremy and now Jermaine leaving the crimegame for good. My first taste of Nigerian food, and I feel like I'm definitely goingto be coming back for more. The only thing left to make this a truly indelible night, would be for the two of you, former crime lords, to give us information on who would be taking over your various operations, now that the two of you are leaving."

Jeremy and Jermaine muttered something unintelligible, and then proceeded to delve deeper into their various dishes; Jeremy had settled on Fried rice and chicken; searching for some mysterious condiment at the bottom of all the food, prompting an exchange of knowing glances from the law enforcement officers, followed by outbreak of laughter from the two, and then joined by Obi and the twoconverts to legalized livelihood.

"Sorry guys." Jack said, after the laughter had died down. "I was only kidding. We, Derrick and I, would never expect you to do that, not after everything we've done on both sides of the fence, and we wouldn't hold it against you, either. The guys and girls, over there in Grahame Park will have their own decisions to make,just like you two have. I just hope they will be smart enough to get out before it's too late for them to."

"I don't mean to be rude or anything." Jermaine said, while wiping his lips with a napkin. "But the two of you have been in quite a cheerful mood since you picked us up. You had no idea about either my decision or Jeremy's, before the last ten minutes, so is there anything we need to know, or had it already been a good day, regardless?"

"Well," Derrick answered. "You guys are not the only ones heading off in a new direction. When Jeremy rang us up on that fateful day, not only did he save Jermaine's life and possibly yours, but he also led us right into the biggest human trafficking syndicate bust in a long, long time. We actually arrived too late to stop them from taking Jermaine from the station, but that mistake turned out to be fortuitous, in the end. Because Jeremy had been quick to get off the train unseen, and therefore able to observe the abduction from a safe, undiscovered distance, hewas able to see the vehicles that bore Jermaine away and get some registration details, which allowed us to track the vehicles to Maida Vale. That was where our good fortune paid off. We have no idea why Eric wanted Jermaine taken there, maybe it was the closest apartment that they had. Whatever the reason, once we got to the location, with Jeremy in tow, he let us know that he knew the building,and the possible apartment that Jermaine might have been taken to, thereby enabling us to dispense with any time-wasting effort needed to interrogate that info out of the heavies we found in the lobby. We got to the apartment door, with some of our surveillance equipment, just in time to hear Eric and his gang, inadvertently admit to complicity in Delia's murder, handing us a multi-charge arrest coup, the type of which you could wait years for, and never achieve."

"I'm not sure if you guys catch the news regularly." Jack added, "But with all the effort made to disrupt human trafficking, our bust was greeted with a lot of hoopla in the media, we've been transferred to the Central human trafficking enforcement division in the London Met, and promotions to boot. A lot of the underlings rolled up on the head honchos in the syndicate, to try and beat the murder rap, and the ripple effects have been felt all around Europe. It's actually been a very good week for us, actually."

Obi wondered if there had been some liquor- facilitated celebrating going on between the two as well, before they had proceeded to come over to pick, first Jeremy and then he and Jermaine, but decided to keep his own counsel on that subject, for now.

The banter around the table went on for another fifteen minutes or so, as the police officers and the former crime bosses, exchanging stories on their times on each side of the fence and their perspectives and each side's operational view, onthe events and activities that brought them head-to-head, in the battles for dominance and order in Grahame Park and its environs.

Obi joined in too, as they all filled in the gaps in the narrative of their most recent ordeal's storyline, pausing at intervals to wonder yet again, at how things could have ended up in the fashion in which it did, when you took into consideration where each of them came from, philosophically, ethically, and strategically, position-wise.

Eventually though, it was time for the inevitable goodbyes. Jack and Derrick were after all, still London Met officers, and they still had duties and responsibilities to attend to, and after exchanging greetings with the rest of the party and asking if anyone needed a lift home, to which all replied in the negative, excused themselves and proceeded to be on their way.

A short while later Jeremy followed, after exchanging phone numbers and contacts with Obi and Jermaine and thanking them for having him, made his way home, leaving the two best friends to ruminate on the events of the day.

"Are you coming home, tonight?" Jermaine asked.

"No. Not tonight anyway." Obi answered. "It's been a truly special day, so far. But I still wish she was here to witness it, you know, Delia. I still feel like I want to spend some more time outside, till almost the wee hours of the morning, just like she and I used to do, and I don't want to really bother you guys. You've been through quite enough in the past few weeks, for me. I'll pass for tonight, bro."

"You'll be staying at that temporary place, then?"

"Yes. The police were kind enough to provide me some shelter, temporarily, untilI get back on my feet, fully. Or at least, until the compensation package, arranged through Derrick and Jack, is finalized. Shoot, I forgot to thank them for that, too."

"Don't worry. I think you'll be seeing them soon, regardless. Everything still ago, for next week?"

"Sure thing bro, the final autopsy on Delia body will be concluded by tomorrow, Ithink. Thereafter, I'll escort her body back to her family in Bucharest, for a proper burial. You're coming, right?"

"I wouldn't miss it for the entire world. It's our last chance to pay proper respects to the lady. Mum and Salma would have liked to come too, but business doesn't wait, and someone needs to mind the store."

"Thanks Jermaine. I'll really need your support to get through that funeral and meeting her family."

No worries, Obi. You never even really needed to ask, I was already there, waiting. Now, if there's nothing else bro, I'll be pushing off. You'll be alright,though?"

"Yes Jermaine, everything will be alright. Go home and get some sleep. The fact that I don't have a girlfriend doesn't obscure the fact that you do. Now go home and keep her company."

"All right, then." Jermaine replied laughing. "Catch you later, bro."

"I'll see you tomorrow, then." Obi said, as he stood up and bumped fists with the erstwhile lord of Grahame Park. "Goodnight, bro."

Jermaine left Obi alone at the table, and after a while he too decided to exit stage left, the night air catching him in the face as he strolled downhill, unsure as to where he wanted to go, but knowing that he didn't want to head home, yet.

As he passed what looked like an Indian fast-food shop, he paused and made his way in; remembering that he hadn't bought anything to cook at his new abode, feeling that he might as well get some takeaway food, to deposit at his apartment,for later.

Looking around for the order procedures, he noticed that order numbers were being called at the counter, after which the customers came forward to collect their orders. He located the ordering point, and after collecting his ticket number for his order, went back to the eating area to wait at an empty table for his number to be called.

It seemed that the food was of really good quality, judging by the clientele that trooped in and out of the establishment, as Obi observed. The fact that there were multiple other more established brand name shops, on either side of the lesser- known eatery, only buttressed the fact that it was the locals preferred destination for food.

Obi, being the only one at his table, made himself comfortable, sitting back and thinking on the momentous events of the day, and in fact, the past week. His mind played back the events, as he thought of the way his life had turned from a normal career working path, to becoming embroiled in the illicit drug trade, or at least associated with those who pedaled the illegal stuff.

It was as he thought about the events of the last few years, that he remembered the reason that his life had taken such a dramatic turn for the worse. The human trafficking ring, the Grahame Park underworld, they had only come after the first disaster of his life. Like a domino effect, they had come one disaster after the other,taking a sledgehammer to the various pillars of his life; pride, faith, ambition, happiness, and belief in the purity of the human spirit; shattering them like they were constructions of diseased and rotting wood.

Hendon… This was where everything had started going wrong in his life, and it seemed like perfect symmetry that his life, had also started to right itself here, like the hands of a broken clock being pulled back to reflect the correct time of day, before the batteries were inserted, to make continue on in its correct motion.

Talia… Obi had met the teenage girl, only a few minutes from where he sat waiting for his takeaway meal. Of all the things that had happened in his life, it was the one thing that had never been resolved, in terms of his psyche and belief in the goodness of his soul. Delia, Jermaine, Jeremy, and everyone else he had met in the aftermath of his conviction, he believed that he was destined to meet, each encounter proving life changing for everyone involved, both known and unknown to him.

Each of those afore mentioned encounters, Obi could cherish, both for the good and bad memories that would forever remain with him, believing through his Christian faith that it was ample sacrifice, if it meant to happen to bring good to the lives of people embroiled in much greater suffering than him.

He could accept that.

Men and women had been given a chance to be freed from the bondage of drug addiction, because of the decision of Jermaine and Jeremy to exit the scene. Eric Kalinsky's looming incarceration would free plenty of young women to look for more legitimate ways to earn money and survive, now that they had been brought to the attention of the various organizations that had sprung up to counter the scourge of human trafficking in the world. He had a small part to play in that.

Even his beloved Delia, he thought, as tears came to his eyes, had always hated what she had to do to survive, and had always dreamed of getting out of the world's oldest trade. Her death was the one cost that he wished that he could avoid, even if she got her wish in the end, and still, in her instance the ultimate cost has not been his to pay, apart from the cost of never being able to see those beautiful green eyes, ever again. Somehow, he could rationalize those events and encounters with the fact that if made a lot of people better, at no permanent cost tohis person.

His encounter with the Zimbabwean girl though he could not rationalize. It had made an incalculably negative impact on his life, had cost him almost everything, and done no good to anyone apart from the lawyers he had paid and the prosecutors and police officers that had claimed a conviction from the farcical circumstances. All of that personal collateral damage, from a misplaced "hello".

Delia had started his rehabilitation of rebuilding his relationships with the opposite sex, starting the massive repair job of restoring his self-confidence and belief that there wasn't another demolition job waiting for him, behind the façade of a beautiful face.

Sometimes, even more so during his recent incarceration, he thought that maybe there had been something wrong with him then, maybe he had deserved all the things that had happened to him. Probably even, the version of events that he remembered was the version that he wanted to remember, and maybe the poor girl's version had been actually what happened. It had to be the only explanation, for God letting him go through all that, for no reason. Maybe, he had been a bad person.

It was the thought going through his mind, as an order number was announced. Obi looked at his own number and found out that his would be the next one. He shook himself out of re-entering his reverie, and decided to get ready to claim his order, as the person whose number has been called, who had been obviously hanging around the door behind him, came forward to claim the takeaway meal.

He noticed the fur-like coat worn by the lady, as she moved past him and collected her food. As she stood for a minute, checking to make sure that her order was indeed complete, Obi looked at her face, and saw what looked like the same familiar face from back home in Nigeria, that he had mistaken Talia for, a few years ago.

"Amazing how tonight of all nights, I see that face again" Obi thought, but as she completed her check of the bag's contents and started to move back past him and towards the door, Obi thought he recognized a familiar gait, one he had not seen for a long time, but what he couldn't possibly forget. His order number was called as she walked past him, oblivious to his presence.He got up and headed towards the counter, to collect his food from the attendantthat held them.

"Are you alright, Sir?" The attendant asked Obi.

"Yes I am." Obi replied, wiping tears from his eyes, "Something got into my eyes back there. I'll be just fine."

Obi picked up the food, checked its contents and headed out the door. He changed his plans of staying out late and decided to go home instead, heading to the bus stop just up the road.

Tears again streamed down his face, unseen by passers-by in the night light. They were, however, not tears of sadness, but instead of relief, for a memory fully restored and vindicated. Things, everything, had really come round full circle tonight in Hendon.

His bus came and he alighted into its almost empty interior, went towards the back and sat down. As the 326 sped off into the night, Obi looked out the window, his spirit at rest for the first time in years.

He was not a bad person, he thought smiling. Things were going to be alright now…

IHEANYI ANUNUSO

www.ingramcontent.com/pod-product-compliance
Lightning Source LLC
Chambersburg PA
CBHW060625310726
48982CB00003B/683

* 9 7 8 1 7 3 9 7 7 7 2 1 0 *